SET PIECE

DOCTOR WHO - THE NEW ADVENTURES

Also available:

SET PIECE

Kate Orman

First published in Great Britain in 1995 by
Doctor Who Books
an imprint of Virgin Publishing Ltd
332 Ladbroke Grove
London W10 5AH

Cover illustration by Tony Masero

ISBN 0 426 20436 0

Typeset by Avocet Typeset, 19 Church St, Brill, Aylesbury, Bucks.

Printed and bound in Great Britain by Cox & Wyman Ltd., Reading,
Berks.

For James, Laurena, Andrew, Edward, and Amy

Thanks to:
Nathan Bottomley for French translations – *absolument fabuleux!*
Kyla Ward for permission to quote from *The Traveller*
Niall and Craig, whose joke it was in the first place

The House has set the rules for this, the game is very sure.
Air to kiss your fingers, cooled in cavern darkness sweet.
The memory of a feather-moon within the deep azure
and dreams lose their distinction as the trees in shadows meet.
But still the travel keeps you from becoming lost as well
you go and you keep going, going, closer than you tell.

(Kyla Ward, The Traveller)

SET PIECE

Introduction

'Are you sitting comfortably? Then we'll begin.

'Once upon a time, the mighty and wise general, Sun Tzu, made an unusual proposal to the Emperor of China. Sun Tzu claimed that he was so wise and so mighty that he could teach anyone to be a soldier, no matter how weak or foolish they were. Why, even the Emperor's own harem could become a crack fighting squad.

'The Emperor, laughing at his general's folly, ordered the one hundred and eighty ladies of the court to attend Sun Tzu's military lessons. The general lined the women up in the palace courtyard and began to teach them how to respond to the drums of war. One drumbeat meant they should stand at attention, two drumbeats meant a turn to the right, three meant a turn to the left.

'No, no, no. This *is* relevant.

'When he had finished explaining, Sun Tzu gave the signal for the practice to begin. But as soon as they heard the drums, the courtesans started laughing.

'Sun Tzu, managing to stay calm, explained everything to them again. Once again the drums began. And once again, the harem fell about laughing.

'Still calm, Sun Tzu announced that the courtesans had broken the rules of war, and that he would execute the Emperor's favourite concubines as punishment. He cut off the two princesses' heads with his own sword.

'Now, when the drumbeats started, the concubines marched in silence.

'Yes I have finished.

'Now tell me: what do you think is the moral of the story?'

1

First Piece

To Break a Butterfly upon a Wheel

Wa-ma yinub al-mukhallis illa taqti' hidum-uh.
All the intervener gets is torn clothes.
(Arab proverb)

Chapter 1

Initial Conditions

> Run! Run! As fast as you can!
> You can't catch me, I'm the Gingerbread Man!
> (Traditional)

Ms Cohen remembered.

It began with a hissing sound. It grew louder and louder, penetrating the blackness, a stinging rush of noise pressing on her eyes and ears. Her lips and toes began to feel the cold.

Those were the first things she remembered.

She blinked eyelids still half-glued together with frost, and looked out through a curved wall, made of some translucent, rough-looking material, covered in condensation. The cold liquid sparkled, blue light refracting through it into icy rainbows. Her eyes locked onto one of the droplets as it fattened, swelled, finally ran down the glass in a chilling flash of light.

And when the muscles in her eyes had thawed, she focused through the droplets, through the wall, and saw the Ant.

Ms Cohen screamed a frozen scream.

Then the door began to open.

The man wore a uniform made of thick dun fabric, topped with a little peaked cap. He had a face you wouldn't remember, fringed with pale blond hair. He took her out of the capsule, away from cold storage, and into the medical laboratory. He checked her blood pressure, her reflexes, her liver function. And then he left her, surrounded by glistening green walls which looked like the inside of a huge pepper. He didn't say a word.

Ms Cohen huddled in a silver heat-reflective blanket, shivering with cold and fright. She wished she had a cup of cocoa. She wished she knew where she was and what was going to happen to her. Marshmallows were all she could think about, white smears of sweetness bobbing to the surface.

Ms Cohen remembered the *Cortese*.

The starliner had been cruising at eight times the speed of light, the universe bending around its hull. If you wanted to watch the relativistic effects, there was the observation deck, where tourists starbaked and argued armchair physics and saw something they wouldn't be able to describe to their grandchildren.

Ms Cohen spent her time reading, playing computer games, brushing up on her zero-gravity squash. One of her opponents teased her that she was missing the whole point of the trip. 'If you don't want to see hyperspace,' he said, 'you take a cheap fridge ship. Otherwise, why bother?'

But Ms Cohen was as afraid of suspended animation as she was of hyperspace. She had to take this trip, but she didn't have to enjoy it, and anyway, the corporation was paying. So she stayed below decks for two months, until boredom and peer pressure drove her up to the deck.

The *Cortese* was the last word in luxury; it had to be, for a trip that could take half a year. The floors were carpeted, the walls studded with video screens and hung with real paintings. Ms Cohen could imagine that she was in an office building, back on Terra Firma (and the firmer the better, ha ha). But not when the doors to the deck slid open with a hydraulic sigh of resignation.

She had hovered for a moment, eyes adjusting to the brighter lighting. Holographic video games flickered and danced in the air. Deckchairs were scattered about at strategically random locations. The smell of chlorine came from the Olympic-sized pool.

It was a beach, a five-kilometre, sandless beach. The crowd was a beach crowd, tipsy and aimless. Reassuringly normal. Unlike the view.

One entire wall and the roof of the observation deck were transparent. It looked as though the entire area was open to space. Ms Cohen stood gawping at hyperspace until she started to feel self-conscious. No-one else was bothering with the view. Blinking, she moved into the crowd.

It was like jumping off a cliff and discovering a mattress at the bottom. Hyperspace was just a black blur, not even any stars. Unless you looked at it for long enough. Then you started to notice . . . the black had colours in it, sort of . . . blurring and jumping and . . . doing the thing they were doing, whatever it was. Ms Cohen had no words to describe it, so she stopped looking at it.

She had a swim and joined a game of shuffle and drank cocktails with some of her acquaintances. She wished she had a friend with her, someone she could discuss her work with. She couldn't even keep up with the journals; communications travelled more slowly than the ship. There'd be a lot of catching up to do after planetfall.

She stood with a Martini in her hand, slowly scanning the crowd, looking for a single upturned face. Nobody cared. When someone worked out how to put non-Euclidean images onto postcards, the passengers wouldn't bother even to come up here any more. In five kilometres, she found one man looking at the sky.

Had he seen the other ship as it dived towards them, moving thirty-two times as fast as light?

The crowd on the deck had swelled as the word passed around the ship. There was a long streamer of light in hyperspace, like a smudged line on a blackboard. It was beautiful, a tinsel comet, following them through the night.

There was no announcement, no sirens. Just a lurch in the pit of her stomach as they dropped back into normal space. And a second lurch as she saw the huge ship looming above the deck, dwarfing the *Cortese*. It didn't look like a ship. Its shape was curvy and irregular. It looked alive.

She had been one of those sensible enough to get off the observation deck. When the other ship had crushed the viewing wall, a thousand people had found themselves riding a tornado out into space.

Life support failed an hour later. The last thing she remembered was hiding under the bed in her cabin, her unprotected

7

arms just beginning to freeze to the floor.

His name was Meijer. His uniform was crumpled and stained. It looked comfortable on him, as though he'd been wearing it for a hundred years.

'The Ants,' explained Meijer, 'are collectors. Some species go about the galaxy collecting minerals, or slaves, or exotic foods. The Ants collect minds. That's my theory. We're certain of this much: they siphon off knowledge and thought patterns and use them in the construction of new Ants.'

An Ant was watching them. It was four foot high at the shoulder, made of some reflective metal, silver with bronze highlights. Its eyeless head was festooned with antennae and jointed tools that pivoted and twitched, like a Swiss army knife brought to life. Why was it metal when the ship was flesh?

'The Ants claimed five hundred and six people from the wreckage of the *Cortese*,' Meijer was saying. 'They're in cold storage now. Thirty-nine have been processed, and processing is continuing.'

Ms Cohen's head spun with questions she was too scared to ask. Is that why you've thawed me out? Does anyone know you're doing this? Why are you helping them? Did you build the Ants? Or are you working for them? What happens to the people who are processed? Why me? Why is this happening to me?

When she didn't speak, Meijer went on. 'We need your help with subject 24,' he said. 'We know you're a neurologist. Now, if you help us to process 24, we won't kill you.'

Why is this happening to me? Why do you need my help? How do I know you'll keep your word?

'How does the process work?' asked Ms Cohen.

The space-craft was full of Ants, scurrying across the textured floors, their metallic bodies scattering the dull bioluminescence of the ship's veins. There were more men and women in uniforms like Meijer's. Had he been a prisoner, like her? Could she strike a deal to stay alive as long as him?
She got a uniform too, beige and long-sleeved like Meijer's,

8

but without the stains and the peaked cap. Now she followed him through the corridors, past rough walls built out of enormous oblong cells covered in a tough organic sheath.

The stuff was cool to the touch – plant, not animal. Even the computer screens were alive, irregularly shaped membranes lighting up from inside with alien symbols.

While Meijer stopped to chat with another hired hand, she watched a butterfly the size of her fist crawling up the wall. When she looked closer, she saw the metallic sheen of its wings, the tiny tools built into its face. It was repairing a piece of damaged organic circuitry, uncurling a proboscis into a slit in the stuff of the wall.

The design of the ship was economical, a doughnut sliced into sections – one computer room, one processing area, cold storage, a shuttle bay, the kitchen and storage areas. Everything was interconnected by short, low, narrow corridors. It was an Ant farm, not designed for human occupants.

'Where do the Ants come from?'

'We don't know,' said Meijer. 'They've been doing this for a long time. There are thousands of alien minds in the computer.'

'They're still alive in there?'

Meijer shrugged. 'The process draws out memories, information, thought patterns. But in pieces. We don't keep the whole mind.'

'What do you do with, what do you do with the subjects when you've finished?'

'We don't keep the whole mind,' said Meijer again.

They had come to one of the pale-coloured sliding panels that indicated a door. It looked like a two-inch slab of skin stretched across the doorway, a complex growth of controls embedded in the stuff. There were two more hired hands outside the room, one smoking a cigarette with the *Cortese* logo, the other sitting on the floor with her back to the wall, watching the door. Ms Cohen saw that the clump of controls was – loose? Damaged? Meijer said, 'We've had to replace that three times.'

He touched the panel and the door slid open. There was a shimmering in the doorway, like air over bitumen. Meijer did

9

more things to the panel, and the force shield vanished.

She had expected something else. Something more, some hero resisting his captors with fierce defiance, not a pitiful lump under a silver blanket. Subject 24 huddled in the middle of the room, staring into nothing.

With a jolt, she recognized the man who had been staring into hyperspace.

Ms Cohen remembered.

He held a glass of sparkling mineral water in his hand. He lay in a deckchair with a blanket draped over his legs as he stared up at the see-through wall. From time to time he took a sip of the drink, keeping his eyes on the view.

She watched him for a while. A woman came up to him, and they exchanged a few words. For a moment, the woman swivelled her neck skywards to follow his gaze. She was wearing a red jacket that Ms Cohen had seen in the ship's stores that morning, window-shopping to pass the time.

And here he was in this featureless, egg-shaped room. No – there was a sort of bunk, a recess in the organic stuff of the wall, and some sort of facilities in the corner . . . but he was sitting in the middle of the cell, staring, not focussed on anything. Focussed on nothing. He didn't even know they were there.

Meijer passed her a handscan. The little machine had come from the *Cortese*, but the Ants had done things to it. Metal and plastic had been fused with whorls of cellulose. There were three abortive legs growing from one side of the monitor screen, dry to the touch.

Number 24 had been scanned when he was defrosted. She had calibrated the handscan according to that initial data. Now she knelt down, perhaps ten feet from him, and activated the little machine.

'You do realise he isn't human,' she said.

Meijer grunted. 'The Ants have processed dozens of different species. But they've never come across one of him before.'

Ms Cohen let her eyes slide from the bleeping scanner to 24. He was wearing the same kind of uniform as the Ants' hired hands. There were laugh lines around his eyes and mouth; that face had done a lot of smiling. He was not smiling now.

'How many times have you tried to, to process him?'

'Seventeen.'

'What?'

'No, eighteen, including this morning. How is he?'

She stood up, faced Meijer. 'He's exhausted, dehydrated and malnourished. His blood volume is down. There is a great deal of subcutaneous bruising, especially on his back. There's a greenstick fracture in his left humerus, as though someone tried to break it with their bare hands.'

Meijer met her stare until the accusation dribbled out of it. 'I meant, how's his head?'

'This thing doesn't tell me much about his psychological state. I'll need to do an electroencephalogram, some other tests. And I'll need to know everything.'

'Everything?'

'About the process. About the computer. Plus,' she said, and her voice quavered as she heard the way she was talking, 'plus I want him back to full health before we do anything else to him.'

Meijer went on staring at her. She took back the scanner, her eyes groping at the data on its screen. At last he said, 'How long's that going to take?'

'I don't know, he isn't human. But he's in poor shape. Unless you want to kill him outright, he needs some time to recover. And proper medical treatment.'

One of the guards outside swore, kicked the wall, boot crunching against the cuticle. Meijer sighed. 'You know what that's going to mean? We'll have to install force shields in the lab. And I'll have to roster people in there, around the clock. We're busy enough as it is, with this new crowd.'

'Force shields and guards?' said Ms Cohen. She gestured with the scanner at the tired little lump on the floor. 'For this?'

'You don't understand, lady,' said Meijer. 'That's the Gingerbread Man.'

'How long was I in cold storage?'

11

'About a month, lady. Why?'

Meijer was checking the preparations in the medical lab. They had ripped chunks of tissue out of the walls and grafted in slimy cubes of living machinery. The pulsing cells and veins in the wall and the mown lawn smell turned Ms Cohen's stomach. She sat on the edge of the medical bench, a great raised slab of plant tissue, and closed her eyes. 'What about him?'

'Maybe a week. We're doing two, three subjects a day. I guess you'll want to see that.'

'I guess I will,' said Ms Cohen faintly. 'How much do you really know about the Ants?'

'They don't say much. We just keep the wheels turning.'

'Where'd they come from? Who built them? Why are they doing this?'

Meijer moved his head from side to side, as though shaking her questions out of his ears. 'My guess is that the Ants used to be people, and they put themselves in robot bodies.' He shrugged. 'Why does it matter how long he was frozen?'

'The cold might have damaged his neuroreceptors.' Or eighteen doses of your process might have left him with no mind to read. 'Have you ever encountered this, this problem before?'

'No-one's given us this much trouble before. Sometimes it takes a couple, maybe three zaps to sort them out. Sometimes we use drugs or electric shocks, things like that.'

'Or a little physical therapy.'

'Yeah,' said Meijer, grinning. His face was unshaven, an ugly colour in the pale green light.

'I don't want you to use that kind of therapy on this subject,' she said, surprised by how firm she sounded. 'I want him in the best possible shape – as close to his condition on defrosting as we can manage.'

Meijer shrugged.

'You don't have to manhandle him.'

'Lady, you still don't understand. Do you think we give every subject the VIP treatment? Guards and shields and stuff?' He had finished his check of the lab's security. Now he sat down on the medical bench, displacing her. 'Subject 24 has been thawed for nineteen days now. In that time, he's escaped twenty-six times.'

Ms Cohen blinked at him.

'Knocked out guards. Busted doors. Shut off force shields. Opened locks. Do you know, he got out of his capsule in cold storage? We couldn't believe it, he should have been frozen stiff. No matter where we put him, he gets out somehow. It's like he's magic.'

'And you've never had that kind of trouble either?'

'No. So I can't guarantee that the hired hands will be wearing their kid gloves. He nearly killed two of us, one time.'

'Really?'

'Me and Groenewegen. We found him in the shuttle bay with somebody's gun. He had the drop on us, would've been easy for him to shoot us and take one of the shuttles. Some of them'll do FTL, wouldn't have taken him long to find help.'

'But he didn't.'

Meijer shrugged again. 'I guess he just didn't know how to use the gun.'

They brought Number 24 to the lab strapped to a metal trolley. It must have been salvaged from a space-craft, perhaps the *Cortese*. Three armed guards followed Meijer as he pushed the trolley along. 24 took no notice of it. The ceiling slid past his eyes, ignored.

'Right,' said Ms Cohen, trying to sound professional. 'Put him on the medical bench.'

There were metal clasps crudely grafted into the living stuff of the bench. The three guards lifted 24 onto the slab and fastened the clasps around his wrists and ankles. It looked like a dissection set-up. Ms Cohen wondered when she would throw up.

'I can't see him getting up and walking away,' she said to Meijer.

The hired hand just smiled sourly, wiping his forehead with his cap. He sat down on the floor, cradling his gun in his lap. 'Groenewegen, Caldwell, you're on first shift. And nobody better fall asleep this time.'

'I give him four hours,' Groenewegen said.

'Five'll get you eight he's gone in two,' said Caldwell, closing the door. There was a low hum as the force shield kicked in.

Ms Cohen unclipped her patient's left arm from the bench. Meijer was watching like a hawk, but the arm was limp, the hand cool and soft, relaxed. When she probed the fracture with her fingers, he didn't wince or flinch.

Dissociation? Catatonia? Deep shock? Police psychic probes had tended to have that kind of effect, which is why they had been made illegal. Or it might be something about his diet, or some medicine he ought to be taking. Whatever it was, he was completely unaware of what was happening. And perhaps he was better off that way.

But the escapes – now, that was atypical. Some part of his mind was still working, watching for opportunities, solving problems. It might be some variation on obsessive/compulsive disorder. She found herself writing an abstract for the paper.

She pushed a drip into his arm, hoping that her educated guesses about his blood chemistry were accurate. Meijer said he'd hardly eaten since they'd brought him here – he wouldn't eat when they were watching, even if it was through hidden cameras, and he wouldn't eat when the food was drugged. He knew, somehow.

She used one of the Ants' machines to heal the fracture. Another device adapted from Earth technology, but simplified and improved. How many human beings . . ? They were obviously putting their stolen knowledge to good use.

A soft hum came from the device as she slowly ran it down his arm, watching the fracture heal, the screen showing the structures hidden under the skin. She wished the machine would show her his mind as clearly.

She gently laid his arm down on the bench, and picked up the handscan.

He sat up, twisting, his other arm still clamped to the bench, and his hand came up and his eyes met hers and he was so angry and he caught the skin of her forehead between forefinger and thumb and he was so *angry* and a cold fizzing erupted through her face and ate into her brain and then

* * *

and then Meijer was shouting in her ear, shaking her. 'Come on!' he shrieked. 'There's a hunt on. You need to see this.'

He pulled her to her feet. Her legs were asleep. She looked around dazedly, leaning on the bench. The drip hung from its stand, still spattering nutrients into a puddle on the floor.

The right clamp had been wrenched free from the bench. There was blood on it, and a small swarm of butterflies, intent on repairing the wrecked component.

'Whudee do?' she said, her tongue thick inside her mouth.

'He cost Groenewegen fifty thousand,' said Meijer. 'Whenever he gets in a fix, he reaches into his bag of tricks.'

'How'd he get past you?' Ms Cohen asked, but Meijer was herding her out into the narrow corridor. An alarm was sounding, a ping-ping-ping that echoed angrily through her head.

'A heat sensor picked him up in the shuttlebay,' said Meijer, breaking into a run. Ms Cohen followed. The smooth vegetable walls flickered past, bizarrely, as though they were running through the middle of a stalk of celery. 'They've got him cornered in the kitchen.'

They burst into the shuttlebay. Ms Cohen slowed, trying to take in the huge area, the shuttles suspended in the air, large as houses, a hodge-podge of vessels stolen from hijacked space-craft. And then they were back in another corridor in the Ant farm.

The kitchen was a jumble of freezers and ovens, some of them probably from the *Cortese*. Four hired hands had pinned Number 24 to the ground. Two others stood by, their guns shivering in their hands as they kept them trained on the captive. 'You missed the fun, boss,' said Groenewegen.

'Give me that,' said Meijer. The hired hands stepped back. 24 was switched off again; he lay loosely on the floor, eyes as blank as the screen of a crashed computer. Meijer reached down and wrenched him to his feet, twisting the damaged arm behind his back. 'I don't believe it,' he hissed into the prisoner's ear. 'Fifteen crukking minutes! You'd better be more polite to the lady, or I might let Groenewegen take his fifty thousand out of you in chunks, yes?'

24 didn't look at him, didn't respond. Slowly, slowly, Meijer started to twist his arm. The hired hands watched, hungrily.

'I just set that,' said Ms Cohen.

And then she saw it. Just a flicker, just a tiny flicker running across the subject's face, as Meijer tried to break his arm. He wasn't catatonic. He wasn't in shock. He wasn't insane. He was completely aware of everything that happened to him.

'Oh, and that's another thing,' Meijer told her, smiling. 'He never screams.'

Ms Cohen threw up.

Chapter 2

Run! Run! As Fast As You Can!

En skulde aldrig ha' sine bedste buxer på, når en er ude
og strider for frihed og sandhed.
You should never have your best trousers on when you
go out to fight for freedom and truth.

(Henrik Ibsen, *En Folkefiende*, 1882)

'Meijer?
  'Will Groenewegen ever collect his fifty thousand?
  'Well, will he?
  'Meijer?
  'You're from New Haarlem, aren't you?
  'When was it you learned English?
  'How do you know what the Ants want you to do?'
  '*How* was it you learned English?
  'Meijer?'

The electroencephalogram didn't tell her anything either.
  'It looks like the workings of an active, aware brain.
Beyond that – '
  Meijer sighed, tucking his arms behind his head as he
watched from a corner of the lab. 'He is an alien,' Ms Cohen
protested.
  Meijer had been watching her for hours. Not Number 24.
Her. Her palms were alive with sweat as she manipulated the
EEG's controls. 'I'll need more time to calibrate the monitor.
And – and I need to see the process .'
  'On him?'
  'On somebody else, first,' Ms Cohen whispered. She put
her damp hand on her mouth. 'Somebody else.'

17

Number 24 was watching her from the bench. Actually, he was staring at the wall; she was just in his line of sight. She moved around the other side, away from his eyes, and started to pluck electrodes from his hair.

He was so *angry*. It was worse than Meijer's ugly, hungry stare. It was worse than the silent Ants. She felt it when she touched him, when she pressed electrodes to his throat or spine, when she felt his re-set arm. She wondered if Meijer felt it, if that was why he wanted to hurt him, to get him to scream so he'd be scared and not so *angry*.

'Did you keep any of his clothes, or personal effects?'

'No. Yes, maybe. I'll find out. If you reckon it's important.'

They put the boy into a chair, an abbreviated version of the medical bench, built from slabs of plant tissue, fat seams at each edge where the pieces had grown together. There were thick, bony clasps for his wrists and ankles. It had been designed with humans in mind.

They pulled his head forward and installed the Leech on the back of his neck.

They switched on a computer screen. A geometric shape rotated on the screen: the patterns of the boy's mind. It pulsed with strange, mathematical life.

'The Leech,' lectured Meijer, 'stimulates each part of the brain in turn. It records the response, converts it, and passes it on to the computer. That way it gets not only memories, but also skills, thought patterns, sensory impressions. When it's finished, it severs the brainstem. Quick and painless. But of course, with Number 24, the process never reaches that stage.'

He activated the Leech. There was a gentle humming.

The boy went into spasms, biting his lips and tongue. He spat blood, his limbs smacking against the skin of the chair.

The shape on the screen flared with light, each part distorting and changing colour as his mind was ripped out a piece at a time.

It went on for fifteen minutes. The boy gave a final spasm and died. Blood and clear fluid trickled from his nose and ears. His head hung down on his chest. The hired hands dragged what was left of him out of the chair and wheeled it away.

18

Ms Cohen exited the processing room and returned to the laboratory.

Meijer found her there, pacing in tiny circles, fingernails plucking at her face. He put his arm around her, and she jerked away, stumbling backwards across the rough floor. 'You've done *that* to him? *Eighteen times?*' she screamed, pointing at the figure on the bench.

'It doesn't last so long with him,' said Meijer. 'The thing barely gets started when he – '

'Oh Jesus!' said Ms Cohen. 'Oh Jesus, I don't think I can do this, I don't think I can do this.'

Meijer's hand came down on her shoulder and gripped, hard. 'You better listen, lady. Either you get him in the chair and you get it to work, or you end up in there yourself.' He shook her, not gently. 'Understand? Do you understand?'

'I'm going to throw up again.'

'Understand. It's him in there or it's you. You're just surviving, right, you're just surviving!'

'Oh Jesus. Don't do it to me. Please. Please. Oh Jesus, please.'

Meijer shoved her towards the medical bench. 'You'll find a way.'

They put Number 24 in the chair and put the Leech on him. Ms Cohen turned it over in her hands first. It was a curved bit of vegetable matter with a few irregular bumps, innocuous, like a courgette. But there was circuitry etched on the inner side, and it felt warm. Alive.

It fit snugly along the base of 24's neck. Ms Cohen thought she saw it move, settling into place.

The image of his mind on the screen was a seething fractal, twisting and curling in unexpected ways. An alien brain, an alien mind.

Meijer watched her watching the screen. 'The Leech can handle just about any form of intelligence. It can scan his mind, it just can't process it.'

Number 24 was staring into nothing again, his hands hanging limply over the arms of the chair. But she could see the tiny beads of sweat on his forehead, and she wondered if

19

Meijer had guessed.

'I'll be sad to see this one go,' said the hired hand, grabbing a handful of the subject's hair. 'He's really brightened life up on this tub. Isn't that right, Gingerbread?' He gripped the man's throat in his other hand, pressing his thumb into the windpipe until the sound of his breathing changed. 'Been a while since we had a challenge.'

'Meijer,' said Ms Cohen. 'Please let go of him.'

The hired hand straightened, looking at her with brute surprise. 'What?'

'I told you. We need him in the best possible physical condition.' Her voice started to tremble. Meijer was staring at her again. 'If you keep – if you keep applying your physical therapy . . .'

'Look, it's been a long voyage. And it's only getting longer.' 24 was wheezing, trying not to struggle. 'We need a bit of entertainment. The escapes are a nuisance, but they're fun, they're something to do. Back on New Haarlem I used to go motorbike racing. You know what a motorbike is?'

Ms Cohen had no idea what he was talking about. Meijer's stolen English took on a wistful note. 'I used to be the best damn racer in the whole East quarter. It was great. You learnt how to look after the bike, how to fix it, as well as how to ride it. There was always something to do. But here . . .' His stare dropped away to his prisoner. He let go of the man's throat. 'We need something to do.'

24 gulped air. Ms Cohen said, 'I mean it, Meijer. Leave him alone.'

'Cruk off.'

'You wouldn't have woken me up!' blurted Ms Cohen. 'You wouldn't have made me do this if the Ants didn't want his mind. They'd have just dumped him out the air-lock like all the other useless bodies. They didn't kill me because they needed me. Meijer, they want to know what he knows. And I want you to stop brutalising him!'

Meijer stood there, staring at her. She bit down on her lip and stared right back at him, hoping he couldn't see her hands shaking and the blush that was spreading across her neck and ears.

'Ah, shit,' said the hired hand at last. 'Do you want to see this process or not?'

He slapped the controls beneath the computer screen. The Leech sizzled into life; Number 24 gasped, convulsed, went rigid in the chair. His eyes were wide, the pupils contracting to points. On the screen, part of the fractal flared as the Leech stimulated the first area of his brain.

His mouth was open. He did not scream.

And then he went completely limp, his head lolling onto his chest.

The Leech spluttered angrily and gave up. The screen went dark. Only the vital signs readout remained, a tiny bunch of squiggling lines.

'That's it?' said Ms Cohen.

'That's all,' said Meijer. 'We've never gotten further than that in nineteen tries.'

Ms Cohen took 24's face in her hands. His hair was wet with sweat. She levered one of his eyes open, carefully. It was a solid disc of blue, the pupil shrunk away to nothing. 'I'll need time to study the results,' she managed. 'Will the Ants give me access to the computer?'

Meijer puffed out his cheeks. 'Don't want much, do you?'

The Ants provided her with an interface based on the starliner's computer – a lap-top with a fleshy mess growing over the back and sides. It took her a couple of hours to get used to it, as information was passed back and forth between the electronic and the organic systems. Once or twice, the link cut out completely, and the lighting dimmed and returned. She wondered what that was supposed to mean.

She played back the EEG readings from the process. 24's mind had simply shut down 2.7 seconds after the Leech had begun primary stimulation. It had to be some sort of defence mechanism. Something built into the alien brain – to prevent him from being interrogated in just this way?

The alarm started its ear-splitting pinging. She didn't even startle this time. That had been a slow one; he must've been recovering from the process. She folded up the lap-top, put it on the bench she was using for a bed, and followed the alarms to their source.

21

Hired hands jogged past her, ignoring her, guns gripped in sweating palms. They came in all shapes and sizes, all ages – all human, which made her wonder. Who had they been before they became the Ants ' servants? Each of them must have been offered the same deal: help us, and stay out of the big chair.

That was why Groenewegen and Caldwell bet fifty thousand, fifty million. She'd heard Caldwell win the Eiffel Tower, the Empire State Building, the Mars Arch. They were going to spend the rest of their lives on this ship. Frightened of the chair, the way Meijer was, the way she was. Just surviving.

She found herself in a storage area with leathery white walls, like the inside of an apple core. Huge cabinets had been dragged into the room and left at untidy angles. A number was scrawled onto each drawer. She found the one labelled 24 and opened it.

A very small pile of things: a slingshot, some coins, a dog-eared paperback. Debris. The debris of a life that would never be completed. A jade brooch and a toffee wrapped in paper. A life that had been stolen by the Ants

Ms Cohen went through everything they'd taken from the subject's pockets and cried and cried and cried.

Meijer found her, much later, crumpled in a corner. 'We got him,' he said. 'Kitchen storage. Hiding in a fridge. A force field failed, let him out. We're still trying to work out why.'

She didn't reply. Meijer squatted down beside her. She held a drawer in her lap, labelled 39. It was empty.

'You didn't keep anything,' she said. 'There's nothing left.'

Meijer didn't say anything. He reached out and put a hand on her leg, just above her knee.

'Why do you bother keeping any of it at all?'

'The Ants like to go through the stuff, see if there's anything worth tinkering with. We decided to keep his things in case there was anything important there.'

'You better not have hurt him.' She shuddered. 'You better leave him alone. I want him to stay alive. I want to stay alive.'

She put the lid back on the box. Meijer took his hand away.

'Don't worry, lady,' he said. 'They're just having a quiet

22

word with him. They won't do too much. I promise.'

They killed him, of course.

Meijer woke her up to tell her. She was curled on the medical bench, arms wrapped around the modified lap-top.

'I'm sorry,' he said. 'It was an accident.'

She started crying again.

'I told them to be careful. They were careful. Caldwell says he just keeled over. I guess it finally got too much for him.'

'No.'

'He was dead as a Dalek, lady. I checked him myself.'

'No.' She sat up, and the lap-top fell, crunching on the floor. 'No. He's not dead.'

'Cruk it, lady!'

'Listen to me.' She grabbed his collar. 'This is just another escape. Don't you get it? The process. His mind turns off automatically when you try to scan it. Meijer, he can switch himself off.'

'Oh,' said the hired hand, 'shit!'

Ms Cohen walked forwards slowly, holding the handscan at arm's length, keeping it close to the wall, almost touching the cuticle.

They were right at the edge of the doughnut-shaped ship. The hull was two layers of the same stuff as bacterial spore walls, close to indestructible. They trapped a layer of air between them. It wasn't the most efficient insulation. She could feel the cold of space leaking through outer wall, air blanket, inner wall. A sandwich. Just big enough for a man to fit inside.

Meijer watched her, his arms folded tightly, his sweat-soaked cap gripped in one hand. 'Is it –'

'Shhh.' She put a finger to her lips.

There were places where meteorite strikes had dented the hull, even a dirty scar where living sealant had flowed in to plug a hole. Ms Cohen had heard about life-forms that lived in space, but she had never believed that life could be strong enough to handle the vacuum, the cold, the sudden impacts and changes in gravity. But then, life could take a lot.

23

A hired hand came running up, panting in the silence. 'She was right. A panel's gone from the air-lock – some maintenance alarms went off when it cycled.'

Meijer and Ms Cohen exchanged glances. Either 24 had been blown out into space, or –

The scanner shrieked. 'Here!' she snapped. A trio of hands leapt forward, carrying long squeeze-tubes like pointed squashes. You couldn't cut through that wall with tools – even a laser would take hours. The squeeze-tubes spat blobs of enzyme on to the wall, and the hired hands spread the sizzling stuff around with fat gloves.

They caught the chunk of wall as it came free, blood or sap oozing onto the floor. A gust of freezing air blew into the corridor. Ms Cohen dropped her handscan and caught 24 as he tumbled stiffly out from the dark space inside. His hair and eyebrows were full of frost.

'He's still with us,' she said, snatching up the scanner. 'Oh Jesus, his lungs are a mess.'

A single butterfly flickered down and landed on 24's shoulder, touching its antennae to his face. 'Where's that trolley?' snapped Ms Cohen.

None of the hired hands moved to help her. Their faces were pale and taut. Groenewegen was looking everywhere but at the subject.

No matter what they did, he always escaped. And this time they'd killed him, and he'd escaped that too.

Ms Cohen sat cross-legged on a bench, eating the nothing-flavoured stuff Meijer had brought her in a plastic bowl. She watched Number 24.

He was comatose, a tube coming out of his nose, draining away the fluids from his damaged lungs and throat. They had fastened the shackles around his wrists and ankles, covered him with a silver blanket as though to hide the fact that they'd bound a dying man.

It had been his most desperate escape. He had been nearly frozen to death. He had been exposed to hard vacuum for at least thirty seconds. When they'd dumped him in the air-lock with the other corpses, he'd pried loose a maintenance panel and climbed out through the wall. And the airlock had cycled before he'd been able to get the panel back into place.

Ms Cohen had borrowed the Leech in order to study it. It sat on a shelf. She was certain that it moved from time to time, that it was watching them, waiting, greedy but infinitely patient. Watching 24. Watching her.

The crystal shape on her monitor changed. His eyes came open, just a little.

He had been the one watching the sky on the starliner. He had been waiting for the Ants. And now here he was on board their ship, immune to their process, escaping and escaping over and over. He was not just a prisoner. There was something he wasn't telling them.

'You planned this, didn't you?' she said aloud.

'Think I . . . planned . . . ?' His voice was almost inaudible, a painful whisper. 'Didn't plan *this*.'

Ms Cohen's spoon clattered onto the floor.

Meijer chose that moment to enter the lab, stooping under the low door. 'How is he?'

Ms Cohen looked from her silent patient to Meijer. 'It's touch and go,' she said gently. 'Meijer, I need access to the computer again.'

'Now what?'

She got up and moved out of the lab. Meijer followed, looking puzzled. 'Normally,' she said, when they were in the corridor, 'I'd study the behaviour of a patient. The way they relate to people, the sorts of things they like to do. In this case, the only behaviour exhibited by the patient are the escapes. I want to study them.'

Meijer thought for a moment. 'There's a security report for each of them,' he said slowly.

'There is?'

'Something to do,' he said. Watching her.

'I can't fly a shuttle,' she said. 'Let me see the reports.'

'Tomorrow.'

She slept curled around the lap-top again. The Ants wouldn't care how much computer time she had. It didn't matter what she did, really – what could she possibly do?

25

She was woken by the sound of low voices. No, of one voice.

She opened her eyes, staying perfectly still.

'You promised,' he was saying, in a fragile whisper. 'Had a bargain . . . need . . . little bit longer. It's not that bad. Really . . . not that bad.'

She moved her head, just slightly. He was looking up at an imaginary someone standing over the bed. 'I've survived worse . . . Just one more week. One more day. Just one more day – just one – no, don't – oh –

The rotating fractal on the screen flared and vanished.

Ms Cohen leapt from her bench and snapped on the lights, fumbling frantically with her handscan.

Dead. He was dead.

How the hell was she supposed to do CPR on a man with two hearts?

She unclipped the cuffs around his left wrist and ankle. She grabbed 24 and rolled him onto his side, dislodging the tubes in his face. She snatched up the Leech. It twitched in her hand as she slapped it into the back of his neck and activated it.

He convulsed, shouted, started to breathe again. Ms Cohen wrenched the Leech off his skin, threw it onto the bench. He was shaking violently, spitting blood, but he was alive.

The guards shoved open the door. 'What the hell?' shouted Caldwell.

'It's alright,' said Ms Cohen, kneeling beside 24. 'It's alright. He'll be alright. I've saved him.'

Meijer was nodding sagely, as though he knew something about medicine. Ms Cohen said, 'His vital signs are stable now. Double cardiac arrest. Vicious. But I don't think it's done any damage that can't be healed.'

'I'm not worried,' said the hired hand. 'He can take anything.'

They were hunched over her lap-top, looking at a map of the ship. They'd pieced together the data from the sensors and from the hired hands' reports. Now she was slowly superimposing the routes of 24's escape attempts, looking for what they had in common.

'He's tried everything you can think of,' Meijer was reminiscing. 'He impersonated one of us once – only worked that one time, there aren't that many of us. He's jemmied four different kinds of door-locks, including a padlock. He's fought a few of us – he used some kind of nerve pinch on Groenewegen once. That's why we carry him around on the trolley. Once, he deactivated a force shield with a *spoon*. And there were other things.'

'Like what he did to me.'

'Stuff from his bag of tricks. You never know what he's going to come up with next.' Meijer wiped his forehead with his hat. 'It's so dumb. He can't get away. He's been in that shuttle bay half a dozen times, and he's never managed to get away. We just keep catching him and processing him, over and over. Twenty crukking times. I mean, is he enjoying it? Why doesn't he just give up and get it over with?'

Twenty times, without ever getting the result they wanted. Completely single-minded, doing the same thing over and over –

'I'll need more time to, to study this,' said Ms Cohen. It came out as a gasp. Because she knew. She knew.

Was her breathing really as loud as it sounded? She shifted, stretching cramped muscles, trying to not make any noise.

It was what the escapes did *not* have in common that made her realise. Fourteen times, he had been caught in the kitchen or one of its storage areas. Ten times, in starboard engineering. Eight times in the corridors between the two. Three times in the shuttle bay.

Almost every escape had taken him through the shuttle bay, slung beneath the hub of the ship. Not once had he tried to take one of the shuttles.

He must know how to pilot a shuttle. Same as he knew how to use the guns – he just wasn't going to murder anybody. He wasn't trying to get to the bay.

He was trying to come here. Here. Cold storage.

The cryogenic capsules were terrifying in the pale blue light – tall, fleshy sarcophagi, their inner surfaces coated with frost, the shapes behind the doors barely suggesting faces, limbs. She tried to imagine her own face behind that glass, her own heart beating once per minute as she slept the sleep of the dead.

Cold storage was a circle at the very centre of the ship's doughnut shape. The capsules curved away in a long wall, circling around a great shaft that stabbed through the middle of the Ants' vessel. In the centre of that shaft was a hideous, actinic light, hanging in the air, a long line of energy threaded through the centre of the craft. Whatever the hell it was, it made the Ants' ship go.

Somewhere, a door slid open.

She checked her lap-top again. The sensors in the immediate area were still shut off. Good. She wondered how much longer it would be before the Ants noticed.

Number 24 came into her line of sight. He was moving slowly, one hand pressed against his chest, his other hand holding some small piece of machinery. At every tube he paused. She could hear his ragged breathing in the frozen silence, see the cold plumes of steam coming out of his mouth.

At last he found the tube he wanted. He knelt down at its base, activated the control panel there. A great puff of steam erupted from the capsule. Machines hissed into life as he manipulated the controls.

He lay down on the floor in front of the tube, waiting. A greenish light was beginning to glow inside the capsule, and fluid was dripping behind the glass. As the light grew brighter, Ms Cohen recognised the woman who had been with him on the starliner.

As she had known she would.

She stayed in the green shadows, the cold, waxy cuticle of the wall pressing against her back. Stayed silent and invisible.

'What are you . . . going to do?' he asked.

The tiny rasp of his voice fluttered through cold storage. Ms Cohen's fingers were frozen to the gun as she stepped out, keeping the weapon between them.

'Ship knows what you're doing,' he wheezed. 'Interested to see what will happen.'

'I don't understand.' Her fingers hurt.

Still think the Ants . . . in charge?' He didn't move as he spoke; his voice just drifted into the cold air. It was like listening to a corpse. 'Meijer . . . far from the truth. They're just Ship's hands.'

'Who's, who's the pilot?'

'No-one but Ship. Perhaps, once . . . now it's just following orders.'

The capsule had completed its thawing cycle. Now the translucent lid began to hiss open, condensation puffing into the air. The woman inside made an incoherent sound and fell out.

Meijer caught her.

He looked at the woman for a moment, holding her in the crook of one arm. She lolled, her teeth chattering in her head. He dropped her onto the floor.

'The whole time,' he said, turning to Ms Cohen. 'The whole time he was trying to get in here. Because of her.'

Ms Cohen was shaking, keeping her gun trained on 24. Half a dozen hired hands were following Meijer, flashlights pushing through the mist of condensation. The beams intersected at the crumpled little figure on the floor.

Meijer reached down and grabbed him. 24 made no attempt to resist as he was dragged to his feet, the same arm pulled behind his back again. The hired hand looped his other arm around 24's throat in a mugger's grip. The machine he had been carrying rolled away on the floor, pulsing with some internal light.

Meijer twisted his arm behind his back, wrenched until he felt muscle start to tear. 'Scream, curse you!' he spat. 'Why don't you scream?'

'Doctor?' said the woman on the floor. She squinted into the flashlights, limbs twitching dully. 'What? What?'

'So that's what the game's been about,' Meijer hissed into his captive's ear. 'Her. What was the point? What was the crukking point?'

He tightened his grip. 'We processed a four-year-old this morning. Subject 51. We'll make her number fifty-two.'

With a movement that was almost graceful, Meijer twisted the arm he was holding one more notch. There was a *crack*.

The Doctor screamed.

The sound was cut off by an explosion. Ms Cohen forced her hands away from her ears, snapped her head around in time to see the glass cylinder smashing outwards. The light inside roared and spluttered.

Something had jumped out of the light and through the glass wall, spraying fragments in all directions. It was shaped like a human, but it glowed violently, covered in seething light, like some sort of toxic angel.

The hired hands shrieked and ran.

The light around the figure was changing as it came towards them, shading down through blue and green to a hot yellow. Ms Cohen thought she could make out features behind the light – eyes, hands. It was a woman, it was just a woman, not even armed. She had long blonde hair and a satchel slung across her shoulders.

Meijer shot at the figure, a finger of energy stabbing out of his gun to connect with the cocoon of light. The field flared and exploded upwards and outwards. The glare caught Meijer in the face and chest. His uniform and hair burst into flames. There was a sudden movement on his face — his eyes, melting –

Ms Cohen ran from cold storage, screaming and screaming like a banshee.

And now, Ms Cohen had finished remembering.

She gave one last spasm and hung loose in the chair. The Leech settled itself into a more comfortable position on her neck, waited a few seconds, and bit her spinal cord in two.

And Ship continued on.

Chapter 3

Interesting Times

> *Egestatem*
> *Potestatem*
> *Dissolvit ut glaciem*
> [Fate] dissolves poverty and power like ice.
> (Carmina Burana, thirteenth century)

Near Akhetaten 1366 BCE

After a while she realized that she was lying on something warm. Some half-memory rose in her, and she shuddered upwards, making sure it was not a corpse, or 'worse, the half-living chutney of human flesh that high-tech weapons spread over the ground.

But it was only sand. She breathed out, hard, hitting the desert warmth with the length of her body. She was trembling all over, the flesh of her arms and legs frozen through and through, drenched in cold. Her fluttering fingers made painful movements in the sand.

She rolled over, gasping night air, clean and dusty, almost as cold as she was. She pressed her back into the sand, willing her frozen skin to suck out the stored heat of the sun.

It was black, jet black, but the sky was an explosion of stars. They spun and jittered as her eyes tried to focus on individual suns, tracing the thick line of the galaxy's hub, a blast of smoky light across the sky.

Relax. Relax and wait for the disorientation to wear off, for her brain to thaw the way her body was thawing.

After some time she realized that the sky was changing colour. She rolled her head loosely, in poorly controlled arcs.

There was nothing to either side of her, no shadows, nothing but sand.

When the sun came up, she was going to die.

She tried to push herself up onto her knees, but only succeeded in rolling onto her side. She panted, feeling the chill deep in her belly, the stabbing of cramping muscle. Kitten, she thought, helpless as a small kitten.

She'd been in dozens of deserts, had stayed alive in a desert with blue sand and a green sun, drinking ground water and eating lizards and beetles cooked by the noon. But she'd had a couple of advantages then. Like being able to move. And think.

Maybe she'd be lucky. The sun might bring her body temperature up to normal before it could bake her. She might be able to crawl somewhere, find water, find people. If there was water. If there were people. She might be anywhere, from the deepest chasms of the mind to the furthest alien world. A dozen suns might come up over the horizon and roast her like the Sunday lamb, the fat sizzling under her skin.

She arched her back against the sand, her limbs spasming, not even knowing she was shouting into the dawn.

'Why doesn't anyone come to rescue me?'

The first time they went to the cafe, the air was humid and cloyingly hot, but a breeze had come in through the windows, cooling the room with the scent of garbage, human sweat, rain on asphalt.

'Take careful notice of the details,' the Doctor had said. The walls were white plaster, decorated with antique dirty postcards in tiny frames. The place was full of students, eating cheap pasta and arguing semiotics.

The Time Lord charted a path through the thin crowd to a table in a corner, stepping around the pot-plants in their brass holders. Ace eyed them as she passed. There was something alien about the leaves, about the way the stems seemed to twist, just perceptibly, to follow her.

Their table was set up with three chairs, linen napkins, drinks already poured (mineral water, tequila, vodka and Coke). Ace sat down and immediately drained her glass; she

32

hadn't seen anything interesting yet. Benny traced the graffiti on the tabletop with the tip of her finger, initials scratched into the unfinished wood. Whose?

'Where are we?' asked Ace.

'Glebe,' said the Doctor, watching the bubbles rise in his mineral water. 'Sydney, Earth, 1995.'

'Nice place.' said Benny. 'It doesn't look like anything special.'

The Doctor shrugged. 'The eggplant parmigiana,' he said, 'is outstanding.'

'Yeah, but . . .'

The Doctor put a finger to his lips.

The second time they visited the cafe, the same table had been set up for them, the same three drinks. Condensation ran down the outsides of the glasses.

Only this time, they were in Bellatrix City, and it was the Twenty-fifth Century.

'Home,' said Benny, smiling. She spread salt along the joint of her thumb and licked, sipped, sucked.

'Alas,' said the Doctor, 'There's a stranger in the house.'

Ace scanned the room slowly. The crowd was not much different – more diverse, and the fashions were different, of course. There were aliens mixed in with the humans, and the humans themselves came in thirty-one flavours. But they were still eating cheap pasta, and still arguing post-post-modern *auteur* theory. The same plastered walls, the same framed postcards.

'Yes?'

'Ships have been disappearing from one of the less-used interstellar traffic lanes. Passenger ships.'

'Any black holes lying around where they shouldn't be?' asked Ace.

The Doctor shook his head. 'In one case out of three, the ships are found some time after their disappearance – minus the passengers and crew.'

'Ransom?'

'Slavers?'

'No demands. Slavery isn't economically viable any more,

33

not really. Robots are cheaper than people.'

'Is the cafe a re-creation, then?' Ace wanted to know. 'Or just a very well-preserved slice of Earth?'

The smile that normally flickered below Benny's surface was extinguished. She was thinking about her father. 'How do we stop it?'

'Ah,' said the Doctor. 'Well.' He slapped down a handful of change on the table, a random mixture of denominations and centuries. 'Come on.'

The sixth time they visited the cafe, it was on Argolis. The wood-framed windows had been replaced by hard plastic sheets, giving a good view of the burning sky. Now the clientele were tourists, every conceivable body shape crammed around tables and into corners. But the tables were the same, down to the initials carved into the wood.

'I've got a simple idea,' said the Doctor. 'We allow ourselves to be taken along for the ride.'

'Get ourselves arrested,' said Ace.

'And let the villains tie us up and tell us their plans,' said Benny, six tequilas deep and still sober as a judge. 'Someone would have to stay behind. Stay free, in case of emergency.' She laughed. 'I'll come and rescue you when you've messed it all up.'

In Ace's memory, the Doctor had developed a livid scar under his left eye, a great purple blotch with a red line running crossways through it where someone had hit him. She felt a hot lump of badness in her stomach as he watched her drink, as though she were responsible for the damage.

'But we don't know who's doing the capturing,' she said. He shook his head again. 'Doesn't matter,' said Ace, as the memory echoed away into nothing, ''cos we're experts at escaping.'

They'd paid their money, hadn't they? Now they had to take their chances. That, as the saying went, was the way the cookie crumbled.

She was sitting up now, leaning forward, trying to support the upper part of her body against her knees. She was wearing

34

some sort of overalls, made of rough synthetic cloth, a lifeless beige that blended into the dawn light. Who had stripped off her combat suit, taken away her tools and weapons? What else had they done to her when she was naked and helpless? Why had they frozen her?

She leaned her head against her knees, taking deep breaths. Her body was full of pins and needles. Did she only feel like she was shaking?

The sun was a searing thumbnail of yellow pushed up above the horizon, lighting the emptiness: honey-yellow cliffs, scattered rocks like a Martian landscape, shadows sharp-edged and glowing black. She didn't even have her shades. Would the force shield generator clamped to her wrist provide any protection against the sun? She'd save the batteries, wait until the heat became intolerable.

She needed to get up and start walking, but she could barely stay upright. She needed to sleep for a hundred years, but if she lost the day she'd never wake up. And even if she did get up, where would she walk to, her bare feet slipping in the burning sand?

Don't care. Her heart was still frozen, her stomach was a lump of ice. The rough defrosting should really have finished her off anyway. By now the three of them must have used up most of the spare luck in the universe. But after everything they'd been through, dying here would be slightly – embarrassing.

She hoped the Doctor and Benny had landed somewhere soft.

The Doctor had had a sort of map with him. It was a flat plate of some white substance, ceramic or plastic, perfectly smooth. He'd passed his hands over it, and at the gesture a hologram had leapt out and up into three dimensions. A chart of their portion of the galaxy.

Benny's remembered hair had grown out, become blonde, dark roots peeking through the straw-coloured strands. She stared through the hologram cube, sucking on a slice of lime.

'How many dimensions?' Ace asked.

'Just four,' said the Doctor, his eyes sharp and bright over the dark scar on his face. 'It charts the cafe's appearance through the continuum. A single space-time event, repeated over and over at different points and epochs.'

'Why?' said Benny.

'There are a handful of occurrences which could cause such an effect. All of them have potential ramifications for the entire cosmos. Look.' He made another magician's pass over the hologram, and a line jumped from point to point inside the cube, electric blue.

Ace squinted at the diagram, following it. Each four-dimensional point represented an occurrence of the cafe. To people living in three dimensions, moving through time in a linear fashion, the cafe's repetition would be invisible. But not to time-travellers –

'The disappearances don't form a pattern unless you're looking at them in four dimensions,' said the Doctor, echoing her thoughts. 'Many in the one location, but spread out at great intervals of time. Or many disappearances at once, but scattered through the galaxy.'

'Something punched through space and time,' she said. 'It burrowed through it.'

'Leaving a trail of cafes behind it,' said Bernice.

'Like breadcrumbs in the forest,' said Ace. She traced the line with her finger.

'Yes,' said the Doctor, and there was a touch of indignation in his voice. It was like coming back to the car-park to discover someone had left a dent in your fender. How dare someone muck about with his universe? 'Now,' he said, 'here's a plot of the spaceship disappearances.'

The electric blue line vanished, and was replaced by a livid green line. Not the same track as the cafe, but dead straight through four dimensions. Deliberate. Artificial.

Ace met the Doctor's eyes over the cube. There was a brilliant spot of blood running down out of his nose, tracing its own straight line across his skin. He didn't seem to notice.

'There's a fracture in the universe,' said Ace.

'Someone's using that, that fracture, like a secret passage-way,' said Benny, 'stealing people.'

'Well!' said Ace, pushing her drink away. 'Let's go get stolen.'

* * *

36

She had never smelt water before. Water had no smell or taste. Drinking the pure stuff, the recycled water given to soldiers in space, was like drinking metal polish; on the better ships ions were added to convince your tastebuds there was no flavour.

But she smelt water now, nearby, making her stomach rumble and cramp.

In the end, unable to stand, she rolled. Sand got in her hair and inside the beige coveralls as she rolled slowly over the stony ground, keeping her elbows close to her body. It felt ridiculous, but it was movement.

She came to the edge of a drop. The world continued to spin even when she had stopped, her guts spasming. She bit her teeth together and tried to see down the hill.

Down the slope was a patch of even ground. It was rocky, white and red, tiny evil-looking plants elbowing their way through cracks in the dry soil. There was a pool of water in the middle, creamy mud built up around the edges. She let herself half-slide, half-roll down the hill until she fell with a splat into the mud.

There was more mud than water. She didn't care. She let her coveralls get soaked in the ooze around the pool while she sucked at it, splashed filthy water onto her face and hair, mud smearing her fingers.

When she looked up, there was a lioness watching her from across the pool.

'Oh shit,' said Ace.

Her head whirled with useless advice. Run away. Don't move. Scream for help. They can smell fear. Instead she found herself staring at the animal across the water, taking in the smooth rolling of muscle under her tawny skin, the elegant shape of her head, those huge eyes regarding the muddy human being across the small diameter of the pool.

Ace could smell the lioness's breath, the hot musk of her skin. She tried to get up, fell over, splattering a wave of water and mud on to the animal's face. Huge eyes were raised to regard her, lazily, as she struggled like an overturned cockroach. The lioness was in no hurry.

Get up and run away, get moving, get up, get up!

37

Ace's hands closed around a stone, but her fingers were shaking with exhaustion and she couldn't hold onto it. Quick death, then, with the lioness' great paws slapping her into the sand and those massive jaws breaking her neck.

Then a tremendous cry split the valley, and the next thing she knew the predator was under attack.

The animal's roar went right through Ace's head. The bird was huge, the size of a human child – some kind of eagle or hawk, diving repeatedly at the lioness. The beast's paws kicked great puffs of dust into the air as she dodged and wheeled, trying to get at the bird. Ace just watched, panting.

She ought to be afraid. But she couldn't feel anything. It was as though she were still frozen, frozen to the core.

When the chariot appeared, she didn't even feel surprised.

It skidded to a halt in the dust, barely twenty feet from the water hole. It was just large enough for the man standing in it, who was struggling to restrain the pair of horses which stamped and tossed, panicked by the scent of the lioness. Ace shouted for help, wordlessly, knowing he wouldn't understand anything she tried to say.

He was carrying a bow. In a fluid movement, he plucked an arrow out of his quiver and shot the lioness dead.

The big cat screamed and fell over in the dirt, her weight making a tremendous sound. The harrier matched her raw cry and perched on the corpse, bounced up and down by its final convulsions.

Ace stared. The arrow had pushed in behind the lioness' ear, penetrating her brain. It was one of the neatest bits of shooting she'd seen in her life.

Rescued.

There were other chariots drawing up now. The man jumped down from his vehicle, strode over to her. His skin was the colour of copper, his head shaven, a stubble just showing on his chin. He wore a white kilt. He was much taller than the other Egyptians, and he had big brown eyes like a deer.

He looked down at her, probably wondering what the hell this pale-skinned woman was doing lying in the desert dirt miles from anywhere, trying to get herself eaten by the lions.

He held out a hand to her, and she took it. His palm was smooth and warm. 'I can't get up,' she said.

With a single movement, the same fluidity with which he'd shot the lioness, he bent down and picked her up.

By now his servants had come into the valley and were collecting the harrier, tying the lioness's paws together to slide a wooden pole under her feet. With a grunt three of them hefted the body, balancing the pole on their shoulders, the arrow still trailing down from the animal's neck.

Ace was looking at their clothes, their skin, half-remembering school videos and trips to the British Museum. Such a long time ago. 'I'm in Egypt, aren't I?' she asked.

'You've come a very long way to die in the desert,' he said, with the hint of a smile in his voice. She let her head roll against his broad chest, let him carry her like a bride in his powerful arms. Then she laughed, just once, a sharp bark from the bottom of her lungs.

'What's funny?' he said, carrying her to the chariot. His servants gazed at her curiously.

'Sorry,' she said, 'this is embarrassing.'

'Eh?'

'Take me home, Lawrence.'

She was sunburnt and frostbitten, and she was exhausted and hungry, and her hair and mouth were full of dirt. Her white knight had his women servants bathe and dress her. His personal physician paid her a visit, armed with a surgical papyrus and a box full of amulets.

She let it all happen, let them scrub her with some thick paste that lathered like thin soap, just stared at the ceiling as the physician checked her joints and eyes. There was nothing to do, there was nothing she could do.

'Well,' she said to the plaster roof when they had finished with her, 'here I am in Ancient Egypt.'

She laughed once more, another hoarse bark. She wanted to laugh until the tears rolled down her face, while the women servants peered at her from behind the curtains. Rescued in the desert by some macho nobleman, who swept her into his arms and carried her off in his chariot.

She had nothing. Nothing at all. Even the clothes she had been dressed in had been taken away, the woman servants intrigued by the curious, heavy fabric. She did not have her combat suit nor any of the things from her room in the TARDIS. She didn't have so much as a tube of toothpaste.

She wished she'd paid more attention on those trips to the Museum. She had no way of working out what year it was. No-one would know where or when she was. There wasn't going to be any rescue from this trap.

But she was alive, and, once she'd had some sleep, she would be in reasonable shape. And somehow, she could understand Ancient Egyptian. Funny. She frowned slightly, her eyelids already starting to flicker as her thoughts started to tangle together. The wooden headrest was surprisingly comfortable. It felt good to be lying down.

They had both been lying on the floor. Ace could not feel the texture of the weird stuff it was made of, some rough material that looked like scales or bark. All she could feel was the deep cold spreading up from it.

The Doctor's eyes were closed. There was a great purple bruise on his left cheekbone, from the impact of a human fist, the skin split open with the force of the blow. He lay on his left side, facing her, his broken right arm curled against his chest. She was seeing him from a crazy angle, unable to move her head.

He opened his eyes and looked at her blankly. A drop of blood, brilliant red against his white skin, ran out of his nose. Some message pressed at her from behind his eyes, like an optical illusion she couldn't quite make out.

Often she had hoped he couldn't read her thoughts, but now she hoped that he could. *Just know that I'm here*, she thought, *just know that you're not alone*.

Hands strong with panic dragged Ace up from the floor. 'Come on, move! We have to get out of here!' Bernice was still glowing faintly as the energy from the space-time rift drained out of her force shield. She looked like an angel, a guardian angel come to save them.

Ace tried to grab at Benny, but her muscles wouldn't work.

A sharp, deep ache was working its way from her shoulders to her fingers. Benny grabbed her wrist and snapped a force shield generator onto it.

Then she bent and grabbed the Doctor by the scruff of his overalls and stumbled backwards, trying to drag both of them at once, cursing with frustration. Ace wanted to apologise for being so useless, but all that happened was her head lolled to one side and a rough moan came out of her mouth.

An incredible light was sleeting through the cold chamber from behind them. Ace recognised the signature of the space-time fracture. Benny dropped her and swore.

The light was coming out of the fracture, flickering, exploding in pops and sparks from a patch of air that hurt her brain to look at. There was broken glass or plastic all over the floor.

Benny was stooped over the Doctor, frantically trying to get a response out of him. Blood was trickling from his mouth and nose, sluggishly. His eyes had flickered shut.

Ace wished she could tell Benny that the Doctor was dead.

But the light from the rift was echoing inside her head, and she felt herself being erased, wiped away until there was nothing left at all.

Chapter 4

Rent

> More nonsense has been written about the Amarna
> period than any other in Egyptian history.
>
> (Margaret Murray)

Ill.

You don't have to do anything when you're ill.

Sometimes, when Ace was very young and she had a cold, her mother would stay home from work to look after her. Little Dorothy would play with Lego, crashing the spaceship set into the police station set. She had a jigsaw puzzle of a family at the beach, their little dog running away across the sand. There was a piece of the puzzle missing. No matter how many times she put the picture together, there was always a piece missing.

Mum came in when she was looking under the bed for the third time. 'Into bed with you,' she said. 'And stay there.'

Little Dorothy lay tucked between the laundry-smelling sheets, listening to the rain on the window, listening to the sounds from downstairs. In Ace's memories the men's voices blurred together, blending into the sound of the television, a muttered buzz as comforting as the warm clasp of her bed.

Tiny hands gripping the bedclothes. Listening to her own heartbeat. Convinced that any second the internal sound was going to stop.

Ace slept around the clock twice, her skin peeling off. When she awoke, there was coarse, bitter bread, with tiny bits of stone mixed into the dough, and pale-tasting onions. When she was able to sit up properly, they brought her roast duck and a bowl full of beer that tasted like sandpaper.

She lay in bed, eyes tracing the wall paintings, and listened to the sounds of the household. The servants wandered in and out of her room without taking much notice of her. They were short, shorter than her in most cases. Her rescuer's nutrition was better, evidently.

In other rooms people spoke in liquid syllables, the words rolling in their throats. Outside, there was the honking of geese, shouts and laughter, the incessant grinding of stone on stone as flour was made from grain.

One night there was a party. Ace lay in the bed, listening, the wicker pressing into her back through the linen. The music was unfamiliar, but the sound of people getting drunk wasn't. Half-asleep, she half-expected to hear the sound of her mother's voice rising into an angry whine, and the muffled thumps that might be furniture or fists.

After a week, she stumbled out of the room, wandered into the walled garden, and fell into the pool.

When she surfaced, plucking lily pads out of her sodden hair, the Lord Sedjet was watching her.

He didn't seem to understand her urgent need for clothing. After all, the servant girls who brought her a shift and tunic went about naked all the time.

He was seated by the pool, tickling a pet monkey under its chin, politely waiting. She tugged on the foreign garments, embarrassed by her embarrassment as Sedjet watched her. It wasn't an unfriendly gaze, not like the rake of restaurant eyes over her body.

The servants brought her a stool and she sat on it awkwardly.

Silence for a bit. Sedjet's monkey jumped into his lap, yawned pinkly and went to sleep.

'Is it always this hot?' she said at last.

'It is much colder where you come from,' he replied, formally. The physician who had visited her twice had spoken like that, when he'd said anything, in between feeling her elbows and peering at the whites of her eyes.

'You want to know all about me,' she said. 'My name is Ace. I come from a distant land called Perivale. My friends and I travel from place to place. We were attacked in the

43

desert, and the bandits left me for dead.'

Sedjet took this in, nodding to himself. She'd been rehearsing it, taking it from the servants' gossip. Desert brigands were apparently a serious problem. 'I am sorry,' he said, 'but we did not find anyone else in the desert. Nor any bodies.'

'You didn't find anything, er, unusual?'

'Only you,' smiled Lord Sedjet. It was a good smile. She had to admit he rated at least an eight. There were muscles under that skin – not the iron muscle of combat, but the firmness of exercise. He was wealthy, and had a lot of leisure time. He wore nothing but a kilt and jewellery – armlets and collar of semi-precious stones.

A servant brought Ace breakfast, bread and dates. 'Tell me,' said Lord Sedjet. 'Where is the land of Perivale? Is it very cold there?'

'Yeah,' said Ace, around her mouthful of food. *What year is this? Where the hell are the Doctor and Benny?* 'People from Perivale don't feel the cold. But this heat!'

'Why did you leave?'

'Long story,' she said. 'I was bored.'

'Are you married?' he asked.

Ace almost dropped her goose wing.

I don't believe it. I don't mind older men, but this is ridiculous. Go on, tell him you've got a hubby and two point four children waiting for you back in the mystical land of Perivale.

'No. I'm not married. I'm a soldier.'

Sedjet started to laugh.

Ace put her plate down on the ground. The monkey jumped down to investigate. Sedjet was still laughing, great whoops of hilarity coming from his belly.

So Ace picked him up and threw him in the pool, dunking him until his wig fell off.

When she let him up for air, he was still laughing, his shaved scalp glistening in the morning sunlight. He twisted around to see how angry she was. But she was looking back at him without emotion. Just making the point.

That afternoon, he made her one of his bodyguards.

The scribe's name was Sesehaten. He wrote tiny pictures

across a bit of papyrus, dipping his brush into a palette of black ink, his hand flashing over the coarse paper from right to left. Ace stood beside him in the foyer, watching as the little jackals and owls and people lined up on the page. Hieroglyphs were just something you saw on jars or in photos of tomb walls. She had never imagined anyone actually writing them.

Sesehaten was a slender man, around the same age as she was. Like Sedjet, he was taller than the other Egyptians – more money, better diet, thought Ace. He was still short, though, and not very threatening – but the four thugs in Lord Sedjet's central hall waited politely for him to finish adding Ace to his records.

She'd broken a jug of beer over the head of the Assyrian, jamming the flat part of her foot into the ex-soldier's groin. That stopped him laughing. She'd been through it on a dozen worlds, when she was an Auxie, smashing bottles over alien heads and kicking Privates in the privates. Childish, really, like proving herself with scraped knees and bloody noses in the playground. But it gave her a chance to test out her body, see if anything wasn't working properly, see if anything had been done to her.

What the bloody hell had happened?

She remembered the giant ship descending on them, remembered fighting her way through crowds of panicking passengers as the *Cortese* went into emergency mode. Containment bulkheads were slamming down all over the place, while men and women in lightweight spacesuits were running up and down with equipment.

Then blackness. In the confusion it was entirely possible that she'd run smack into a bulkhead and knocked herself out.

Then a bad taste in her mouth, and cold so bad it stung. Then she was lying on the freezing floor, its coarseness scraping her cheek – what was it made from? – trying to get her eyes open.

There was a great purple bruise on his left cheekbone, the impact of a human fist, the skin split open with the force of the blow.

Shit happens, as the T-shirt says, and a lot of shit had hap-

45

pened while she'd been playing corpsicle.

At least she'd landed on her feet. She could look after herself here while she searched for the Doctor and Benny. They had to be here somewhere. She'd find them or they'd find her, they'd sort out who the enemy was, the Doctor would have a plan. And his plans always worked.

A drop of blood, brilliant red against his white skin, ran out of his nose.

Cruk it! What had happened?

She shook her head. Sesehaten was saying, 'You'll be provided with weaponry. A bow, plenty of arrows, and a *khopesh*. You do know how to use the weapons, Tepy?'

First One, they called her Tepy, 'Of course I do. What's a *khopesh*?'

The ex-soldier and the half-Hittite grinned at each other. The Assyrian started laughing again. Out of his belt he pulled a heavy copper sword, shaped like a sickle – a long straight piece with a wicked curve and a pointed tip. It looked like a question mark.

He threw it at Ace. She caught it, awkwardly, feeling the weight drag her wrist down. The tip thumped into the floor with a crack.

'I'll need some practice,' said Ace, shrugging. She flipped the sword up, gripped the hilt in both hands and had it at the Assyrian's throat before he could move, the flat of the sword thwacking his shoulder as it landed.

He stopped laughing. Ace started laughing.

Sedjet knelt, stroked the sand with his hands, long fingers sifting through the grains. 'We may have left it too late,' he said. 'Anything the bandits left behind may have been swallowed by the desert.'

Ace shaded her face with her hands, slowly swivelling her gaze around the valley. It was a narrow crack between eroded cliffs, the water-hole an oval smear at the very bottom. The mud she had rolled in on the day she arrived was hard and cracked now, fired into wavy shapes by the sun.

There was nothing out of the ordinary, just rocks and sand. Nothing to indicate that a dimensional portal had ripped open the air and disgorged a woman from the future. Even the animals were gone, hiding from the noon.

Suddenly the TARDIS did not materialize.

'It's been a fortnight,' said Ace. 'They would have found me by now if they were here in Akhetaten.'

'Perhaps the bandits kidnapped them,' said Sedjet. 'Or maybe they just went on their way.' He wandered over to a boulder and sat down in its shade. 'There's nothing here.'

Ace was shaking her head. 'They wouldn't just leave me here.' There was an itchy panic in her stomach. 'They must not be able to find me. But they'll come. They'll come for me.'

'Maybe they think you're dead,' said Sedjet.

Ace turned to squint at him. He looked up at her, his doe-eyes round, staring. He seemed to be looking at every part of her body at once.

'What're you thinking about?' she said, after a while.

'I'm hungry,' he said.

Ace shook her head again. 'I'm just going to have to wait it out. The Professor says patience is a virtue, right?' She stalked the sand, agitatedly, wanting to find something she'd missed. 'Patience.'

She felt Sedjet's eyes on her movement. Don't say anything, she prayed silently, don't say anything at all.

Ace wasn't sure which of the nobles was hosting the party. She probably wasn't the only one; everyone was plastered. Someone fell out of one of the boats with a massive splash, and his friends hauled him back aboard, laughing, before the crocodiles could get him.

She was lying back in the canoe, working her way through a whole roast chicken. Sedjet stood in the prow, a throwing-stick raised in one hand. He wore only a kilt, and his muscles rippled, glistening in the morning light.

It had been a pretty typical party, one of dozens she'd been to over the last two months. They'd been up all night, stuffing themselves with food, drinking beer and wine because Nile water was full of mud and parasites. She was one of several foreigners at the party; the Pharaoh's predecessor had been busy conquering the world, and business and people had flowed back into Egypt from its new colonies.

The smell of perfume and lamplight clung to Ace's white dress. In one of the boats, a lone musician still played a flute, blind eyes half closed with fatigue and booze.

A dozen waterfowl jumped into the sky from a clump of rushes, frightened out by a gang of servants. Sedjet hurled his stick with surprising precision, given the amount of wine he'd drunk, and a bird shrieked and hit the water. A servant came splashing out through the shallows to collect it.

The big man turned those doe-eyes of his on Ace, hoping for her approval. She waved at Sedjet, and he gave her a little-boy smile. She had last seen Sedjet's wife snoring on the mansion floor, someone's pet monkey eating dates off her back.

There was a whoop and a giggle, and someone else's boat collided with them. Sedjet stooped, grabbing at the sides of the canoe to keep his balance. 'Tell us another story, Tepy!' chorused the half-dozen men and women on board.

Ace rolled her eyes. Sometimes she didn't care for the weight of history at her back, going over it again and again. But she was singing for her supper. 'Where did I get up to last night?'

'You were being held prisoner by the traitor.'

'Oh, yes. That's right.' Ace pressed the heels of her palms into her eyes. London was an eternity away. Such a long time ago. 'Someone rang the doorbell. Mike went to see who it was.'

'Who was there?'

'What's a doorbell?'

'Never mind,' sighed Ace. 'It was the little girl, the one the demons had given magical powers to. She struck Mike down with a bolt of lightning.'

'Oh! '

'That's a shame, I rather liked him.'

'Served him right for serving the demons, didn't it.' They were like children, lapping up the tale.

'I like these stories.' Sedjet held his kill by the neck. 'Lots of action.'

'We like them with a bit of sex and violence!' hooted someone else.

'You might not have liked it so much if you were there,' growled Ace, looking Sedjet in the eye. 'Men I like have the bad habit of dying.'

Someone passed her a bowl of beer, and she splashed it in her face. 'It's so hot!'

'It's always hot, here,' someone snorted. 'Did you hear about that letter from what's-his-name, you know, that prince? "Let Pharaoh perish in the sun if he wants, but let my ambassadors stand in the shade!"'

Someone hissed for them to be quiet, while others tittered. 'I like Akhetaten. Thebes was mouldy and full of beggars. I like living in new buildings.'

'If they didn't lean over at funny angles!'

More giggling. Thankfully, they had forgotten about the story.

'You want to go hunting?' asked Sedjet.

'You're too drunk,' said Ace. 'You'll fall out of the chariot again.'

They both laughed. 'She,' Sedjet was trying to tell the assembled company, 'she is the best hunter I've ever seen. Besides myself, of course.'

'I'm a better hunter than you,' she scolded, 'and a better *senet* player.'

'I always win!'

'Only because I let you.'

'She shot a jackal running at full speed,' Sedjet boasted to his friends. 'I mean, the jackal was running, no, wait a moment, she was running as well. But what I mean is – '

'Shut up, Sedjet,' muttered someone. 'I'd like to meet this Sinu of yours. My own physician's magic is pitiful. He couldn't cure a stubbed toe.'

'Maybe you can meet him when he comes to get me,' she said.

Sedjet's mouth pulled into a line, and he rolled over, rummaging in the remains of the feast for a chunk of mutton.

'What happened next?' said the blind flautist.

'Yes, tell us more about the places you've travelled to!'

Ace closed her eyes. How many more parties was she going to have to attend? How much longer?

The sun banged down on Akhetaten, bashing against the white walls of the closely packed houses, making the sandy streets hot enough that you had to wear sandals.

Even at night it was still hot. It had been dusk when she took a horse and chariot from Lord Sedjet's estate, leaving the wide plain of the city behind and travelling over the rocky desert until she came to this place. Now she sat with her legs dangling down over the cliff edge, the warmth of the stone soaking through her sheath dress. Two months and she still wasn't used to the heat.

Her torch had long gone out; there were spares in the chariot. Her bow and quiver were slung over her back. Sometimes she looked up at the sky. It was more stars than black. She'd seen skies like that in Sumer, travelling through the countryside after dark, the Industrial Revolution five millennia away. The air was pure, you could taste it, taste the desert, hot dust and hot rocks. If there were animals, Ace was sure she'd be able to smell them. Assuming, of course, Lawrence of Arabia hadn't already shot them all.

Suddenly the Doctor did not walk up and say hello.

Chief Scribe Sesehaten had helped her with the library. She'd peer at the hieroglyphs over his shoulder, tidy rows of writing on long papyri. She was illiterate. All those years of school for nothing. A tiny frown crossed her face again, but she put it out of her mind.

They had searched histories, business records, religious writings. There had been no sign of the Doctor.

She didn't believe it. He'd been everywhere, man. He must have visited Egypt. There must be something. The whole country ran on written records, ledgers, receipts, letters. Everything counted; everything recorded.

There was one fragmentary papyrus that had made her laugh. The Daleks had been to the pyramids. Now, that was just bizarre. But the fragmentary account didn't make it clear whether the Doctor had been there too.

They searched through the writings from Sumer. Any

record of their visit had become so intermixed with the general muddle of half-truths about Gilgamesh that it was lost to time. They searched through stories from Punt and from Syria. There were hints from time to time, stories of gods or heroes that made her think of him, or imagine Benny.

– trying to drag both of them at once, cursing with frustration –

Smiling as she read about her own adventures on a fragment of pottery five thousand years her senior.

But there were no messages, no hints as to what she was supposed to be doing. So she sat on a cliff overlooking the place she'd woken up, every night she could, the personal force shield generator tight around her wrist.

It was shaped like a wristwatch, a tough elastic band with a small, solid disc of machinery attached. One evening, working by the light of a smoky lamp, she'd used a sliver of wood to peel open the casing. Then she'd stared blankly at the insides for half an hour. *Sorry, Captain, but I can't bypass the warp phase dilithium diagnostic coils.* Without the proper tools, all she'd be able to do was break the thing.

The boiling light in the organic ship must have been part of the space-time fracture. She'd seen spatiotemporal anomalies, knew the headachey geometry that surrounded them. Benny must have travelled through it, breaking the glass wall inwards as she arrived, spat out of the rift like an irritation in reality's mouth.

She must have planned to escape the same way, and had been expecting them to be ready to leave.

So the desert outside Akhetaten was one of the rift's endpoints – one of the places it bit through space-time, creating a sort of gateway. It made sense that the Zargoids were using one of those gateways to steal the passengers off spaceships. And then freeze them.

Why?

And was there anything for them to steal in the desert?

So Ace sat on the cliff watching the blackness.

There was a sound behind her, and she was turning before she thought about it, the bow coming instantly into her hand. She'd nocked and aimed an arrow before she realised it was Sesehaten the scribe.

51

'Jesus in a rocking chair,' she said. 'I could have perforated you.'

Bad, bad, bad. She should've heard him coming, should've seen the dim flicker of torchlight coming up over the ridge behind her. She gingerly pointed the arrow at the ground, letting her cramping hands relax, feeling the crick in her back from sitting still for too long. She had goosebumps. Sesehaten did that to her sometimes, for whatever reason.

'I'm sorry I frightened you, Tepy,' said Sesehaten.

'You didn't. What the hell are you doing here?'

'I wanted to be sure you were alright.'

'You should know that I can take care of myself.'

Sesehaten nodded, the torch bobbing up and down slightly. 'I hadn't realised you were coming out here at night.'

He didn't ask why. Ace sat back down again, holding her bow across her lap.

'The Red Land is very beautiful, especially at sunset and sunrise,' Sesehaten said behind her. 'It's so different to the Black Land around the Nile. So untouched. It seems so simple, but it's so complex. All those ripples in the stony cliffs, all those particles of sand . . .' His voice trailed off into the night air. Ace had never heard him speak like that, all he ever talked about was bills and receipts.

She turned her head to look at him, half-expecting yet another proposition. She knew by now that foreign women were fair game. On the other hand, being a foreigner meant being able to bend the rules – at least, a little more than a native Egyptian woman might have been able to bend them. She still had to prove herself nearly every day, demonstrating over and over that she could wield the weapons and that she wouldn't shrink with fear.

She and the Assyrian had been boozing one night when he'd decided she had to get married to the next serving boy who came to their table. The poor waiter hadn't been able to work out why they broke into drunken giggles.

'That's all women are good for,' growled the Assyrian, chugging the black stuff down. 'Making bread and babies.'

'Ah,' snorted Ace, 'but all men are good for is braining one another with swords.'

'Which job would you prefer?' he said, spilling beer down his front.

Ace laughed. 'I can do *both*.'

Her laughter echoed inside her head, like the laughter of Chinese women lined up in a courtyard. Sesehaten was looking out at the desert, the immensity of the Red Land, cloaked in the blackness of the sky.

Out of nowhere the storm came, as desert storms come. Pink lightning cracked, the air stank of ozone, and the water came down. Ace stuck out her tongue to catch some. The valley rattled as the sudden flood swept through crevices and down alleys, boulders and chips flying in the torrent.

She wanted to show it to the Doctor, hear him say clever things about weather and butterflies and grains of sand. She kept thinking of things she wanted to tell him; she kept wanting to ask Bernice questions about Ancient Egypt.

They watched the storm, listening to the roar of the water. Water and movement in the silent, dusty desert. They were lucky to catch this rare moment of chaos. 'You don't really have weather here, do you?' said Ace. 'The same forecast every day. Hot. Nothing changes.'

'How much longer?' asked Sesehaten.

'While there's life,' she said firmly, 'there's hope. Just as long as it takes.'

'Race you to the top!'

Ace craned her neck back. The sun was behind the top of the Great Pyramid, creating a halo of harsh light around the tip. Sedjet was already clambering agilely up the first few steps. He sat down on one of the sandstone blocks, looking down at her.

'I thought you said you'd climbed the Pyramid before.'

'Only about a dozen times,' the Egyptian grinned. 'We always come here on holidays.'

'It's true,' sighed Mrs. Sedjet. 'He has to climb to the top every time.'

'The view is great!'

'View? What view?' Ace waved her hand at the desert. Look, why don't you go ahead?'

53

'Are you feeling alright?' Sedjet said, pouting. 'The climb isn't that hard.'

Ace shook her head. 'I'm fine. You go ahead. Go on.'

After a bit he did, leaping up over the ruined face of the Pyramid. Ace sighed, sitting down on the sand with her back to the sandstone.

Suddenly one of the tourists did not turn out to be the Doctor.

One of Mrs. Sedjet 's servants brought her a stool. She gave Ace a maternal smile. It occurred to the time traveller that Sedjet's wife was not much older than she was. People grew up fast here, same as they had in Uruk and Tenochtitlan. They grew up fast and died young. They were short and had terrible teeth and died of little things like dirty water and small scratches – stupid things.

There were some compensations, though. No-one here was going to die of fall-out or air pollution or too much junk food. If they wanted to kill one another they had to do it the old-fashioned way, eye to eye, shoving forged metal through one another. And you couldn't destroy a whole country, let alone a whole planet.

Life was lived on a smaller scale here, she thought, leaning back on the Pyramid.

Mrs. Sedjet said, 'This is a pleasant place to visit. Though there are a few too many tourists for my tastes.'

Ace laughed shortly. 'They're really old, even now, aren't they?'

'The Pyramids? They're the oldest thing in the world. I suppose Egyptians should be proud of them.' She folded her hands in lap, looking a bit lost without her daughters. The servants were looking after the infants back at Akhetaten. 'Why didn't you care to go to the top?'

Ace blinked up at her, shading her eyes with her hands. 'I don't know. I guess I'm not that interested.' She blew out a sigh. 'Sedjet's probably going to sulk for a week.'

'He does like to take you everywhere.'

'Yeah.' Ace squirmed against the warm stone. 'I've been meaning to say to you – um, well – there's nothing going on between us,' she blurted.

54

'Oh, I know that.' The laugh lines around Mrs. Sedjet's eyes stood out as she spoke. 'He's always had a passion for foreign women. I won him away from a Babylonian, a very exotic lady. He was smitten with her, but there was one difficulty.'

'What?'

'He can't speak a word of Babylonian.'

Ace grinned, despite herself. 'Look, there really isn't anything going on. He's a married man, right?'

Mrs. Sedjet nodded. 'Yes, I was aware of that. It doesn't bother me when he has the occasional affair. I even had one myself – that came as a shock to him, I think. Ours is a business relationship: not only can't he speak any foreign languages, he can't add up to save his life. I supervise the books and the foreign traders.'

'Where I come from,' said Ace, 'people are supposed to get married because they're in love. Doesn't always work that way, though.'

Mrs. Sedjet nodded. 'I do love Sedjet. He's a good man, Tepy, a gentle man.'

A gaggle of children wandered past, following their mother and father, tripping over one another as they gawked at the Pyramid. Ace folded her arms. 'So if he did – I mean, I keep expecting him to say something, but I – if he did say –'

'I would not be offended. After all, if he's serious about you, he can always take you on as a concubine.'

'Oh.'

'You don't look very happy, my dear.'

Ace shook her head. Mrs. Sedjet, looking a little puzzled, peered up at the receding form of her husband.

It was a seething hot day when Sedjet decided to visit his uncle. He chose four of his bodyguards for the trip. Only one of them came back alive.

They took a short-cut across the desert in chariots, the horses' hooves kicking up great plumes of dust. The thugs were dressed in loin-cloths and not much else, showing off their muscles and scars. Ace wore what any leisured lady might wear: white linen, the pleats ironed carefully into place by servant girls going cross-eyed with the precision, and half a kilo of jewellery.

The arrows came showering down from the cliffs, killing one of the horses, scattering the chariots. Something slapped Ace's face, hard, and she realised there was an arrow caught in her hair.

When the thieves ran down to attack, waving clubs and swords, they mistook her for a harmless noblewoman. She killed two of them before they realised what was going on.

Centuries in the future, when the art of damaging human beings was honed to fine technological precision, she could have left them alive. But a *khopesh* is a bloody great lump of soft metal with a nasty hook, and all you can do with it is hack out your enemy's guts and hope he dies quickly. That was how the half-Hittite died, groaning in the sand, hairy hands pressed against the gash in his armour.

The *khopesh* had a clumsy swing and a lousy recovery time, but if you hit with it, it was very palpable. Ace came silently up behind one of the bandits as Sedjet tried to fight him off. Whoosh, wallop, sounds of parting air and parting flesh, head rolling on the ground. *Next*? She dragged the hooked sword through the side of the largest bandit, feeling organs tear like paper against the force of her swing.

Something hit her, missing her face but crunching into her collarbone She screamed, enraged, striking out gracelessly with her *khopesh* and her foot. One or the other connected, sending the luckless bandit stumbling back into Sedjet's hands. He twisted the man's neck until it made a satisfying crack and dropped him.

Ace discovered she sat down hard in the dust, a ferocious line of pain spitting blood from her left shoulder. Sedjet loped over. 'Sister! Does it hurt? How bad is it?' His face loomed over her like a dark-skinned sun, eyes black as night-time, their corners creased with concern.

Ever so romantic, she had thought, as the pain thumped up into her skull and laid her flat out against the sand. *I be Benny's having an even worse time.*

* * *

Benny was eating grapes. She was lying on soft cushions in a voluminous drawing room, a silken sheet drawn up to her neck. Flickering candles illuminated the room, picking out Vivant's features.

'Do try to hold still,' he admonished, waving his charcoal stick at her playfully.

'*Excusez-moi* .These are delicious. Do you want one?'

'*Non, merci.* now stop wriggling.' His charcoal moved quickly over the paper, tracing the lines of her body. 'You're an excellent subject – or would be, if you didn't move about so.'

'I'll bet you say that to all the girls.' She lobbed a grape at him. It bounced off his nose. His features were ruddy with Egyptian sunlight, well-fed and pleasant, small mouth hooked into a permanent smile. He was handsome in a comfortable way. He didn't look all of fifty-one.

'*Je cède.*' He put his unfinished sketch to one side.

Benny picked up a sheaf of the day's earlier work, gripping her sheet. Mostly the pyramids, which Vivant had fallen hopelessly in love with. The Sphinx, buried to the neck in sand, tiny savants crawling over it with plumblines and notebooks. All drawn in tiny, precise pencil strokes.

She raised her head at the sound of distant cannons. 'Perhaps you'd better put on your clothes,' said Vivant. He gripped the case of pencils under his arm and stepped outside.

Benny waited until she was sure he wasn't going to pop his head back around the door. Smiling to herself, she tugged on her battered trousers and loose brown shirt. They were good clothes, working clothes, the sand and the dirt ground into them so deeply they'd never be washed clean.

She picked up the half-finished sketch. The picture had been her idea; while Vivant had been showing her some of his earlier works, she'd found a copy of *l' Œuvre Priapique*.

'*Ah, oui,*'he had said, not quite blushing as Benny casually flipped through page after page of drawings of the sex life of the citizens of Pompeii.

'No wonder the volcano erupted,' she had teased.

'The reception of that work was somewhat mixed . . .'

She considered her portrait, done in light, almost playful strokes. A flick of charcoal showed where the dark roots were starting to peep through her long blonde hair. Her hair felt as grubby as her clothes. She'd never get another colour treatment in an eighteenth century desert, but she'd settle for a decent shampoo.

Vivant Denon was about due for his great southern expedition with General Desaix. Ol' Boney was pretty impressed with Denon, and didn't mind him nipping down the Nile to sketch a few antiquities – all for the greater glory of *La France*, of course.

That was why Napoleon had brought over a hundred of his favourite savants to Egypt. Denon had made sure that his strange (English?) assistant was among their number, charming Bonaparte into letting him bring a woman along.

To the rest of the savants, the scholarly gentlemen in their scholarly suits, she was merely Denon's latest conquest. Their conversations stopped when she approached, and they wouldn't let her attend the seminars. When they gave her those glances, condescending, almost pitying, she wanted to spit in their faces.

But she was a guest here, on her best behaviour. She had no choice; after all, she wasn't going anywhere. It bothered her more because, despite his reputation for charming the ladies, Vivant treated her better than any of them. And hell, he was charming.

There was a knock at the door. 'Are you decent?'

'Never,' giggled Bernice. 'Come in.'

He reappeared, his eyes politely averted until he was sure she was dressed. 'Everything's ready for our departure,' he said, and coughed. 'Perhaps we can finish our studio session once we return.'

'Perhaps,' said Benny mischievously. 'Crack open another bottle.'

'Ah,' said Vivant, fishing a flask of absinth out from a hamper. 'It's rather warm, I'm afraid.'

Benny made a face. 'Never mind.' She unzipped her travel bag, started rummaging inside. Vivant eyed the zipper curiously. Benny turned her back slightly, so he couldn't see what she was doing.

Everything inside was mixed up. She pulled out a plastic box with a red cross on it made out of two sticking plasters, some clean underwear, her diary, and a hat.

She turned the hat over and over in her hands. Her diary fell into her lap. 'What is it that you are writing?' Vivant asked, easing the cork out of the bottle.

'A history of booze,' she said. 'Any booze gets near me, it's history.' But she was massaging the felt of the brim with her fingers, frowning.

'I haven't seen this before,' said Vivant, taking the hat from her hands. Benny snatched it back from him, with more force than she had intended. 'It belongs – it belonged to an old friend.'

He nodded, seriously, not wanting to intrude on her privacy. 'It's the only white Fedora ever made,' she explained, incomprehensibly. 'And it's all I've got left of him.'

She closed her eyes. She remembered the violent tugging, the burning lights inside her skull. Losing her grip. Feeling Ace and the Doctor being wrenched away from her. She remembered screaming, her voice swallowed by the hurricane noise of the rift.

'It's all I've got left,' she said again,

Vivant passed her a glass of absinth, and she downed the bitter stuff in a single gulp.

For a while things were a bit fragmented, like jumping channels on the telly. Grating pain as the physician messed with the wound, Ace trying to slap him away, swearing. Sedjet waiting by the bed, smiling at her as she wandered in and out of consciousness.

When she woke up properly, the room was full of lamps, filling the air with golden light and the smell of cooking fat. Sedjet was snoring in a wooden chair by her bedside, scaring off the evil spirits. Ill again, safe again, tucked into bed and watched over.

The scar was a long one, shallow but ragged. She explored it gingerly with her fingers, wishing she could see it properly.

It burned dully when she moved her arm. She'd had far worse, but she was nervous as hell about being treated by people who were twenty centuries away from penicillin.

But if anything nasty got into the wound, the little machines inside her would gobble it up, running around in her blood like teenage gangs, leaving Gallifreyan graffiti on the walls of her arteries: THE DOCTOR WAS HERE.

She watched Lord Sedjet sleep for a while, his arms knotted over his chest. He had a terrific-looking five o'clock shadow. Normally he had his chin and head shaved every morning. Now there was a tiny blur of black stubble on his scalp. Sweet. He had been worried about her.

Pity he was such a bore.

She had been here six months. Half a year on automatic, doing the things she did in any new environment: getting her bearings, finding ways of surviving. Searching for the Doctor and staying in one piece until he could explain the plan. And going to parties. And wearing pretty clothes. And playing games.

Sedjet's generosity was too convenient. Not that she didn't deserve some good luck after all the crap she'd been through. But surely it had been set up, was part of some plot going on just outside the range of her perception?

He wrote her love poems, sometimes, sketching out the hieroglyphs in his own hand – slower than Sesehaten, but with firm, broad strokes. The scribe read them out to her, blushing. 'Let me see you step into the pool again, your white dress clinging to your body. Bring me a red fish from the pool, or a spotless lily.' Thank goodness Sedjet's wife couldn't read.

He was reasonably wealthy, sympathetic, and he had genuine affection for her. He could keep her alive in this alien world. And, after all, he did have a nice arse.

But she didn't want any babies, not here, where the women screamed and died in childbirth. There was no contraception. At least, no contraception she was planning on using. There are some places you just don't put crocodile dung.

She wondered if the little machines in her body would let her get pregnant.

Sedjet woke up. 'Sister,' he said. 'I hope you are feeling well.'

60

'I've been better,' she said, remembering not to shrug. 'Looks like you got away without a scratch.'

He smiled. It was the same old bland smile. 'Sister,' he said, 'I've been thinking again about the possibility of a marriage contract.'

Ace felt a great weariness descend on her. She shook her head, gently.

'I am wealthy enough for two wives,' he was saying, too quickly. 'I would not make you a mere concubine. You would spend your time playing music and *senet*, and the servants would bring you date wine. I would give you anything your heart desired.'

'No,' she whispered. 'No, Sedjet, no. I can't stay here, I can't stay in this place forever. I have to find my friends. I have to leave.'

'Don't you understand?' said the nobleman. 'Your friends aren't going to come back.'

'I don't belong here. I have to go, I have to get out of here!'

'Tepy, listen to me. Listen, sister. They are not coming back for you.'

Benny was stooped over the Doctor, frantically trying to get a response out of him. Blood was trickling from his mouth and nose, sluggishly. His eyes had flickered shut.

Oh, God.

Oh, my God.

The icy certainty she had known on the alien ship came back into her.

He really had died, hadn't he?

'It doesn't hurt.' She squeezed her eyes shut, trying to find some part of herself that wanted to cry. 'Why doesn't it hurt?'

Sedjet looked at her, his smooth face crumpling with very real grief.

No ruby slippers. 'I just feel cold,' she said.

'People from Perivale don't feel the cold.'

'I'm not from Perivale,' she whispered. 'I'm an Egyptian.'

61

Chapter 5

Yesterday, When I Was Mad

> [Paris is] the only place in the universe where one can relax entirely.
>
> (The Doctor, *City of Death*)

Paris 1871 CE

Normally, when he woke up, it was very sudden: snapping from oblivion into consciousness, sometimes so abruptly he had to think about it to be sure he'd slept at all.

But this was a slow return from the darkness. The first flickerings of awareness, becoming aware of awareness. He was drifting up through murky water, some dim light above him or below him, the weight of the ocean pressing against his eyes. There were doors he couldn't quite reach.

With an effort he forced them open.

The light made him blink. He tried to take in all the details. But it was gibberish, charivari, chiaroscuro, *son et lumière*.

He closed his eyes again. Stick to the basics, one thing at a time. He was alive. Always a good start. He was lying down. There was a restrictive weight on his chest and arms, something plastic clinging to his face. His breathing made a noise. Plastic over his mouth and nose.

He rolled over and out of the bed, out from the heavy covers. The floor was cold. The respirator mask jerked part of the way loose and he batted it free of his hair.

The room reeled around him as he tried to catch his breath. He could see a door, upside down. A way to get out. He pushed himself to his knees, grabbed the bed and dragged himself to his feet. Keep moving.

He fell against the door and scrabbled at the knob. Locked. Simple lock. It wouldn't take long to pick it.

But there were sounds, sounds coming from behind the door! Someone was coming! He needed to get out, get out quickly.

He made it the few feet across the floor to the window, ripping the curtains open as someone put a key into the lock. The window was not locked. He wrenched it open, dragged himself through. Keep moving.

He found himself on a tiled roof. The sun! He raised a trembling hand against the physical force of its light.

The sky and the dancing buildings waved up and down like the ocean. He crawled across the roof, clinging hard to the tiles, tasting blood. He wasn't sure where he was heading, what he would do next, but it didn't matter. Keep going, keep moving, get away!

There was a shout behind him. He twisted his head around. Someone was leaning out of the window, yelling at him to stop, to stop being an idiot. She snaked out of the window and landed on the tiles, graceful as an animal, and came after him.

He lost his grip, rolling down the roof, snatching at the tiles as he fell. There was a lurch as he went over the edge, a fierce jerk in his shoulders. He opened his eyes, squinting against the burning sky, and realised he was holding onto the gutter. Perhaps someone was shouting below him. He didn't look down.

He remembered something falling out of the orange sky, falling, falling –.

His pursuer appeared over the edge of the roof, throwing a cold shadow over him. 'What the hell do you think you're doing?' she shouted, and reached for him.

He let go of the gutter.

She snatched him out of the air, both hands gripping his left wrist. In a single heave she pulled him onto the roof.

He struggled, but her grip was like iron, and already the sun was ringing in his head like a funeral bell. She was behind him, one hand across his chest, the other clutching his wrist. 'Relax,' she said into his ear, 'Relax. I've got you.'

With a sound like a camera snapping, reality clicked into

place. He melted into her grasp, his head falling back against her shoulder.

This was Earth, and he was safe, and there was no need to escape. No need to get away. Some part of his mind was broken like a renegade piece of a pocket watch, rattling loose inside the casing.

He was out of his mind.

He opened his mouth to cry out with the horror of it. But then he remembered, and was silent.

Two weeks later. Kadiatu Lethbridge-Stewart sat curled in a wicker chair in her underwear. She was watching the Doctor sleep.

The bump that indicated his toes was a good three feet from the end of the canopied bed. His arms were folded neatly on his chest above the covers. She'd never seen anyone alive look so relaxed.

Weeks ago she'd got out of the nervous habit of checking whether he was still breathing. He took a couple of breaths a minute. His skin was cold enough that condensation sometimes formed on it.

He slept with a tiny smile on his face, as though sleeping were a new and exotic luxury he was determined to fully explore. As though spending several weeks comatose was something he'd intended to do.

Never stand when you can sit, never sit when you can lie down, never stay awake when you can sleep. Kadiatu had dropped off in the big wicker chair. The upstairs bedroom was gently scented with pot-pourri, almost enough to overwhelm the distant smell of burning.

With the curtains carefully drawn, she could imagine she was anywhere, that she could walk down the stairs and into any street she chose. Not into the stinking Paris midnight, the hot air and the shouting.

She was awake before she was sure what had awoken her, uncurling from the chair onto her bare feet. The cold wooden floor made her shiver. She rubbed the back of her neck. A clock on the mantelpiece was ticking like industrial machinery.

He was blinking in the candlelight. 'Ruby?' he muttered, squinting at her. 'Ruby Duvall?'

She padded over to the side of the bed. 'Oh,' he said. 'Fancy meeting you here. Small world, isn't it? Where's Ace?'

Kadiatu unlocked a drawer and removed a handscan. 'She isn't here. It was just you.' She ran the scanner over him.

'Two psychics meet in the street. One says to the other, "You're fine, how am I?"' His voice was a little hoarse, which wasn't surprising, given that most of the epidermis of his throat had had to grow back.

'All things considered, you're in pretty good shape. What do you remember?'

'Useless things, mostly. I remember drinking coca leaf tea in a hotel on Cloudcuckooland, above the cumulus on a mountain twenty miles tall.' His eyes darted around the room like searchlights. 'They said I could have my breakfast at any time, so I said I'd like to have it in Nineteenth Century France.'

'Eighteen seventy-one,' said Kadiatu. 'The furniture?'

'Your clothing.'

'You were just wearing some sort of coveralls.'

'Not much style,' he said.

'Where did you come from?'

'Where did I arrive?'

'At a friend's house.'

'This is your house?'

'It belongs to the friend. A black foreign single woman is conspicuous enough without also being propertied.'

'How long ago?'

'About two months.'

'I'm grateful.'

She shook her head. 'You're my exit visa.'

'Ah,' he said. 'Sans my TARDIS, that might be a bit tricky.'

'You'll think of something. Is there anything you want?'

'Universal peace. I'll settle for a glass of water.'

She brought him a glass of water. He sat up, shrugging his left shoulder awkwardly as though it pained him. He was wearing a brand new set of English silk pyjamas: She sat on the edge of the bed and watched him drink.

He found himself in the vanity mirror. There was a nasty scar across his left cheek, bright red, surrounded by a mass of bruised purple tissue. 'Odd,' he muttered. 'The peripheral damage should heal first.'

'You're lucky to be alive. What happened?'

'I hate it when a plan falls apart,' he said, slowly drinking the water. His gaze was reflected from the mirror and onto her. Her hair was short. Her eyes were shaped like almonds, sharp windows in her serious face. She was more than a head taller than him, long-limbed and muscular.

'I feel like eating,' she said. 'Are you hungry?'

Bernice closed her eyes. They felt like a desert, seared by the noonday sun and full of sand. She lay back under the canvas, in the shade, praying for the premature invention of air conditioning.

She and Denon had taken a detour, leaving Desaix to his forced marches for a few days. A short boat trip down the Nile and they'd be in Amarna.

She'd arrived in France months ago. She had fallen out of the rift alone and glowing like a light bulb, scattering the terrified peasants who had been picking apples. All she had had was her travel bag.

She unzipped it and took out her diary. Stuffed inside the bag were antibiotics, camping equipment – things which might help to keep her alive, assuming she landed somewhere that didn't kill her instantly.

She'd spent almost a month aboard the TARDIS waiting for the Doctor and Ace to signal her. She slept in her clothes, the bag under her head, ready at a moment's notice to home in on the beacon.

The signal had jerked her out of sleep. The TARDIS automatically locked in on it. She bolted into the console room, the bag slung across her shoulders, force shield clipped onto her wrist. The TARDIS doors were already opening, a great spiralling corridor of light leading out into the Vortex. She could see a flickering portal at the other end.

She ran out of the doors, felt herself propelled through the time corridor, picked up at the last moment by the forces inside and flung out through the portal. Somehow she managed to keep her feet as she crashed through a temporal barrier, then a real one.

The corridor's energies surrounded her in a rapidly dissipating halo. Bits of shattered glass melted into droplets, falling like rain at her feet.

The Doctor and Ace had been there. Somehow, things had been worse than the nightmares she'd been having.

Bernice pulled the Doctor's Fedora down over her eyes. She wasn't sure why he had left it behind – or why she had stuffed it into her travel bag. She was glad she had it with her. After all, it did keep the sun off.

The gold and the vodka had gone in the first month. She'd spent that time just surviving, struggling to polish up her high school French. The TARDIS' telepathic circuits had spoilt her rotten as far as languages were concerned – but puzzling out ancient tongues was an archaeologist's skill.

She had needed every bit of that skill. At first, everything had been totally alien – the money, the food, the clothes, even how the loos worked. She couldn't hope to blend in, so she'd kept on the move, working her way towards Paris with a crazy plan in mind. If she hadn't spent part of her youth living in a forest, she'd have starved. As it was she'd been eating bugs by the time she made it to the capital.

Denon was the obvious choice. He more or less invented Egyptology and was one of the first archaeologists. She'd studied him; she'd be able to impress him. He had money and connections. He was a life preserver in the ocean of history.

It was good to get out of Cairo. Egyptian rebels were harassing French soldiers daily, the French had burned down mosques, and both sides were already responsible for shocking massacres. Napoleon had even poisoned all the dogs to stop them barking a warning to the rebels. Fairly standard stuff for a war, in fact.

Benny frowned sleepily. She didn't care to be on the conquerors' side, but there wasn't much she could do about it. It wasn't as though the French were the Hoothi or the Daleks –

67

no, this was just another dull stretch of human military history.

Even in her century the history books tended to be long, boring descriptions of battles and wars, lists of dates that didn't tell you much about the people who had lived and breathed in those times. To the average peasant, it probably didn't make a *sou* of difference who the Emperor was.

Denon had been intrigued by the bizarre, ragged woman who had turned up on his doorstep. He wasn't impressed by her knowledge of Egypt – he was astonished by it. French education was full of the details of Ancient Greece and Rome, but Egypt was still a mystery, its language untranslated and its monuments standing unnoticed in the sun.

Napoleon had set up the Egyptian Institute in a palace in Cairo, wanting everything in the newly conquered land measured, catalogued sketched. Denon was just one of the team, gathering the details and illustrations that would eventually become *Voyage de la Basse et la Haute Egypte*. When he was done here he would go on to help Napoleon pinch European art treasures to stock the Louvre. He was taking everything in his stride, which wasn't too surprising for a chap who'd been sent on secret missions for the Emperor and had cheated Madame Guillotine.

Benny felt herself drifting off into sleep. Her salary was good, her belly was full and she had managed to become part of the very invention of archaeology. She could not have asked for a softer landing.

The Vortex had flung the three of them in entirely random directions. They could have exited anywhere, in empty space, in the far future or the distant past. The Doctor had been beyond help, she told herself for the thousandth time; it didn't matter where he landed. But Ace – Benny had a pretty good idea of where Ace had ended up.

She dipped into her mind again, dredging up the jarring memory. An Academy classroom, a lecturer's soft drone, a hologram of the Amarna cliffs.

Vivant popped his head under the canvas. She could read him like a book; the nobly restrained interest. We should arrive later this afternoon,' he said. 'And then we can begin

68

the business of locating this Egyptian mystery of yours.'

Benny nodded. 'There's such a huge area to search. But I'm guessing that some of the locals will know exactly what we're after.'

'A three thousand year old sentence written in English?' laughed Vivant. 'I would imagine someone would have noticed by now!'

Benny frowned again. The Amarna Graffito was a famous archaeological puzzle, still much-discussed in her century. The thing was, there was something strange about that classroom memory. As though she had dreamed it. Or as though it hadn't been there before.

Kadiatu got through four courses and a bottle of red wine while the Doctor slowly ate a bowl of vichyssoise. Her *gens de maison* hovered anxiously. The maids were country girls, healthy and muscled, who stamped across the waxed floors in and out of the dining room. As much as they resented being in the service of a *Noire*, they were grateful for a mild employer – even one who decided to have *dîner* in the middle of the night. But the Doctor's abrupt resurrection had unnerved them.

Kadiatu had dressed for dinner, which took half an hour, even with her chambermaid's assistance. One of the servants brought the Doctor a jumble of clothes – frock coats, hats, laced boots and fashionable French shirts. He had long since lost his taste for frills. He ended up in a slightly oversized shirt and trousers, a long black coat and a white scarf, re- minding the servant girls of practical relatives on Bourbonnaise farms.

'You could've just erased it all,' she said, watching him spread butter on a white bread roll. 'You erased everything in the Stone Mountain archives, which was where I got my information in the first place. You had the chance to destroy my work as well.'

'I was curious.'

'Curious,' snorted Kadiatu. 'I destroyed it myself on my way out. The human race wasn't ready for time travel yet.'

'Except for you.'

'I was curious.'

'So you solved the problem of initial conditions. Your school science project worked.' He dunked the roll in his soup. 'A train that travels in time instead of down tunnels. You could solve the problem of late-running passenger services forever. What did you use for a power source?'

'A thermonuclear explosion.'

'Hmm, batteries not included.'

'I carried four spare nukes.' The Doctor looked alarmed. 'I haven't irradiated Paris. I didn't even irradiate Arizona, though the explosion destroyed all my research. I'll explain how it works later.'

The Doctor nodded slowly, wiping up the last of his soup with the remains of his roll. Two months unconscious with only drips for lunch, and he wasn't even particularly hungry. He seemed a little weary, but that wasn't surprising.

She wondered what it would take to kill him.

'What day is this?' he asked.

'May 3rd,' she said. 'You arrived the day they proclaimed the Commune.'

'The glorious harbinger of a new society,' said the Doctor, 'or was that the other Commune? All these revolutions tend to blur together. Paris was one of my earliest tastes of Earth, you know. What do you think of space-time?'

'Big,' said Kadiatu, waving a hand, 'long. I'm glad I brought some books.'

'I told you you wouldn't like it.' One of the maids dipped in and took his bowl away.

'I could make the shuttle go,' explained Kadiatu, 'but I couldn't make it go where I wanted.'

'Ah,' said the Doctor. 'A not unfamiliar problem.'

'And it's so hard to compensate for the solar system. It's like rattling around inside an enormous watch. Each time I jumped I'd end up days out from Earth. At least I could calculate my temporal displacement from the movement of the planets.'

'You must have compensated. Otherwise you might have ended up billions of kilometres outside the solar system.'

'Once I arrived above the surface of Mars, falling at an

angle through the atmosphere like a meteor. I had to jump a second time to stop myself from crashing.'

'I'm sure the locals appreciated that.'

'I checked the external camera record later. There was no sign of habitation. I had no chance to check which epoch it was.'

'A wasted experiment.'

'The very first jump took me to the twenty-fifth century.'

'And what did you make of it?'

'Not much. I filled up a lot of videotapes. I had to leave when they started to ask too many questions.'

'Steal anything?'

'Not much. Information.'

'Planning to go home?'

'I don't care where I end up,' said Kadiatu, 'as long as it's not here. If I hadn't packed all that gold, I'd be nothing here. Money talks. A historical constant.'

'I expect Karl would agree.'

'I'm thinking of writing a paper about it. Where did you come from? And what happened to Bernice?'

'And what about Ace?'

'It was just you. You turned up in the same place I crash-landed. There was an explosion in the night and Thierry found you in his orchard.'

'You knew that Ace was female,' he said, catching her eyes. 'You said "she".'

'I read my grandmother's history of UNIT. And there was more in Stone Mountain. Dorothy McShane was still listed in a pan-European database of missing persons in 2006.'

The Doctor nodded. It was a good answer. 'How do you imagine I got here?'

'I was rather,' said Kadiatu, drumming her fingers on the tabletop, 'hoping you'd tell me that.'

He held his wine glass between his palms, rolling it back and forth. 'I came through a transdimensional rift. A linear breakage in the continuum. A crack in the ice cube of time.'

Kadiatu knocked over her wine glass.

'Someone has carelessly punched a series of holes through the universe,' he continued. 'Those tracks form unpredictable connections between separate pieces of space and time. The holes can drift in unexpected ways, and the rifts can open up at weak points anywhere along their five-dimensional length. A really quite astonishing amount of damage to reality can result.'

'So you're here as Mr Fixit?' she asked, breathlessly, getting up, getting away from his eyes. The Doctor picked up her wine-glass.

'They can't be fixed,' he said. 'They're quite permanent.'

With a sudden snap of his wrist, he threw the glass at the wall. One of the maids shouted.

Kadiatu stood stock still. 'You might have mentioned something about it. My equations didn't show any – '

'Your equations are the scrawling of a little girl,' said the Doctor. His arms were folded, holding onto himself. He was very different to the man she remembered. 'They are precocious, crayoned nonsense. And if I'd had any sense I'd have taken away your matches before you could burn yourself- or anyone else.'

'Fine. What are you going to do about it?'

'There's nothing we can do about the temporal fractures. I have to stop – you must tell me everything, everything that might be important. Everything you know.'

'I'll show you the ship,' she said.

'Good.'

'Not now. In the morning.'

The basement was much larger than it should have been. There were rough lines across the ceiling and floor, where internal walls and floors had been knocked down and ripped up to make room for Kadiatu's equipment. The resulting space was two stories high and several metres across. Everything was covered in dust, and brickbats and rubbish filled the corners; the *domestiques* didn't come down here. The Doctor kept catching cobwebs in his candle flame.

Kadiatu's time vessel took up most of the basement. It was a cargo shuttle, three-quarters storage space and one-quarter life-support. The surface, painted a drab military green, was marked with streaks of mind-jarring colours, silver and heliotrope and cerulean; iridescent go faster stripes formed where the vortex had licked the paintwork. The hull was pocked with micrometeoroid strikes. The phrase WHOSE IDEA WAS THIS???? was spraypainted in dripping red across its nose.

The life-support section was a flattened bulb at the bottom of the ship, with room for one suited occupant. The Doctor leaned in and flipped a switch, and a panel obligingly opened in the side of the cargo portion of the vehicle, exposing the hold.

There was a thick, square patch of something sticky next to the cargo hold door, just above eye level. He scratched at it with a fingernail. Something organic, dried in wet blobs on the spaceship's hull. Vegetable, not animal. The surface shrugged, shrinking away from his touch.

He leaned into the cockpit, brought the computer online, read the flight program most recently entered into it. Read it again. A bit drastic for an anti-theft measure. Or was it?

There was a radiation gauge above the cargo bay door; the Doctor flicked his eyes across it. The interior of the ship was a little hotter than the background, but not enough to stop him. He popped his head inside for a look.

The hold was mostly equipment, machinery stitched together into a jury-rigged time-space engine. The main section of it was a modified field regulator from a subspace train, the public transport system of an Earth twenty minutes into Ace's future.

Ace. Covered in frost, lying on the floor an inch from his nose like an enormous fish finger. Watching him bleed to death while Bernice struggled to save them both.

A dreadful urgency rose up in him, and he didn't really care how Kadiatu's toy TARDIS worked, he just needed to get to Ace. Benny must have dragged them both into the rift. She and Ace could have ended up anywhere that the fractures led. Including several hundred miles above the surface of Mars.

His left collar-bone suddenly erupted with pain, and he sat down hard against one curving wall of the shuttle, little flashes going off in his field of vision. He blinked hard and pressed his fingers against his chest above the left heart. There was no scar there, no bruise, nothing to indicate an injury. If the welt on his face hadn't healed, what might be broken on the inside?

Ace could take care of herself, and so could Bernice. He pushed the panic down along with the pain and forced himself to concentrate on the machinery.

The big gold-coloured things were power baffles, designed to soak up huge amounts of energy. Such as a hydrogen bomb going off in the immediate vicinity.

The design was rough and ready – everything was covered in welding lines – but it had a functional elegance. The train engine wrapped the capsule in a self-generating, dimension-warping field. That field protected the physical vehicle from the thermonuclear explosion, shunting the power instantly to the baffles, which sucked it up and pushed it back into the field in a huge positive feedback loop. When the field strength got above a certain level, the whole thing was booted unceremoniously into another part of space and time.

No wonder she couldn't control its flight; it would be like trying to steer a car that ran on dynamite. And it was just as damaging to the road. Kadiatu had managed to invent a whole new form of pollution.

Every remaining inch of the hold had been stuffed with useful things: medical supplies, weapons, food preserved in various inedible ways. He flipped open one box and discovered neatly stacked bars of gold. The only empty space had been left by her spare bombs.

'What'd they do to you?'

The Doctor jumped, banging his head on the curve of the wall. Kadiatu was a flickering silhouette in the cargo hold doorway, her nightdress hanging heavily around her. Her eyes were empty hollows in the feeble light of her candle. 'I am presuming you didn't beat yourself up.'

The Doctor got his breathing back under control. He rolled his shoulder back and forth a couple of times. It seemed to be alright again. 'If you make a hole, something will probably decide to live in it.'

'Like weeds growing in cracks in the road.'

'Even a non-Euclidean theoretical construct is a habitat, if you look at it the right way. Something's living in the fractures.'

'What's it up to?'

'Travelling around. Hunting and gathering. Flexing its muscles, making a bit of noise, seeing if anyone notices.'

'And you noticed.'

'Yes. And they noticed I noticed.'

'Who are they? What was their technology like? Advanced? Did you understand it?'

'I don't – I don't remember it very – I don't remember . . .' He frowned, as though he'd forgotten where he'd left something. 'I . . .

Kadiatu hunched back, uncomfortable. 'One thing I can tell you,' he said, looking her in the face, 'they don't treat the people who work for them very well.'

'Do you know how I can get out of here?'

'Oh, that's easy. Dive your shuttle into the sun.'

'What?'

'When you hit a hot enough section of chronosphere, the temperature should trigger dimensional transference. And you're on your way. An effectively unlimited power source. You can keep making jumps until you end up somewhere you like.'

'I can't do that. I'd do more damage. I'll have to think of something else.'

'That's better,' smiled the Doctor.

Kadiatu looked like she wanted to hit him.

Chapter 6

In Taberna

> Life is just one damned thing after another.
> ('Kin' Hubbard, *A Thousand and One Epigrams*)

Ace held up her left arm. It was covered in bangles, tight rings of gold glistening dully with lapis lazuli. They didn't go well with the loop of the force shield generator. The maid servants were wondering if she were ever going to take it off.

Sedjet hosted two or three parties a week. There didn't seem to be much else for him to do. Tonight the servants had more important things to worry about than Ace's strange ornament; they were slapping dough on the outsides of smoky ovens, unsealing jars of beer and wine and arranging flowers about the house. Overseeing it all, Mrs Sedjet moved about in her finest garments, a crimson cloak knotted over her white dress.

Ace sat in the corner, like a vase of flowers: pretty and useless, slowly wilting.

It had been a week since Sedjet's proposal. She'd asked for time to think, trying to get her head around the fact that she wasn't going to be rescued. Perhaps he was a little hurt that she needed to be rescued from him.

But Sedjet's patience was great, even if his intellect wasn't. So now she sat on a stool, watching the servants preparing scented wax cones to perch atop rich guests' wigs, and tried for the hundredth time to make a decision.

If her Sergeant Major could see her here, going soft in a nobleman's estate. Sedjet hadn't even put her on guard duty since their little chat – such work was below any future wife of his.

For a moment she was off amongst the stars, soaring in crazy loops in a one-seat fighter, trashing Dalek platforms as they buzzed towards her in clumsy squadrons. The electrodes in her helmet passed information back and forth between her brainstem and the ship, so fast she could feel the nuclear heat in its belly, its nausea at the high-g turns.

She forced herself out of her memories and back into the real world. Which consisted of Sedjet bounding in and pecking his wife on the cheek. His pet monkey scurried up to him and his daughters called their greeting. *Hi, honey, I'm home.*

He came over to Ace, his eyes weighing up her choice of dress and jewellery. 'I think,' he pronounced, 'you should wear something more open. Something that would reveal your scar more clearly.' He fingered the long mark on her left shoulder. It was quite visible under the flimsy linen, a ragged blue-and-red line at odds with the geometry of the pleating.

She caught his hand. 'Sedjet,' she said, 'would you come with me for a moment? I want to talk to you. Just come right this way.'

He followed her, bemused, out into the entrance courtyard. The sun was just setting; the servants were lighting torches beside the path to the front gate.

Ace faced Sedjet and said, 'You've shown my scar to your wife. You've shown my scar to your scribes. You've shown it to visiting dignitaries and generals. You've even shown it to your three nephews when they came calling.'

'But,' protested Sedjet, 'I thought you were proud of the scar.'

'I was proud of it,' said Ace, 'until you started showing me off like a bit of jewellery.'

Sedjet opened his mouth and closed it, like a goldfish. It looked really stupid. He said, 'Do you expect to be a woman warrior, and not attract any attention? Look at you!' he waved a hand, taking in her pale skin, her long brown hair, her hard muscles, her scar.

'I just want to get on with my job. I don't want to do weapons practice in front of your business associates like I was an acrobat. Right?'

He shook his head. 'I have not asked you to bear arms for

77

the past week.'

'And I'm going stir crazy! I'm not your bloody dancing girl. I just want to do my job, okay?'

'Listen to me, sister,' said Sedjet, starting a slow burn. 'I plucked you out of the desert like a fading flower. I saw to it you were nursed back to life, fed, clothed. Even though you were a woman, even though my friends raised their eyebrows, I gave you employment. I even desired to marry you. I saved your life!'

'And I saved yours, toe-rag,' and suddenly she was laughing, 'so we're even, aren't we?'

'Tepy,' he said sharply, 'what do you want?'

She stopped in place, suddenly silent, her mouth still open.

The feel of soaring through empty space, the *pock* of Dalek shrapnel on her wings.

Slowly, one by one, she took off the bangles and dropped them on the floor.

Her naked feet slapped across the faience tiles. He followed her out into the courtyard, shouting, scattering the servants. 'You never play by the rules!' he yelled, pushing past his wife, stepping over a necklace as Ace let it fall to the floor. 'You always break the rules!'

'And I'm going to go on breaking them,' said Ace.

She went into the street, not expecting him to follow. But he stood at the gate, shouting out into the night.

'You're one of Set's, do you know that, you irritating little slut? You're a woman of Set!'

Ace turned, suddenly, holding the last of her bangles in her fist. She looked down at it. It was the personal force shield generator.

They stood a little distance apart, quivering in their anger.

'You're just scared to admit you're not leaving,' he growled. But now he looked like a hurt little boy, instead of a furious, wealthy, powerful man.

'If I'm stuck here,' she said, 'I'll spend my life the way I want to.'

'You're a woman of Set,' he said again.

'And you're too crukking used to getting your own way,' said Ace, more gently.

78

She held out the generator to him. He looked at it, that idiot expression slowly covering his features. Ace rolled her eyes and pressed it into his hands.

'Just so you don't forget me,' she said, and walked away into the gathering evening.

She didn't know whether he kept it, or hurled it into the dusty road.

She also didn't know that she would never see Sedjet again.

They were thieves, cut-throats, kidnappers, criminals of every kind. They were scarred and dirty, grinning as they downed pottery cups of raw home-made booze in the oil lamp dimness of the tavern.

The songs faded into a murmur. The ruffians looked up from their games of dice and their back street deals. They gaped at the woman standing in the doorway.

She was pale-skinned, tall and well-shaped. She was dressed like a man, in brown shirt and trousers, a leather satchel slung over her shoulders. On her head was a white hat, pristine, lacking the mud and the miscellaneous stains on the rest of her clothing.

She walked in, smiling nastily as she realised every eye was on her. There was a French pistol on her hip; she moved her satchel away so that everyone could see it.

'Ah,' she said out loud, 'a wretched hive of scum and villainy. Just what I'm looking for.'

She walked right up to the dice game, half a dozen low-lifes on stools around a badly-constructed wooden table. She picked up the beer mug of a staring one-eyed man and drained it at a gulp. 'Tastes like camels smell,' she said. 'I think I'll have another.'

She picked up an overturned stool and sat down at the table. The two thugs to either side of her moved a little to give her space. Excellent.

Vivant would have had a fit if he had known she was coming here – a lady exposed to scum like these: a fat thief and his wife, fanning herself in the smoky atmosphere; the man with the eye-patch, his working eye running over Benny's body; a tall man and a short man in black clothes, almost a sort of uniform, with tiny bulges that suggested hidden weaponry; a drunken French soldier chewing on a cigar. She wondered who was winning the game of dice. Probably whoever was cheating the most successfully.

In Benny's experience, the second best archaeological information came not from textbooks or learned professors, but from the locals – people who had lived with, and perhaps even lived in, the ruins or remains or tombs you were interested in. If they didn't know where something was, they could find someone who did.

A bored waiter slammed another mug of beer down in front of her. Benny grinned and hefted the glass in a toast. 'Right,' she said. 'Who's for a little bet, then?'

Sesehaten the scribe took his leave of Lord Sedjet – who had been in a foul mood for weeks – and went to the local tavern to quench his thirst in black beer and bad singing.

Sesehaten sighed as he trudged through the streets of Akhetaten. He was carrying his sandals in one hand, feeling the intense heat of the day soaking into the soles of his feet through the dust.

He hated this city. He hated its hodgepodge of hastily erected buildings. He thought very little of its lazy inhabitants, courtiers uprooted from Thebes in the great rush to join the Pharaoh at his new capital. Oh, the Lord Sedjet wasn't too bad an employer, even if his skull were thicker than a mud brick. But Sesehaten hated paperwork, and a wealthy man's estate is nothing but paperwork.

There was a lot of paperwork these days. Every time the Pharaoh found some new tradition to skittle, there were more forms and plans and receipts, on papyrus or slates or bits of broken pottery.

It had been, what, seven years since the new king's coronation? And in that time, the inheritance of centuries had been knocked over like so many ducks being taken with throwing-sticks. Just trying to think about the pace of change these days gave Sesehaten a headache.

Worse than that was the thrumming behind his eyes. It came with sunset, not every night, but strongly this evening as

80

the fierce stars began their wheeling in the sky. He knew enough astronomy to pick out Mars and Jupiter, and to name one or two of the brighter stars. But tonight there were darker secrets purring in the sky, trying to push themselves into his brain, as though he had forgotten a skyful of knowledge. When this happened the only thing to do was drink the noises into silence.

So he kept his eyes in the dust, letting his naked feet take him to the tavern.

He plonked himself down on a stool in the corner. One hand automatically went to his shaven scalp, ran down the smooth skin and scratched behind his left ear. He yawned, running his eyes over the clientele. Plenty of foreigners, as there were always foreigners these days. Pretty much the usual low-life knocking themselves out on bad beer. Or good beer, if they could afford it. That was what Sesehaten was here for.

A woman shuffled up to his table, holding a tray full of bowls. She wore a peasant's dress which covered her breasts. Her hands were an unhealthy red colour with sunburn and washing-up.

'Tepy,' he breathed.

She lifted her head, just a little, to look at him. 'What are you doing here?' he asked stupidly.

'I wait on tables,' she said dully. 'I'm a waitress.'

'Oh, no. I've been looking for you for more than a week. Sit down, for – for Aten's sake,' he pleaded.

Ace stood there for a few seconds, as though she hadn't understood what he was saying. Then she dropped her tray on the table and dragged a stool over to him. She leaned on her elbows, looking at him blearily.

It was not the same woman. Not with those soft, empty eyes, those slumped shoulders. 'I thought you planned to enlist,' he stammered.

She snorted. 'They didn't even laugh,' she said. 'Didn't even laugh. They said no woman could fight as well as an Egyptian soldier. So I beat up a few of them.'

Sesehaten laughed, hesitantly. 'That got their attention,' said Tepy. 'So they went off to find their general. He said I fought better than some of his officers. But a woman in the ranks would only cause confusion, break up the boys. A foreign whore in the field would ruin morale.'

'You're no whore,' said Sesehaten.

'It's only a matter of time,' she said simply, and he was suddenly aware of the eyes pressed to her body, furtive glances or overt stares from around the open room of the tavern.

'There are,' said Tepy, waving a heavy hand, 'there are little boxes which an Egyptian man can fit into. He gets one from his father, right, a little box with a label saying SCRIBE or PEASANT or PRIEST or SCULPTOR. For women there are only two boxes. Right? They're labelled WIFE and WHORE.'

'There are women who are singers or professional mourners,' said Sesehaten. 'And musicians.'

'Can't sing,' said Tepy.

'Oh no, that's not true. I've heard you sing, it's quite pleasant.'

'The singers,' said Tepy, 'spend the whole night telling horny boys to get lost. Or not, depending on how strapped for cash they are. They're not married, so they must be open for business, right? Trap's closing around me, Sesehaten. I'm being stuffed into one of those little boxes.'

'Your like a cat herding geese,' said the scribe. 'Out of place. Not part of *ma'at*, the order of the universe.'

There was an explosive sound across the room: wine jar and skull meeting. A quarrel had started up in a corner of the tavern, two meaty soldiers arguing about the fine details of some old campaign. ''Scuse me,' said Tepy.

She weaved over to the two men, who had knocked over their table and were grappling ineffectually. She tapped one of them on the shoulder, and when he turned around she smiled invitingly.

They both gaped at her. Tepy reached up and put her arms around the soldier's neck. Wine dribbled down his face and dripped off his nose while he grinned stupidly down at her.

She locked her hands together behind his head and slammed his body down as her knee came up into his groin. He didn't make a sound – just a thump as he hit the floor. His friend stared down at him, still holding the handle of the broken wine jar.

Tepy gave him her smile, and he hoofed it for the door.

She sat back down with Sesehaten, picked up a bowl of beer from the tray, and drained it at a gulp. 'I double as a bouncer.' She wiped her mouth with the back of her hand. 'One of the reasons the old bastard keeps me on. The other one is he's trying to get into my dress. It's just the same as Sedjet. It's just the same as Sabalom. He pays the bills, eventually he'll get what he wants out of me.'

'There must be some noble who would have you as his bodyguard.'

She shrugged. 'I'm too well known, I've lost the element of surprise. And I've lost my novelty. Sedjet showed me off too many times. So much is changing around here. I thought maybe one more change wouldn't make any difference . . .'

'There are thousands of years of *ma'at* to overcome,' he said, trying to sound consoling. 'Changing that is too great a test for one woman.'

'Who fails the test feeds the Devourer,' she muttered.

'What?'

She fixed him with a dull eye. 'I hear a lot of politics, you know,' she said. 'Just one man's changing all those thousands of years of tradition.'

'Yes, but that one man happens to be the Pharaoh.'

'When I tried to join up, you know what I found out? Hardly anyone's going abroad to fight any more. There was a punitive campaign to Nubia, and a few troops sent to some of the vassal princes. But you know where most of the army is? Right here. Where the Pharaoh needs 'em. Because he's changed everything around. He's messed around with *ma'at*. And nobody's happy.'

She waved vaguely at the tavern's inhabitants. 'You should hear them start on their dreamer Pharaoh, when they've got a few bowls of beer inside them. It's like a huge wheel trying to turn, but it's stuck on a rock and there's friction and sparks. Resistance.'

'I used,' said Sesehaten, 'to be a priest.'

'Is that right?' Tepy ran her finger around the rim of her

83

bowl. 'There used to be a lot of gods, and now there's only one. And you're not allowed to worship any of the ones that Mr. Pharaoh killed. Which god did you worship?'

Why did you mention the Devourer?' asked Sesehaten.

'I had a dream.'

'Tell me about your dream.'

She was walking, descending on a long, labyrinthine path. There was a cold pain in her right wrist, and when she looked up, she realized she was being led by the hand.

The White Lady turned to her, as if wondering why she hesitated. The Lady had no face, only smoothness, like a pearly mask. Ace saw her own features reflected in that mask, and snapped her eyes away from it, worried in case the White Lady tried to take her face for her own.

They went through huge halls, great pillars shooting up towards the roof, the walls covered in the chiselled scrawl of a million scribes. There was incense everywhere, fogging the air, and through it Ace could make out figures, seated in rows, holding knives or busy with papyri. Sometimes eyes looked back at her through the scented clouds, and the eyes were not always human.

They came to a huge hall, huger than all the rest, seeming to stretch away into infinity. At the far end, miles away but perfectly clear and visible, was a raised bier, its roof covered in cobras.

'And inside the bier sat a green-faced man, attended by two ladies, with a lotus at his feet,' Sesehaten whispered.

Tepy had been staring into her bowl of beer. Now she dragged her sleepy eyes up to him. 'What is it?'

'The Hall of the Judgment of the Dead,' said Sesehaten excitedly.

'The pit of hell,' said Tepy. 'I thought all that stuff was banned.'

'It is,' said the scribe, 'but I don't think the law extends to dreams. Go on.'

There was a long, long row of figures sitting against one wall.

Perhaps half of them had human faces. Each one held an ostrich feather – or was it a knife? Ace tried to squint through the smoke at the bizarre jury, but the White Lady's sharp grip was pulling her to one side of the hall.

There were figures standing in the hall, figures that rang tiny bells in Ace's mind. She'd seen them at the Museum, her schoolfriends touching their tiny hands to a fallen arm of Ramesses, ten foot of solid stone.

A man with a jackal's head was adjusting a set of golden scales, while another man with an ibis head wrote something on a piece of papyrus, the way she'd seen Sesehaten do it, moistened brush flicking across the paper.

There was something crouching under the scales, something she didn't want to look at yet.

'This,' said Tepy, 'This is the weird bit. This is the bit where it starts getting really weird. Not just normally weird, mind you.'

She knocked over her bowl of beer.

'Next,' said Bird-brain, who was suddenly wearing a suit and tie. His curved beak peaked out from under a bowler hat too large for his tiny head.

Dog-breath left the hall, stepping past Ace and the White Lady where they stood to one side. As he passed he momentarily became dizzyingly tall, as huge and fundemental as the moon. Names were banging away in Ace's mind: Anubis, Osiris, Horus, Isis. She wished she could remember which was which.

But now each of the forty-two jurors was busily scribbling a label in the air beside them, like subtitles. They weren't human gods any more, even though their pale, lean faces looked human, capped and collared in red and gold and heliotrope. Procrastination, one was labelled, sitting next to Predestination, who was chittering at Anachronism and Lull. Time, they were gods of time.

Ace risked a glance at the White Lady who had dragged her here. Which one are you, then?' she asked. But the Lady put an alabaster finger to her non-existent lips.

When the jackal-faced man came back he was accompanied

by two ant-headed soldiers, marching at double speed, hands firmly gripping the arms of a captive being brought for judgment. The jurors hooted and shrieked as he was dragged in, the hall filling with their cries. The captive's hands were manacled before him, and he wore a beige coverall, and you know perfectly well who he is.

'Your friend?' said Sesehaten. 'The *Sinu*?'
  'Yeah,' said Tepy.

The Ant-soldiers pushed the Doctor to his knees before the scales. The jurors sat up, waving their feather-knives and cooing at the sight of the purple damage to his face. Someone had embroidered a convoluted rose over the left breast of his coverall, where a pocket might have gone.
  A great silence rolled through the hall. The jurors leaned forward, listening intently. Dog-breath stood by the scales, arms folded, looking utterly grim.
  The silence continued.
  'Well, come on, then!' said Bird-brain from underneath his bowler.
  'Yes!' cat-called one of the jurors. 'Let's have the negative confession!'
  'Have you robbed?' squeaked Twilight, waving his feather-knife in an excited circle.
  'Have you destroyed supplies of food?' Blue Moon insisted.
  'Have you stolen sacrificial offerings?'
  'Have you told lies?'
  'Blown up any planets lately?'
  'Tell us!'
  'Have you terrified people?' Ennui wanted to know.
  'Have you been quarrelsome?' shrieked Second Last.
  'You must protest your innocence!' Dog-breath told his prisoner, tiny at the feet of the god of Death. But the Doctor just looked him in the eye and kept silent.
  'Tell us! Tell us!' Haste and Quarter To started a pitched battle with their feather-knives.
  'Who cares for you?' Ace heard herself shout. 'You're

nothing but a pack of pen-pushers! We've faced worse than you!'

The Doctor was smiling, just the corner of his mouth turned up. In contempt of the court.

The bird-headed god glanced at his wrist-watch. 'Isn't there anything you'd like to tell us?'

'He died,' said Ace.

Silence fell like a stone. The gods leant forward, listening.

It came out reflexively from her throat. 'He died.'

'We know that-bit,' said Bird-brain. 'Everyone here is dead. You're dead, he's dead. This – and he gestured with his brush – is an ex-Time Lord. What's your point?'

'He left me,' she said in a tiny voice. 'He didn't come back for me.'

The jackal-headed man stepped forward, carrying something Ace hadn't been able to make out clearly before. Now she saw it was a pair of hearts.

In one of the scale's pans an ostrich feather was sitting, heavy, dragging the balance down towards it. 'The word truth and the word feather are the same in hieroglyphs. *Ma'at*,' the White Lady was hissing in her ear. 'The dead man's heart is tested by being weighed against *ma'at*.'

'What is it?' Ace whispered. Her throat had tied itself in knots.

'Truth, justice, and the Egyptian way. The order of the universe, the order of society. If his heart is heavier, he fails the test.'

'But that's not fair,' Ace was trying to say. 'He has two hearts.'

'Who fails the test feeds the Devourer,' the White Lady whispered in her ear.

Under the tipping scales, the moving thing resolved itself into a patchwork she-monster made out of pieces of animals, her mouth wide and hungry as a crocodile's.

As Bird-brain started filling in a papyrus in triplicate, the guards stepped smartly away from the Doctor, leaving him alone in the centre of the floor. The rose over his left heart blazed.

The Devourer came for the Time Lord.

He started to laugh.

* * *

'You know the weirdest thing?' said Tepy. 'I felt like I was just a bystander, an extra. Like it was his dream, and I just happened to be there.'

'A funeral dream,' Sesehaten said, 'indicates grief. It is good, it means that there is something left of him inside your mind. It is good to dream of friends, especially when we can't see them again.'

'I don't want to dream about him,' said Tepy heavily. 'I don't want to think about him, I just want to get on with it. And I'm not – there's no – I'm not grieving.'

'You don't believe he's dead, do you?'

'You don't know him. He's crukking unstoppable. Crukking unkillable. The only way he'd die is if he planned it himself.' She blew out an angry sigh. 'If he'd have landed here instead of me, he'd be telling the Pharaoh how to tie his shoelaces by now. He'd have the Zargoids eating out of his hand. 'Cept there *are* no Zargoids.'

She rubbed her eyes with the heels of her hands. 'You know, I was always dependent on him, too. And he could always get me to do what he wanted, one way or another. I can't move without him. He never stops moving, only one thing could stop him moving. And I saw it happen, I actually saw it happen. And I didn't care.'

Sesehaten said, 'When Sedjet's first wife died, he hired a bevy of wailing women to tear their hair and throw dust on their faces. He never shed a tear himself. But he had to keep up appearances.' His lip curled. 'Mourning when you feel no grief is just an elaborate lie.'

'Don't I love him? Didn't I love him?' Her voice was cool, even with the rich beer. 'He didn't even die for a good reason. 'Slike the Sarge used to say, anything you can do can get you shot, including doing nothing. And I don't care. I just don't care. I didn't really love him, and now he's gone. And I'm stuck here. Wasted. Because I can't fit into a box.'

'Listen to me,' said the scribe. 'You're a separate person. Are you the eye of your friend? Are you his hand? He's dead, but you are still alive. And not everyone shapes themselves into a box.'

Tepy's eyes were watery with booze. She wasn't listening. 'One thing about the Doctor, wherever you go, he always has powerful friends, and if he doesn't have them he makes them, and if he can't make them he becomes powerful himself. People think he's a god or an official or something. But I threw away the only powerful friend I had.'

'You said you were an Egyptian. But you don't fit in.' Sesehaten sighed. 'I can't imagine you fitting in anywhere.'

'Yeah, I'm a woman of Set,' she snorted. 'What the smeg does that mean, anyway?'

Sesehaten opened his mouth, closed it, then spoke with precision. 'Before our beloved Pharaoh established his new religion and built this city to worship his Aten, Set was worshipped as the breaker of rules, the upsetter of order. Chaos is just as much a part of the universe as order; the Nile swells every year at the same time, but sometimes it floods the villages. We pay our taxes but we get drunk. *Ma'at* says you should be a lady. But some of us have to break the rules.'

'I can break all the rules I like,' said Tepy. 'I'm still stuck in this crukking tavern. I'm off the board, out of the game. I'm going to die here, and someone will paint me with tar and bury me in a patch of sand. Jesus, listen to me. You said you'd been looking for me,' she said abruptly. 'Why?'

The scribe took a mouthful of beer. 'You know that stretch of desert you used to visit? Where Sedjet found you?' She nodded. 'I just wanted to warn you that demons have been seen there. You should avoid the place for a while.'

'Demons?' Tepy let go of her hair, pushed it cut of her flushed face. 'What the cruk kind of demons?'

'Some soldiers saw them. Giant scarabs, or some kind of insects, shining like the sun.'

'How many? What were they doing?'

'I don't know the details. The report was garbled.'

Tepy stood up, grabbing the edge of the table for support. 'Oh cruk,' she said. 'Oh cruk. The Zargoids are here.'

'Tepy,' said Sesehaten, alarmed, 'What's a Zargoid?'

'The people who killed the Doctor. They've come looking for me. Whatever they are.' She pressed her hands to her face, trying to think. 'They'll scan for high-technology equipment. Oh cruk, Sedjet –'

* * *

89

This is the home of the Lord Sedjet.

In the courtyard, torches are burning, sending thinning curls of smoke into the sunset. A soft wind blows the smell of ash over the surrounding fields, carries it through the rooms of the mansion.

Inside the main hall, the braziers have burned low, filling the room with cool red light. In a corner, there are instruments scattered across the floor: drums, castanets, *sistra* with their tiny rattles silenced. A pair of flutes have rolled across a reed mat to stop at a lute with a broken string.

The stools and tables have been overturned, and the floor is covered in food and flowers.

A cat picks its way across the floor, its fur still standing out with fright. It steps delicately over a fallen necklace and picks up a grilled fish in its mouth. There is a single bite missing from the fish.

The cat pads out of the room, silently. There is no sound but the hiss of wind through the grain.

Ace came sprinting up the narrow path that lead to Sedjet's estate, at the very edge of the city of Akhetaten.

She was drunk and unarmed, totally unprepared for combat. But she ran like a leopard, on naked feet with soles as hard as leather, her blood thumping through her. She was sure she could see in the dark. The air was cold and dusty and it tasted like clear water. It was as though she had woken up.

The estate was dimly lit, and silent. She hoped that just meant everyone had gone to bed early.

Slowly, staying in the shadows, she circled the house. Nothing hiding behind the grain bins at the side, nothing in the garbage yard – the first flush of adrenalin was starting to wear off, the bright battle feeling becoming a distant nagging in her belly. She thought of Sedjet's tiny daughters. What had followed her here? Whose fire had she drawn?

The entrance courtyard was on the inside, the mansion had no windows; torches at the corners of the building, created wide pools of light. She tilted her head. Listening. Gathering intelligence.

There was a cat sitting at the front door, chewing on a scrap of meat. It hissed at her and shot into the night, leaving its meal behind. Ace watched it go. Little bugger had the right idea.

She went into the house.

They'd been having a party when they were interrupted. The spoor of panic was all over the place, smashed dishes and trampled fruit.

She went from room to room, listening carefully. She found the armoury, wished for a phased plasma rifle in the 40W range, picked up a *khopesh*.

When she was in the girls' bedroom, someone started shouting in the main hall.

She loped back out, the heavy weapon flashing in her hand. 'Oh, god!' Sesehaten was crying, stumbling about the room. 'Oh, my gods! Was it the demons?' Ace didn't bother to shut him up. She went back to her search.

The place wasn't damaged. It hadn't been empty for too long, either, judging by the torches and the braziers. Some of the meat was still warm. Now, if everyone just decided to leave, they'd run back down the path into the city – and Ace would have seen them. So they'd gone into the desert, or they'd vaporized altogether.

Bandits?

She knew it wasn't bandits.

Sesehaten started to scream.

Ace was back in the hall in a moment. The scribe had fallen backwards over a stool, and was staring up at an enormous metal Ant. The insect turned its oval head to look at her, with complex stalked eyes or antennae whirring.

In that instant Ace's world exploded back to its full size. A high-tech extraterrestrial in the living room. There was a numb tickling in her chest, and she realized that she ought to be laughing.

What was the damn thing packing? Didn't matter. If the enemy is in range, so are you; which means that if you're in range, so is the enemy!

Ace sprang over the table and smashed the thing's face with her sword. There was a delightful sound of metal on metal, even a few sparks, and several antennae twisted into new and interesting shapes.

The robot reared backwards. Sesehaten screamed again. Ace swung her khopesh in a beheading arc, but the Ant's slender neck refused to give.

Now she could feel a fierce humming at the edge of her mind, and snarled, battering at the thing's legs as it distorted subtly, like a dream monster, its bent antennae reaching for her face.

Sesehaten hit it with a stool. It turned, and the droning in Ace's head got worse, like a headache coming on, occluding her vision. The sword trembled in her hand.

The Ant fell over.

The buzzing stopped, as though someone had thrown a switch. Sesehaten and Ace looked at one another over their fallen enemy.

'Where have you been all my life?' Ace asked the machine.

She knelt down beside the insect, put down her sword, started probing it all over. She ran her fingers over its seams, testing the swivelling joints of the antennae. It really did look like an ant, with the wasp waist and the six, jointed legs, though there were far too many things attached to its head. It was a sophisticated little bug. But it wasn't The Enemy, it was just a lackey.

'What happened?' gasped Sesehaten, keeping well away from the machine.

'Someone cut its broadcast power,' said Ace, which really didn't answer his question.

Perhaps when the Ant(s) hadn't been able to find her, it had taken everyone else. Possibly as hostages. Equally likely because it didn't want to return to its controller empty-handed, or empty-mandibled or whatever. They'd snatched the passengers from starliners, and now they were kidnapping Egyptians.

'Right,' she said. She stepped past Sesehaten, who was quivering with confusion. As far as he was concerned, this thing was a demon. 'Where are you going?' he asked.

'The desert. Where the Ant came from.'

'Where you came from,' said the scribe.

They rode a chariot for two, thankful that the sun hadn't quite gone down. Ace knew from practice how dangerous it was to drive the things at night. Especially when you were still half-sloshed. Though finding an alien robot in your former living room was a sobering experience.

Sesehaten grabbed her hips and held on for dear life as they hurtled over the desert rocks. She had sod-all in the way of strategy. Just rock up with one sword and a quivering ex-priest.

However she'd got here, the Ant had obviously come the same way. She should have checked the desert more carefully. Maybe there was a hidden machine or some sort of gateway. Maybe all this time she could have escaped.

Maybe she'd been supposed to work that out for herself. Maybe there was a big clever plan, and she just hadn't seen it before now.

Or maybe not. She was so used to trying to work out what the Doctor was up to, and now he wasn't up to anything except pushing up daisies.

The ridges became more familiar. She pulled up the chariot, Sesehaten clutching at her as they skidded to a halt.

Silence. Desert darkness. 'You feel that?' she said to him, invisible under the starlight.

Sesehaten shook his head.

Ace stepped down and lit up a torch. 'Come on,' she said.

Silence. Desert darkness. 'You feel that?' she said to him, invisible under the starlight.

Sesehaten shook his head.

Ace stepped down, lit up a torch. 'Come on,' she said, and 'What the hell was that?'

Sesehaten said, 'What was what?'

'Didn't I – didn't we –'

Sesehaten shook his head.

Ace stepped down, lit up a torch. 'Come on,' she said, and 'What the hell was that?'

Sesehaten said, 'What was what?'

'Didn't I – didn't we –' Ace spun, the torchlight waving over the ground. 'You didn't notice anything weird just then?'

'Nothing,' whispered Sesehaten, alarmed. 'What's going on?'

'Let's find out.'

She led him down the rough path into the valley. There was the water hole, dried up now. Good. Armed with only her torch and the *khopesh*, she wasn't in the mood for wild animals.

No sign of the Ants. Damn. Where were they? Had they left any tracks? Slow down, slow down. The problem with the easy way out is that it's been mined.

Her hackles were standing up, but it was more than just grunt caution. There was some sort of distortion here, the sort that only someone who's crossed the time field dozens of times can sense. Like a sphere talking to a circle, she thought crazily, I've got perspective.

They were walking up the ridge she had rolled down, all those months ago. She'd been over the place with a fine-toothed comb, looking for clues. How could she have missed something?

There was a popping sound in the air, just ahead, as though something were frying.

Sesehaten grabbed her hand and pulled her backwards.

She dropped the torch, yelling. The red flames went out as the torch rolled in the sand. She struggled with Sesehaten, who was still grabbing at her, trying to drag her away from the sound.

BANG! Pop! Splitch! BANG!

Ace ripped herself free of the scribe's hands and leapt up the ridge. The air was distorting, shafts of intolerable light exploding out of a point perhaps five feet above the sand, Coming out of nowhere as the popcorn noise intensified and the burring in her brain made her stomach twist and her hands ache.

Cornwall, she'd felt this before in Cornwall, when the sky had torn like paper, and she'd felt it on the organic ship, lying on a floor made of flesh while Benny tried to drag her into a rip in space-time.

With a silent explosion the rift opened above her.

Wind screamed into the hole in reality, whipping dust over her crouching form. She couldn't help looking into the hole, like when there was an eclipse when she was a little girl and they told you not to look at it in case you went blind and she spent the whole day staring at her shoes in case she saw the eclipse and her head just couldn't get itself around what she was seeing inside the hole!

She was being dragged across the sand, lifted into the air. Sucked in, she thought dizzily.

Sesehaten caught her ankle and pulled hard. Somehow she struck the *khopesh* into the hard ground, like an anchor.

The rift imploded, and they both dropped to the ground, dust and tiny stones falling onto them in a layer. They lay there, winded and dazed.

Then Ace hauled herself to her feet and ripped the sword out of the ground. 'You son of a bitch!' she screamed at Sesehaten. 'You knew! You knew all the time!'

He scrambled backwards across the sand, out of range of her rage, convinced she could see him in the pitch blackness.

'You knew how I got here! You knew about the rift! You bastard, you knew the whole time! Why didn't you tell me, you – Why didn't you tell me?'

'Tepy!' he screamed.

'Jesus Christ,' she breathed, and suddenly she was on the other side of him, and he couldn't see which way to run. 'If you're working for the people who killed the Doctor, I'll gut you. I swear I'll slice you up. Come *here*.'

'Tepy,' said another voice.

They both looked up.

Torches, a dozen torches, flickering in a dozen hands. Red light reflecting from shaved heads. White robes. Eyes watching.

What Ace wanted to do was come at them with the *khopesh* and wreak havoc. Vengeance for seven months in hell.

Instead, she said, 'Oh, for God's sake. Who are you?'

'The gods are banished,' gasped Sesehaten from the dirt. 'Banished but not forgotten. The priests are unemployed, but they haven't forgotten their duty.'

'Which gods?' Ace asked, but she already knew.

'We are the men of Set,' said the leader of the priests.

'Yeah, and I'm Cleopatra,' said Ace.

'We are the priests of Set, called Sutekh, called Setekh. He is the all high, the all powerful, who holds all life in his hands, who brings death. He is the desert, the storm, the flood. He is the destroyer, the trickster, the chaos-bringer, the law-breaker.'

Ace laughed. 'Sounds like the Devil,' she said. 'But that's okay. I've worked for the Devil before.'

Second Piece

Butterfly Wings

They say that chess, like cards, has Kings and Queens.
What of the Aces? They play too!
                                        (Jan Standinger)

Chapter 7

Opening Flower

Yume no naka ni
Ai-mimu koto wo
Tanome-tsutsu
Kuraseru yoi wa
Nemu kata mo nashi

I was up all night hoping I'd dream about you.
(Anonymous Japanese poet, *Kokin Shu*, tenth century)

The soldier's name was Michel. He was twenty-two years old, tall and skinny, with fair hair and blue eyes that looked perpetually surprised.

But the details aren't important.

Michel had joined the Garde Nationale long before the trouble had begun. He had a dream about becoming a soldier of fortune, marching through France's colonies, writing to his mother and sisters to tell them about his adventures. He wanted to see something amazing, something really unbelievable.

Michel tried to make the war more exciting by imaging it written down in books, being read by scholars and schoolchildren in a hundred years' time, in a thousand. He was part of that history. But the events of the past few months were shuffled inside his head like a deck of cards.

Paris was the City of Light, the centre of the civilised world. It was all about Paris. He remembered the September day the Emperor had surrendered to the Prussians. Like all the Garde, he had no chance to bite the enemy; they stayed in the capital, idle, as the news from Sedan came through in trickles. It was hard to remember that France had started the war in the first place. *Nach Paris*, the Germans were shouting. Paris next!

The very next day the Parisians had elected their own Republican government. There was no way *la ville de lumière* could be made to surrender! But Michel had not been with Flourens when he marched on the Hotel de Ville, demanding that Garde be permitted to attack the Prussians. That was one day he did remember clearly, staying behind as the news trickled through. But no, there was more waiting.

The bombardment and the famine came together, followed quickly by smallpox. The rich were dining on elephant and antelope as the Paris zoo was emptied. The poor were eating one carrot a day and freezing to death in the gutter.

Michel wrote to his mother and sisters in La Bas, scribbled notes tucked into the coats of travelling soldiers. Once, he sent a letter by balloon. That was another moment of clarity: staring at a patch of blue sky long after the fickle thing had flown away. He sighed, hoping his letter wouldn't land in Norway, or the ocean.

Michel spent his days at rifle practice, or drinking, or swapping stories with the other men of the Garde. It was hideously cold. Every tree in the Champs Elysee had been cut down for firewood, old women using picks to hack up the roots.

It was January when they finally sent the Garde out against the Prussians. Michel stayed behind. Michel wasn't one of the ten thousand *gardes* who died. The word was that the government had wanted to see as many of the Garde killed as possible. They knew they were sitting on an army of rebels, half-starved. half-crazy and half-drunk. burning with siege fever. Why not let the Prussians thin them out a bit?

The armistice had come soon after. They'd cut the Garde Nationale pay – you had to beg to get anything. In the popular clubs, the revolutionaries debated the demands on the poor to pay the rent waived during the siege, the fact that the food and aid pouring into the capital was bypassing the starving. Paris seethed under its surface as though the sewers were alight.

Michel wasn't one of the *gardes* who attacked the Hotel de Ville after the January Sortie. The first French blood spilled by French bullets. He stayed behind, reading the Red Poster that was stuck up everywhere: "Make way for the people! Make way for the Commune!".

Barely a month after that the Garde Nationale seized scores of army cannon and took them to Montmartre, storing up arms and ammunition. Suddenly they were the most powerful army in France. Michel had stayed behind, marching in the Second Empire anniversary celebrations.

He remembered a shell striking the pavement close by him and the taste of concrete powder in his mouth. Things after that were a little blurry.

Vaguely Michel was aware of the clock spinning around him, of grains of sand running through the hour-glass too fast for him to count.

He remembered the fumigation of Paris after the Prussian victory parade, the smell of bonfires and disinfectant.

He remembered a little of Montmartre, the screaming of the mob, *gardes* and rabble pressing in around the army. The regular soldiers were abandoning their own officers and joining the Garde. Michel watched when they shot a couple of generals, for really no reason at all. Was it the soldiers, or the mob? He couldn't remember. Someone with guns. Angry faces, shouting.

Things after that were more blurry still. He remembered the election of the Commune, of course – who could ever forget that day? Two revolutions in a row! *'Vive le Commune! Vive le Commune!'* and pouring through the streets before the Hotel de Ville. Red flags waving. Smiling faces, shouting.

But the shelling went on, and the fighting went on, and the Garde were as confused and drunk as the Commune, wandering about Paris with no-one to fight.

And some small part of Michel, a buried human understanding passed down through generations of killing, knew that this war was no different to any other war. The reasons weren't important, the strategies, the economics, the history. It was part of the long-unbroken chain of human violence. It was just another war.

It was a surgeon shot under a flag of truce.

It was an innocent man bound by a mob and hurled into the Seine and stoned until he finally sank.

It was the field of Buzenval, so jammed with bodies that you couldn't walk over it.

It was a grandmother gnawing at a rat's bones because there was nothing else to eat.

It was a small girl sliced in half by a shell on her way home from school.

But the details aren't important.

Kadiatu's ship was well-stocked with antibiotics. In her own time, the whole human race was stitched together by massive public transport; if someone came down with a cold, a million people got it – and got immunity to it.

But the past was a foreign country – or a lot of foreign countries, with no Solar Transit System to homogenize them, separated by trivial barriers: mountains, water, politics. Kadiatu had been expecting to pick up every little bug. She'd brought plenty of tissues along with the medicines.

But Kadiatu had never been ill in her life.

Around her, Parisians were dying in their hundreds as the water went bad and the food started to run out. Or in childbirth. Or from a pinprick. Or a mosquito bite. Sometimes Kadiatu imagined herself taking a shot of penicillin, and some severe French schoolmarm rapping her over the knuckles and saying, 'Well, my girl, I hope you brought enough for everybody.'

She was spending a lot of her time in the basement these days, not so much because of the stored equipment but because of the shelling. A house right next door had been completely demolished; only the joining wall had been left standing. Her own house was completely untouched, except for a rain of brickbats and plaster powder onto the roof.

'How did you get that thing in here?' the Doctor said.

Kadiatu had been going through her morning exercises, stretching and jogging on a bit of carpet in the corner of the basement. She wore the undergarment of her hostile environment suit, grey synthetic stuff that breathed like her own skin. She stopped.

'Nicolas carried it in his cart,' she said, rubbing the back of her neck. She hadn't worked up a sweat; she wasn't even breathing hard. 'In pieces.'

'And then you put it back together?'

'Don't panic. I'm not about to nuke Paris.' She saw an image of a city flattened under a piece of asteroid belt, a Martian warning that howled out of the sky, brighter than Hiroshima. Cribbed from a hundred warvid ads, documentaries her father's description. 'I'm out of fuel, remember?'

'What did you tell the locals it was?'

'I didn't tell them it was anything. People are desperate for money, there's a war on. Don't worry, nobody knows I'm here, it's all under control.'

The Doctor was sitting on the basement steps, the trap-door over his head. From time to time the wooden hatch rattled with the falling of distant bombs. 'So you arrived in the countryside. Why move to Paris?'

'More central, more resources.' Kadiatu tried to start up her exercises again, clumsy and uncomfortable under his gaze. 'And the soldiers were crawling all over Thierry's estate. We couldn't leave it out in the open like that.'

'You must have had help. If nothing else you would have needed French lessons.'

'*J'ai atterri dans le verger de pommiers de M Thierry*,' she said. '*Il sait que je viens de l'avenir, mais tout est en ordre.*'

Someone banged on the trap-door. The Doctor looked up and pushed it open a crack. One of Kadiatu's *domestiques* peered at him. '*Excusez-moi. La voiture de M Thierry est arrivée, et il y a des soldats dehors. Madame, est-elle là?*'

'Soldiers? Hell. What do they want? Hang on, Lili, I'll be up there in a minute.'

Benny smiled, aimed in the direction of her head and perched the glass atop it.

Her opponent, the fat thief, slid silently under the table. His wife squawked and went down on her knees, fanning him frantically.

Benny took the glass off her head and raked in the kitty. 'Anyone else?' she said.

The two men in black were the only sober people left at the table. The one-eyed beggar kept giggling to himself, his

103

stringy beard dripping with beer. Benny was pleasantly sloshed, but nothing more – she could still walk in a straight line, and had even managed to get to the bar and back again with more of the watered-down beer.

The smaller man reached for the jug and poured himself a cup. 'What d'you plan to bet?' she asked.

'You've been talking all night about the French,' said the short man. 'But you are not French.'

Benny shook her head. 'But I want the same thing as the French. Information. About all the old things, the old, old things.'

'Anything in particular?'

Benny nodded, grinning. She took out a piece of paper. Three English words were written across it in bold capitals.

There was a long moment. The taller man shrugged.

'I've seen that,' tittered the beggar.

Michel was with the ragged Garde troops when they went on their doorknock through Paris, looking for horses. Through the haze of cheap wine – he never had been able to hold his drink – he wondered how many doors there were left to knock on.

That morning they'd been helping to put up the scaffolding around the Vendôme Column. They were planning to pull down the old monument, one of these days; there was even talk of destroying Notre Dame.

The Column would make a good crash when it came down, thought Michel. A good, loud crash.

When the lieutenant found him quivering against a wall with his hands over his ears, he'd spat and swore and put him on *Comité* detail. Now Michel trailed behind the other soldiers in his patched uniform, eyes reflecting the details of Paris like broken windows. The morning light was smoky and orange.

The merchants had complained that the Commune put its guns where they would draw the Versailles shells onto their houses. He had no idea whether that were true, but there were houses in ruins – houses with holes knocked in walls or roofs, rich men's mansions reduced to splinters, children and their

104

grandparents rummaging in the wreckage for firewood.

Sometimes they heard a dog bark under the ruins, or a woman weeping. There were people living in cellars, under what was left of their homes. The shells fell in a gentle rain. Each distant *thwack* drove Michel deeper into himself. His feet followed his little group but his head was wandering in the village of La Bas, under a summer sky.

They had come to a yard attached to a house – damaged, but still standing – with a stable at the rear. A single gaping hole in the cobblestones showed where a shell had landed, missing the house by a few feet.

The other soldiers were shouting and bashing at the gates with their rifle butts. Where was the concierge? Killed, or fled, thought Michel. He could see a horse and trap in the courtyard, a man defensively holding a child while he looked back at them in surprise.

The door at the side of the house banged angrily open, and out strode an immensely tall woman. Michel stared at her between the bars of the gate. His head was suddenly full of the musk of the tigers and lions, still alive in the zoo, too terrifying to kill for food even when the elephants' trunks were being eaten in fashionable restaurants.

The Lieutenant was waving about a requisition from the *Comité de Transport*. 'Horses!' he shouted. We want any beasts of burden which you have. Donkeys and large dogs will do as well. We are commandeering them.'

The woman was followed by a small man, scurrying to keep up with her. It was only when Michel saw his paleness that he realized the rich colour of the woman's skin, saw her African face. Even in her skirts she moved with the perfect rhythm of a panther. Some part of his mind imagined the muscles under her dress, the dark skin beneath her petticoat.

The woman unlocked the gate. The lieutenant waved his pistol in her face.

She moved, in a blur of limbs, long limbs as graceful as a ballerina's, too fast for Michel to follow. The lieutenant had fallen onto the ground, and still she was moving, dancing between the *gardes*. Robert fell over, Jean-Paul was skipping backwards, wearing a ridiculous expression of surprise, fumbling with his gun.

Michel unslung his rifle and held it in front of him. She was beautiful, the most *incroyable* thing he had ever seen.

Someone was shouting. Michel couldn't understand the words. Perhaps shouting for her to stop.

He saw that there was a single diamond stud on the right side of her nose, glittering like a tiny fire against the deep colour of her skin.

She twisted the rifle out of his hands and smacked the butt into his face, driving three centimetre-long splinters of his nasal bone deep into his frontal lobes.

But the details aren't important.

The littleboy was eating a biscuit. There were less than a dozen left, carefully wrapped in paper and hidden away in a tin in Kadiatu's kitchen. The littleboy nibbled it all around the edges, carefully, picking up any crumbs that fell onto his trousers.

Monsieur Thierry sat beside him on Kadiatu's chaise longue, hat clasped in one hand. He was dressed as simply as he could manage, but the hat gave him away. His trousers might be worn and the sleeve of his shirt conspicuously ripped, but the hat was expensive and in perfect condition.

One of Kadiatu's *gens de maison* brought him a glass of wine, and he held it in his hat-free hand. The grandfather clock's pendulum swung, its deep *tock* echoing from the wood panelling.

Round and round the littleboy nibbled, red head bobbing, pale eyes watching the grown-ups.

M Thierry was an exceptionally tall man, with unkempt wavy hair, a large mouth, and dark eyes that roamed about the room like an insect's. His arched eyebrows gave him a permanently serious look. At the moment he felt thoroughly uncomfortable, and well he might, given that this strange woman friend of his had just slaughtered four soldiers in front of his eyes. What exactly did one say in these circumstances?

'Are all women of the future like you?' he ventured, half-jokingly.

'Assuredly not,' said the Doctor.

106

The odd little foreigner was examining in great detail a glass bowl of flowers on the mantelpiece, one hand stretched out as though to stroke the dewy petals. Fresh roses from Mlle Lethbridge-Stewart's garden. The little man's eyes were closed. A half-full glass of wine stood on the mantelpiece.

The littleboy bit through the centre of his biscuit with a *snap*.

'I'm sorry,' said Kadiatu. She had washed and put on a new dress, the maids silently taking away her bloodied clothes, their lips pressed together with distaste. 'In front of *le petit*.'

Thierry looked from her to the Doctor and back again, a peculiar half-grin showing the tips of his teeth. She was watching the little man anxiously – well, not watching him, but her eyes kept going back to him. It was as though he was the dangerous one.

Thierry patted the child on the head. 'He doesn't seem any the worse for it,' he said.

The Doctor said, 'Who else knows you're here?'

'M Thierry saw me crash. Er, land.'

'Right in the middle of my apples,' Thierry joked quietly. He had the strangest feeling that he was attending some sort of trial. He got up, still holding his hat and sauntered over to the birdcage that stood in the corner. 'I take it the Doctor is also from *votre siècle*?'

'You weren't too discreet yourself,' Kadiatu was saying, 'not if Stone Mountain is anything to go by.'

'Who have you told about Kadiatu, M Thierry?' asked the Doctor softly.

The song-bird had died through neglect. It lay in a tiny heap on the bottom of the cage. 'No-one. She is too large a secret to share. I want her all to myself.' He half-smiled again. Was it he or Kadiatu who was being judged? 'I helped her to move her vehicle and to conceal her equipment.'

'Why?'

'I saw a human being in need, and I came to her assistance,' said Thierry. He patted Kadiatu on the shoulder, paternally. 'What would you do without me, my dear?'

'That's a good question,' said Kadiatu, but Thierry missed her irony. He opened the package he'd brought with him and took out a sheaf of paper.

'Receipts and records for the house, Mademoiselle,' he said. 'I wanted to make sure you had these papers, as well as a few fresh vegetables. Alas, they were commandeered by soldiers at the gates, wanting to be sure I was not a spy from Versailles. I expect they imagined the parsnips were filled with gunpowder.'

Kadiatu took the papers and locked them in her writing desk. 'You took a hell of a risk coming here,' she said, and her eyes were on the little man. 'It's not that I'm not grateful, but the shells, you must look after the boy –

'I understand,' said Thierry. 'I'll postpone my next visit until conditions are a little more favourable. Please, if Paris becomes intolerable, you must come and stay with me. I will take good care of you. Good care of you both.'

The Doctor looked across at the littleboy. For a few moments their eyes met.

The little man drew his hand back sharply from the flowers, and absently sucked on the finger pierced by the thorn.

He hadn't meant to go to sleep.

The book slowly slid out of the Doctor's hand. He was lying on Kadiatu's chaise longue, head propped up by an embroidered cushion, trying to read Les Misérables. *Outside the sky was golden, shuddering with the sound of cannons.*

Normally he only slept an hour or so in every forty-eight, and wasn't in the habit of dozing off, except when he really needed to conserve his energy, but tonight, after supper, his head was fuzzy and his limbs were heavy. Sometimes it was pleasant to let things take their own course, not to plan every minute.

Sometimes.

Half-awake, he saw the face of the child-soldier whose head Kadiatu had smashed. The thrill of the kill had been hardwired into her genes long before she'd been born. He imagined himself falling past a giant strand of her DNA, wondering if he could change it, rewrite it. Rewrite her. It was because of him she was here, and he could not let her do any more damage.

The book teetered, just held by his fingertips, as the last

108

wave of weariness overwhelmed him. He muttered something
in his sleep about tea.

Like most people, Kadiatu forgot her dreams. But when you
have the same dream again and again, the details build up
layer after layer – until, stirring in your REM sleep atop the
heavy covers in the French summer, the déjà vu kicks in.

Kadiatu had been here before.

She was aware that she was dreaming, in a disconnected
way, as though she were playing a VR game while half-
asleep.

It was absolutely silent. No, there was the wind in the bamboo, the tiny bell-sound of a small stream.

She snapped her head around, eyes raking the trees. She
would be attacked, she didn't belong here! But there were
only trees, and stones, and bushes, placed by human hands in
deceptively natural, random patterns. A path led deeper into
the garden, dark stepping-stones gently curving away through
the yellow gingkos. The air was pure and cool, without the
taste of smoke. An autumn sky wheeled overhead, licked by
cirrus, full of golden sunlight.

It was too real, too untidy to be media memories, a maga-
zine-and-movie Japan. No, this was someone else's memories, someone else's dream.

She walked along the path, the breeze damp against her
cheeks, following the *tobiishi* until they led her to a hut
covered in moss.

Kadiatu looked around again, sharply, straining to make out
some half-heard sound. But there was only the whirring of the
cicadas and the trickle of water into a hollowed-out stone
beside her. A butterfly landed on the rock, a muted flutter of
colour.

Kadiatu picked up the bamboo scoop and poured water
over her hands, rinsed out her mouth. The water was shock-
ingly cold, slightly metallic – spring water, bubbling up from
somewhere inside the garden. As she had done every time,
she carefully replaced the bamboo scoop, bent under the doorway, and went inside the wooden hut.

She hesitated, not wanting to disturb the occupant. At first she thought he was kneeling, but then she realised he was sitting Japanese-style, deep in contemplation of the flower arrangement in the *tokonoma*. She'd seen her father do the same, sitting in front of a soothing hologram he'd bought from an artist on Triton.

The room was bare except for the *tokonoma* and a great iron kettle perched over a fire-pit in the middle of the floor, surrounded by straw mats. Behind the flowers the niche was decorated with an equally simple painted scroll. Kadiatu ran her eye down the calligraphy, wondering what it said.

'Empty your cup,' said the Doctor.

Kadiatu was startled. He'd never spoken before, never been aware that she was there before.

'Who are you?' he said, without turning around.

'An engineer,' Kadiatu heard herself saying. 'A student.'

'Nan-in received a university professor at his temple,' said the Doctor. 'He poured tea into his guest's cup, and continued pouring until tea ran onto the table and dripped onto the floor. "It's too full!" cried the scholar.'

'Listen,' said Kadiatu. 'Can you hear that?'

'I can't hear anything,' said the Doctor wearily. '"Like this cup," said Nan-in, "you're full of your own opinions. How can I teach you the truth unless you empty your cup?"'

Kadiatu's head turned. It was a woman, her face painted chalk-white, kimono, the full works. The butterfly was perched on the woman's hand, its iridescent wings opening and closing softly. 'Where is your steward?' she asked.

'I'm trying to find her,' said the Doctor. 'I'm trying. But it's taking so long. I need just one more week. One more day. Just one more day.'

The woman took something from the sleeve of her kimono. Kadiatu saw it was an hour-glass. The woman stretched out a delicate hand, put the glass in front of the flowers and the scroll. It was very small.

'You're Death, aren't you?' said Kadiatu.

'There is a family resemblance,' said the woman. 'I am Time, and this is my champion.'

'He's mine.'

There was another woman. Kadiatu found herself shrinking

110

back, instinctively. *It's starting to get crowded in here.*

The newcomer (or had she been there all along?) knelt on the floor on a low wooden stool, idly flicking the air with a feather-duster. She was white, absolutely white, a silhouette, a piece of the rice-paper that the artist forgot to paint.

The Doctor turned his head, and Kadiatu saw the spectacular bruise on his left cheek. 'You see?' said the White Lady. Her voice was like swallowing glass. 'He wears my favour.'

There were other figures too, crowding into the tea room. Or perhaps they were only wall-hangings, or holograms in single neon colours: Blue Aztec, silver Sumerian. A glaring Egyptian with the head of some animal Kadiatu didn't recognize, a camel with square ears, or a long-snouted greyhound. Different cultures and times crammed into the one place, all the gods who had lived inside the Doctor's head.

Kadiatu imagined his dreams leaking through the cracks she had made in time, forwards, backwards, sideways. Who heard him, who dreamed his dreams? Did he only exist because so many people dreamed about him? Did they exist because they dreamed of him?

None of these gods had been invited to the tea-party – but then, neither had she. She'd left the door open for them when she'd come trespassing in his garden.

So she shut up, tried to stay inconspicuous. At least, as inconspicuous as a six and a half foot tall black woman can be in a small *chashitsu*. She didn't want the White Lady to notice her.

The Lady ran a smooth white finger along the Doctor's scar. He tried hard not to react. 'I came here to get away from it all,' he said.

'You can't get away from me,' said the White Lady. 'Like a moth to the flame you're always returning.'

Kadiatu tilted her head, trying to make out the sound outside the hut.

'Do you remember the first time we met?' the Lady was saying. 'High on a rocky hillside, and you running out of the house, into the cold air.'

'I remember. I remember watching the outsiders in the valley, with their bows and arrows . . .'

Time put her hand on his shoulder, her butterfly flittering and landing in his hair. He smiled at the feathery touch. 'I remember the flutterwing. I thought it was some sort of meteorological phenomenon; it took up half the sky. It was gorgeous . . .'

'And then?'

'I did not know whether I was then a man dreaming I was a butterfly, or whether I am now a butterfly dreaming I am a man,' breathed the Doctor. 'Or was it a frog?'

'Don't avoid the question,' said the White Lady.

'Don't mind me, I'm playing for Time.'

'Playing to win?'

'She heals all wounds.'

'Wounds all heels?'

'Can't you hear it?' said Kadiatu. 'Someone's screaming.'

The white Lady lifted her head to listen. 'That's my song. I hear the scream, even when you make no sound.'

Kadiatu looked at the hour-glass, but the sand weighed heavily on the bottom. There was no Time left. The hut was empty but for the three of them.

'Scream,' said the White Lady.

She pressed a perfect hand against the Doctor's left collarbone. He met her eyeless eyes and grabbed at her wrist, trying to wrench her palm away. She was irresistibly pushing him back onto the matting, her fingers digging through the cloth of his jacket. The butterfly was crushed against the matting.

'Why won't you scream?'

He moaned through clenched teeth as something green erupted from above his collarbone. Young leaves shot up between the Lady's white fingers. A single, blood-red flower unfurled itself in her grip, its petals pulsing in time with his hearts.

'WHAT DO I HAVE TO DO TO MAKE YOU SCREAM?'

Kadiatu did not want to throw up on the nice straw mats, so she bolted out of the tea-room, fingers dragging at her midriff.

She ran through a hideous green, organic chamber. A group of uniformed men and women were kicking something on the floor, something curled into a protective shape, arms thrown over its head.

She fled into a room full of surgeons, masked and gowned,

112

one stabbing a massive scalpel into the shoulder of a draped figure on a table. The other figures carried garden implements. A nurse filled a syringe with fertiliser. Kadiatu ran, throwing her arms over her head. She didn't remember any of this.

She found herself stumbling over a worn hillside covered in scree, gasping as she looked up into the orange sky and saw the giant insect pitch and yaw, a long arrow shaft embedded in its body, rainbow wings twisting as it glided to earth. Someone cried out, a young voice in this ancient place, but it wasn't pain.

She found herself in a vast chamber, the walls and floor grown in pieces in a vat, cryogenic tubes embedded like neon in the walls.

'What was the point?' snarled Meijer. 'What was the crukking point?' He tightened his grip. 'We processed a four-year-old this morning. Subject fifty-one. We'll make *her* number fifty-two.'

With a movement that was almost graceful, Meijer twisted the arm he was holding one more notch. There was a *crack*.

The Doctor screamed.

But it wasn't pain. It was anger.

Kadiatu sat bolt upright in her bed.

What was that?

The book teetered, just held by his fingertips. He muttered something in his sleep about tea.

He woke up with a start.

There was an Ant not a foot away from him.

He dropped *Les Misérables*.

Its antennae reached for him almost faster than he could react, jolting backwards with such force that he knocked the chaise longue over. He landed hard on the floor, rolling away from the machine.

There was a terrible buzzing in his skull, like a kitchen timer gone insane. The Ant was climbing over the chaise longue to get to him. Soft buzzing. Its attachments whirred like blender blades.

Someone was pouring warm honey into his head.

113

He scrabbled limply backwards across the floor, but his arms and legs were melting, melting into the sweet heat. The droning dragged at his feet and hands. Keep going, get away! He tried to fight, but there was nothing to fight, only the slow unknotting of his muscles, the sleepiness gnawing at his eyes.

There was a paraffin lamp burning low on the writing desk. He grabbed with hands as heavy as treacle.

Somehow he swung the lamp as the Ant lunged at him. Glass smashed across the hungry metal face. There was a flash of flame and a puff of kerosene smell. The robot reared up, struck at him with metal legs, knocking him gently against the grandfather clock.

When it came down it brushed its antennae across his face, softly.

His whole body turned into honey and melted down the wall.

The Ant loomed over him for a moment, its antennae twitching. The metal sensors traced patterns on his face, stroking his mind. It didn't hurt, it was gentle, it didn't hurt it was so soft, tick buzzing, working its way into him gently, tock, it didn't hurt, alarm clock, tick, ringing, buzzing, tock. Get up! TICK. Get up! TOCK. Time to, TICK, get up! TOCK. Get up.

Chapter 8

Mandelbrot Set Piece

> The great god Ra whose shrine once covered acres
> Is filler now for crossword-puzzle makers.
>
> (Keith Preston)

'You ever heard of the butterfly effect?' said Ace.

She and Sesehaten were watching two priests bathe in a small fountain, ritually washing their bodies. They stepped out of the water, and the other Setites handed them clean linen.

Ace had been formally introduced to the group. They were serious men with serious eyes, their mouths set in hard conspiratorial lines. Ex-priests, now clerks – petty officials who had come a long way down in the world. The fountain was behind Senef's house, and behind the fountain was a cave, a vertical slit in the cliff. 'What's in there, Sesehaten?'

'My name,' said the scribe, 'is Sesehset.'

'You had to change your name when Pharaoh brought in the new religion, right?'

Sesehset blew out a long sigh, disturbing the motes of dust swirling in the dawn air. 'He changed his name, and everyone followed suit. He was born Amenhotep, in honour of Amun, the first of gods. I suppose in some ways we should be grateful. Our temples and estates were confiscated, our priests put out of work and the care, the feeding of Set left undone. But Amun's temples –' He shook his head. 'Akhenaten's men swarmed over the land like wasps. Everywhere they found Amun's name, they hacked it out with a chisel. Even in Akhenaten's own father's name. Temples, tombs, royal inscriptions, it made no difference.'

'I've heard the gossip in the tavern,' said Ace. 'Pharaoh

115

won't let anyone else worship the way they want to. Everybody's got to worship his god.' The priests had disappeared inside the cave. 'What's in there?' said Ace again.

'Set.'

'What?'

'His image. The statue from his temple. Each day we bathe and feed it, just as we did when it was in the inner shrine. We saved it from Akhenaten, and when the tyrant is overthrown, we will reinstate it.'

'The Setcave,' Ace laughed. 'Right.'

'The real Set is hidden somewhere else.'

'Is that right?'

'He's waiting. The gods shackled him after he and Horus fought. But he'll be back, back from the west, the land of the dead.' Sesehset leaned closer. 'That's what the doorways in the air are for,' he murmured. 'One day, Set's going to walk through one of them. Maybe sooner, maybe later.'

'Listen, if he's the god of evil, how come you were allowed to have temples and stuff?'

'He's not evil. He's thunder in the desert. He's a hippo trampling the papyrus crop. He's dancing and sex and,' he raised his bowl in a toast, 'good wine.'

He waved the wine about, indicating all of Egypt. 'They call disorder evil. They turn us all into numbers, numbers on the scrolls here. This whole country runs on records and numbers and records and clerks, measuring everything and scribbling everything down.'

'Like we were pieces in a machine,' said Ace.

Sesehset was in full flight, not listening to her. 'He can't be measured by anyone, written down by anyone. He has his place – had his place, before the madman came. "I am Set",' he recited, '"strongest of the gods, and I slay Ra's enemy every day, standing at the front of the ship of millions of years – and no other god can do that." The universe wouldn't work without him. He is chaos. He is the storm.'

Ace nodded coolly. 'A butterfly flaps its wings, making a tiny change in the air. That change gets magnified, right? A breeze turns into a gust, a gust turns into a wind. The wind turns into a hurricane. All because of the butterfly.'

Sesehset laughed out loud. 'That's superb! A hurricane caused by an insect.'

'Every storm starts with something small.'

Sesehset reached out and touched her on the nose. 'Set sends the butterfly to start the storm.'

One of Sesehset's servants brought them more wine, and they sat in the shade of a palm tree, slowly drinking the strong stuff. Sesehset said, 'We had about five years. Then Akhenaten picked up the court and moved it to this blasted desert plain. They hadn't even finished building the palace – he lived in a tent for a year.'

The ex-priest plucked a bit of grape stem out of his teeth. 'No Net, no Isis, no Khepri, no Khnum. No stories, no pictures, no moral teachings, no priests or rituals. Just Akhenaten and his silent, faceless Aten. He just stands around in the sun all day, throwing flowers at it. His brain's probably boiled by now.'

'He's not crazy,' said Ace. 'Or if he is, he's crazy like a fox. What he is is a tyrant. That's why there are soldiers everywhere, right? No-one likes what he's doing.'

Sesehset snorted. 'And meanwhile, foreign princes are taking our lands, and there's plague devouring the Levant. One thing you could say for old Amun, he looked after the wars. Akhenaten's father used to stuff Amun's temples with booty. But now Pharaoh lives in a dream, talking to his Aten, his eyes closed to the real world.'

'You've gotta fight back,' said Ace. 'You can't let him do this, he's wrecking everything.'

'Now I think *you* have been standing in the sun for too long,' said Sesehset.

Ace shook her head. 'Let this go on and you'll have a civil war on your hands. Religion's one of the best excuses for war, right? Belfast, the Draconian jihads. It'll be Egyptian soldiers killing Egyptian people. Our people. Unless we do something about it.'

'You know,' said the priest, 'you're not like any woman I've ever known.'

'You propose to me, and I'll gut you.'

Sesehset shouted with laughter, pouring them both a fourth

bowl of wine – or was it a fifth? 'Copper will be beaten into swords, bread will be bought with blood,' he recited, his voice growing more serious. 'We will laugh like the sick, we will not weep at death. Our hearts shall beat for ourselves alone. We'll sit with our backs turned when someone kills another. The land dies, no matter how many laws you make to stop it.'

The priests had returned from the secret cave, carrying a platter of food, bowls and cloths. Their daily duty was done.

'If we move against Pharaoh,' Sesehset said, 'we could be starting that civil war.'

(a) The drawing room was on fire, and (b) there was an Ant in the corner, which was (c) doing something to the Doctor. Therefore (d) Kadiatu, who had come bolting in clutching a weapon, yelled (e) 'Oh shit!'

The Ant didn't appear to notice her sudden entry. Its front pair of legs were pressed against the Time Lord's chest. He lay against the floor and wall at a peculiar angle, ragdoll-limp. The Ant's face was dipped to his, three of its antennae fixed to his forehead and cheek in a delicate steel kiss.

His eyes were open, his enraged blue gaze reflected in the robot's metal face. One of his hands spasmed, again and again.

Kadiatu had raised her gun, taken a bead on the Ant. Now her conscious mind kicked in and told her she was holding a percussion rifle that would blow a three-metre hole in the wall. The shrapnel would've shredded the Doctor, and probably her too, at this range.

There was an industrial laser taped to the top of the rifle. She slapped a hand over it, sliced down delicately. The red point burned a black graffito down the wall and bit into the back of the Ant's neck.

It reared up, squealing – no, the sound was its antennae, whirring and twitching wildly as they detached from the Doctor's face. Its head hung at an odd angle. The little man raised a hand between him and the monster, rolling limply to one side.

Kadiatu fired the laser a second time, the red beam cutting through greasy smoke, slicing through one of the Ant's legs.

It wobbled, trying to turn its head to find the source of the attack. She fired a third time, and the Ant's head rolled onto the wooden floor with a dull clang.

The body collapsed. For a moment Kadiatu thought it had fallen onto him. But the little man was clear of the metal corpse, trembling in the corner, one hand pressed to his temple where an antenna had drawn blood.

Kadiatu gripped her gun in one hand as she beat out the flames with a rug, urgently. 'Christ, you idiot!' she snarled, 'you might've burned the house down!' He didn't say anything.

She thumped out the last of the fire, still clutching the gun in one hand. 'Why didn't you cry out?' she yelled, striding towards him.

In a single, fluid movement, he pulled his whole body into foetal position, arms thrown over his head.

Kadiatu stopped where she was. 'Christ,' she said again.

Most of the scars, it appeared, were on the inside.

Ace sat in the main hall of Sedjet's house, alone.

Despite Sesehset's words, the Setites were local boys, without much of an idea about history. For them, the world just started with the gods' war and then kept going indefinitely. Egypt's fortunes might wax and wane over the centuries, but the country hadn't changed in any major way for thousands of years.

But for Ace, who'd ridden the back of time, history was more like a series of circles. Empires rose and fell, old religions died and new ones took their place, elections and coups and wars and fashions flowed like the tide. To the Egyptians, Akhenaten's changes were shattering. To her, he was just another fascist.

Ace drank black beer from a bowl, slowly, wishing for a vodka and Coke. She was drinking a lot. Maybe she was drinking too much. It was something to do instead of making up her mind.

Her own home time in the late eighties had seemed like a little pocket of eternity, as though it had always been two minutes past the Industrial Revolution and The Farm had

119

always been the best band out. But turn the page, and you had the Berlin Wall coming down, and the Gulf War, and Nirvana.

Ace closed her eyes, but she couldn't stop the tumbling imagery in her head. Was this the way the Doctor had seen time? Not a straight line, obviously, but a circle, or a spiral, or a hopelessly tangled web.

Or a Mandelbrot set with his name on it. The storm of time that had blown her out of her bedroom and onto Iceworld had been coloured like an insane fractal, the hurricane whipping her faster and faster past every star in the galaxy, accelerating through two million years of patterns, and the patterns got more complicated as you looked more closely, histories inside histories, events inside events. Her head was spinning and it wasn't the beer.

The more you interfere, the more you have to interfere. The treadmill that had kept the Doctor coming back to Earth.

A lump had lodged itself in her throat, but it refused to resolve itself into tears. Why aren't you here with me, so I can do my companion bit, ask you questions, watch your back, be part of the plan? God, why am I so dependent on you? Why aren't you here to help me? Why am I alone?

Once she had dreamed about Jan, in a crazy morphic dreamspace on Belial, her mind and body flowing like wax into Benny and the Doctor. Liquid intimacy, closer than she had ever been with her Traveller man. 'Love is forever,' he was saying in the dream. 'Did you forget?'

'Then maybe I didn't love you!' she screamed. 'I don't love you! I never loved you!'

And now she was screaming into the dusty air, 'You died! You died! What's the point of love if we're gonna die? If i isn't forever it isn't love! If it isn't forever it isn't real! I doesn't count! It doesn't matter!'

She stumbled out of the room, shrieking, and ran a few paces into the desert sand and threw up.

She lay down on the ground, her chest heaving.

Something had untied itself inside her, something heavy was gone from her stomach. Her father was dead. Jan wa dead. The Doctor was dead. Something broken loose insid her skull kept chanting it, over and over – it's over, it's over

120

it's over, it's over.

Listen to me, Sesehset had said. *You're a separate person. Are you the eye of your friend? Are you his hand? He's dead, but you are still alive. And not everyone shapes themselves into a box.*

She was here for a reason. The timestorm had brought her here for a reason. This time she was ready for it, not just tossed into a new world. Not controlled by the world, but ready to control it. She was going to overthrow the tyrant. She was going to bring Set back, back where he belonged. She was going to be history.

'No,' she snarled into the dirt. 'Akhenaten! *You're* history!'

The Doctor woke up in shadow and thrashed, trying to get away from the thing looming over him.

'Easy!' hissed Kadiatu. 'Easy! I'm not the enemy.'

She took her hand carefully away from his mouth, straining to hear what he was whispering.

'I look for butterflies that sleep among the wheat. I make them into mutton-pies, and sell them in the street.'

They were in the back of an empty hay-cart, covered by a tarpaulin, bumping roughly up and down. The smell of farm and animal was overwhelming. Kadiatu sat cross-legged with the tarp just touching her cramped neck and shoulders. Random streaks of late afternoon sunshine leaked in as the tarp flapped up and down.

He had been lying on his side in the straw. Now he rolled over and sat up, plucking hay from his sleeves. '*Chez M Thierry?*' he murmured.

'We'll be there by dawn. Nicolas will get us past the guards. He's been carrying messages between Thierry and I.' The Doctor listened, counted two horses, heard the driver yawn.

'What was that thing?' said Kadiatu. 'What was it doing to you?'

'Looking for something hidden,' he said, running his fingers through his hair to get the straw out. 'You know what Ants are like. You cut off their heads, and the legs come looking for you.'

'It was trying to read your mind?'

121

'It wasn't having much luck.'

'Thick skull?'

'Lots of practice,' said theDoctor grimly.

'What was it looking for?'

The Doctor grinned suddenly. 'You know, I like being asked lots of questions. Ask another.'

Kadiatu sighed. 'So that was one of the things living in the rifts.'

'It was just a servant, a *doméstique* if you like, with no mind of its own. Employed to fetch and carry. What did you do with the pieces?'

'I put them in the cellar. The key is on a chain around my neck.'

'The padlock won't stop a shell.' His mouth was a tight little line. 'About those men you killed.'

'Don't you dare lecture me!' she hissed, almost forgetting to keep her voice down. 'Don't you lecture me. It's your fault I'm here. If they'd come into the house, the basement –'

'Why did you kill them?'

'Desperate expediency,' she spat.

He closed his eyes in the greyness. 'You could have talked your way out of that situation. Bribed them, handed over the horses. You could have persuaded them. I could have persuaded them.'

Kadiatu said nothing.

'You know what you are now, don't you?'

Kadiatu said nothing.

'All the years of your life it had never occurred to you there was something odd about never getting sick, or having to eat so much food. It's possible that blind spot was built into your brain –'

'I don't want to talk about it.'

'– if you see what I mean. It would make the indoctrination easier.'

'I'm some kind of experiment, aren't I? All those modified super-soldier genes cooked up in the one organism, and then left with retired soldiers to grow up into – what?'

The Doctor was shaking his head. 'It wasn't like that.'

'They didn't even tell me. They died without telling me.'

122

Did anyone know about me? Were there others? Did I come with an instruction manual?'

'No and no and no.'

'I'll never know,' said Kadiatu. 'I never know, when I react, whether it's me or my genes.'

'You can choose. You're not a machine.'

'I was designed, programmed. I didn't kill those soldiers, the bioengineers killed them. You killed them.'

The Doctor sat back, leaning against the side of the cart, hands folded in his lap. 'I'm not selling any alibis.'

'I didn't ask to be born,' said Kadiatu. 'It's not my fault.'

The sun was low in the western sky by the time Bernice reached the tomb entrance. It was easy to spot when you knew what you were looking for; peasants had camped inside, leaving potsherds and charcoal all over the place. Bernice smiled to herself, pushing aside a chunk of pottery with her toe. In another thousand years, this rubbish would itself become archaeology.

She made hand gestures until the handlers worked out they were supposed to stay outside. They sat down with their backs to the wall of stone, bundles at their feet. Bernice wished she could talk to them. She wished she had had the sense to throw a computer translator into her travel bag.

There were so many things that she should have done. If only it were possible to put yellow sticky labels over your life.

She slipped in through the narrow crevice and moved inside.

When she was sure the handlers wouldn't see, she took a flashlight out of her pocket, rolling the circle of light rapidly around. The entrance to the tomb proper was a little distance ahead; probably a natural cave which had been enlarged with mallet and chisel.

There was more rubbish inside the antechamber, and the ceiling and walls were stained with soot. Peasants had been sheltering here ever since the tomb had been unsealed and robbed, perhaps for thousands of years. There wouldn't be any fancy artifacts or golden trinkets to please Bonaparte. Benny didn't care, as long as the wall paintings were intact.

123

The entrance to the tomb had a low ceiling and narrow walls. She shone her flashlight inside. The roof was irregular, but the walls were smooth, and unpainted. She would have to go further inside to find what she was looking for.

She took off the Doctor's hat and stooped under the lintel. Claustrophobia tried to take hold of her, the way it always did when she first stepped inside caves or underground chambers. She waited patiently for it to dissipate, listening to the sound of her breathing echoing off the stone.

Ahead, the passageway – which had probably once been filled with funerary goods – bent sharply to the right. She squeezed through and froze – where was that sound coming from?

She stood perfectly still, holding her breath. After a moment she realised the torch was still on and snapped it off.

Her balance went awry in the sudden blackness. She threw out a hand to find the cold stone wall. Her ears rang, filling the empty chamber with random noise. Had the sound come from before or behind?

After a full minute she said, 'Oh, for goodness' sake,' and switched the torch back on. 'Pull up your socks, Summerfield,' she muttered, comforted by the sound of her own voice. 'This isn't *The Mummy* .'

The passageway ended in a wide doorway. There were still ancient fragments of wood lying on the floor, all that was left of the doors that must have once filled the space. They had probably been used as firewood centuries ago. The stone walls had been cut before Sappho taught at Lesbos and before Hypatia taught at Alexandria, before the Exxilons visited Peru and the Celtic chieftains rode across Europe, before the Doctor had challenged Fenric to a friendly game of *Ya Shah*.

On this scale a human life was nothing more than a beat of a butterfly's wings. Benny felt the weight of time hanging heavily on her. Or was it just the musty air?

She ran the beam of her torch over the walls of the tomb. The wall paintings were not only intact, they were in remarkably good condition. She sat down, gripping the torch under one arm, and got out her diary.

She sketched rapidly, awkwardly, peering into the pool of

light on the wall. The pictures told her everything she needed to know, which was handy, because Boney wasn't going to turn up the Rosetta stone until next year.

The tomb had belonged to an official and his wife. The period was dead right: no pictures of the happy couple meeting with the gods, just with Pharaoh. The Aten symbol appeared over and over in the hieroglyphs.

One picture showed the dedication of one of Akhenaten's stelae, a large carving in the cliffs near Akhetaten. And there was something more in the illustration of the cliff. There.

Surely the Amarna Graffito hadn't been present at the dedication of the stela – but the artist, in true Amarna period style, had been trying to represent the area realistically. The lines representing the cliffs formed a rough map. Using that, it would be easy to track down the Graffito.

And anything else Ace might have left behind her.

Benny stood up. She had no way of reaching back through time to her stranded friend. All she could do was try to find out how Ace had fared. Who knew, there might even be a tomb.

There was a footfall outside the chamber. Benny stood up. 'I told you to wait outs–'

There was a flash and a tremendous shove against her left shoulder. Suddenly Bernice found herself sitting down with her back to the wall.

She swung the torch around. There were two men in the doorway, squinting in the unexpected brilliance of the beam.

The man with the gun crouched down. His friend was holding a flickering torch. Tall and short, both in black. 'You were at the tavern,' she said. Her voice had gone all high-pitched and wobbly. She dropped the torch, put her hand to her shoulder. It was soaking wet. Oh, cruk!

'Give me the book,' he said.

Benny didn't move. The man reached up and plucked the battered notebook out of her lap. There was a large ring on his finger, with a glittering, oval green stone.

'Why?' breathed Bernice. 'Why do you care about finding it?'

The man hesitated, spoke in halting French. 'We will find

125

Sutekh by following . . . his footsteps? His footprints. The trail he has left for us. This is how it was written.'

'Oh, the Osiran site at Sheta-Khu'u,' murmured Bernice. 'Are you lot in for a surprise.'

The tall man ignored her. 'Our ancestors fought to sustain the religion of Sutekh. The sacred writings mention this picture.' He pointed at the wall.

The other man was holding a shovel. Now he smashed it into the wall and started levering off chunks of plaster. Benny shouted, 'No!' but in minutes the illustration was gouged out of the wall, falling in a rain of dust and shreds onto the floor.

We do not know what we will find there,' the first man said. 'Perhaps the hidden prison of Sutekh.'

He stood up, put the gun away. 'The handlers,' said Bernice. He shook his head.

'Don't leave me,' she breathed, as the shock started to muddle her thoughts. She tried to rise, but fell back hard against the wall, the pain making her heart skip a beat.

'This tomb shall be yours,' said the Setite.

'Every storm,' Ace said, 'begins with something small.'

They had walked to the edge of the city, where Akhetaten faded into the desert. The rocky Red Land, Set's land, stretched away to the north and west.

The boundary stela was cut into a limestone cliff, twelve feet high, columns of hieroglyphs dangling from an illustration of Akhenaten and his family worshipping the Aten, the disc of the sun. Two of the Setites held a ladder against the cliff as Ace climbed up it, clutching a chisel in her mouth like a pirate biting on a dagger. She had tied the mallet to a rope strung it around her shoulders.

She climbed until she was face to face with the stone Pharaoh. 'You know something, mate? You have an ugly mug.'

'He insists the artists make him look like that,' called Sesehset.

'Can't think why.'

'It's the new style. Another change.'

The ladder shook as she chipped away at the inscription

126

First she hacked out the sun disc, rough strokes digging into the soft limestone. Then she came down two rungs. 'You'll have to read it out,' she called down to Sesehset.

The priest flicked his eyes over the columns of hieroglyphs. 'Well, it's a dedication, promising the Pharaoh won't move the city from this site or extend it beyond the boundaries.'

'No,' she said, 'word for word.' She pointed with the chisel at the top of a row of hieroglyphs. The Priest peered up. 'The Good God – that means Pharaoh – sole one of Re, whose goodness Aten has created –'

'Stop there,' said Ace. 'That says Aten in the oval shape?'

'The cartouche marks a divine or royal name,' said the priest.

'Right.' Ace picked up her mallet once more, and slowly and carefully dug the Aten's name out of the stone. Tiny chips fell to the bottom of the cliff. 'And here as well,' she said.,

'Who exalts Aten, makes his name great –' Sesehset had begun to read, but already Ace was chiselling out the cartouche.

'Heh,' she said. 'I've rubbed him out. That'll do for now.'

She clambered down the shaky ladder. The Setites were glancing around in the reddish dawn, nervously. Ace clapped Sesehset on the back, laughing. 'Just one more thing before we go-go,' she said.

The priests watched anxiously as she scraped a series of curves and angles into the cliff, just above the height of her head. It took nearly half an hour to make a proper job of it. She was sweating in the sunlight when she'd finished.

'Right. Now we can leave.'

'Is it writing?' said Sesehset. 'I don't recognize the language.'

'It's for the twentieth century,' and Ace raised a hand to her mouth, snickering like a child. 'That ought to give them something to think about.'

The priests fled the white cliffs, running for the safety of Senef's estate.

In letters three feet high, in a language that would not be spoken for thousands of years, the cliff shouted: ACE WAS HERE

Chapter 9

Raiders of the Lost Akhetaten

Poets do not go mad; but chess-players do.
(G.K. Chesterton, *Orthodoxy*, 1908)

M Thierry's house was a modest twenty-eight room affair near the Bois de Vincennes, a little outside Paris. It was separated by a wide lawn and a pond from the orchard, with its rigidly defined rows of trees stretching off into the distance.

The lawn had not been cut for months, and weeds grew thickly between the trees. There was a crater of dried earth and grass where a stray shell had come down. The pond was slick with decay. 'I've eaten the fish,' commented Thierry dryly, leading them in through the servants' entrance.

The kitchen smelt of must and dust. 'My servants have left me to fend for myself,' joked the tall Frenchman. 'There is plenty of room for visitors, as there are only the three of us.'

As if on cue, the littleboy came through the kitchen door. He was holding a mouse-trap, turning it over and over in his hands, looking up at them with pale, incurious eyes. Thierry watched the Doctor watching the child. 'Won't you come and have some *déjeuner*?' he said. 'I'm afraid a shell hit the dining-room.'

Kadiatu steered the Doctor around the littleboy and to the kitchen table. From somewhere, a skinny woman in a grey dress emerged; despite the summer warmth, she had a black shawl wrapped around her narrow shoulders. She brought cutlery, glasses, the remains of a leg of lamb. Kadiatu started removing great slices of meat from it while their hostess set down plates and a bowl of apples.

M Thierry did not bother to introduce his wife. 'This poor

old farmhouse has taken more shells than my other home in Paris. Whole trees blown up, *pan!*' He made the explosion with his hands. 'I'm sometimes not certain whether we'd be safer with Mlle Lethbridge-Stewart inside the walls of Paris. I remain here to try to continue running my business, but I sleep in the cellar with the wine!'

He patted Kadiatu on the hand. 'I'm pleased you're here. I feel a little guilty leaving you to the mercy of the Communards – or at least I did before today. I think you would eat the rogues alive.'

The littleboy was playing with his mouse-trap, pulling back the killing bar and letting it snap against the bait.

'It's the Doctor's safety I'm worried about now,' said Kadiatu. 'The Ants found him so easily.'

'Yes,' said the Doctor, 'it makes you wonder why they waited for me to wake up first.'

Kadiatu threw him a sharp glance. 'They would have ways to locate my ship,' she explained to Thierry. 'Anything from another time.'

'There is nothing like that here,' said their host reassuringly. 'The worst we have to fear here is one army or other marching through my orchard in their big boots.'

'Well, then,' said Kadiatu, 'what are we going to do?'

Life in Egypt was one long party. If you had the money. And the King's parties were the best raves of all.

Ace stretched luxuriously, feeling muscles rippling below her tanned skin. She felt at home, no images or memories throwing themselves up into her consciousness. No dreams. No distractions. *Wu wei.* She was an unsheathed knife – and nothing else.

The Setites milled about in the palace courtyard, chatting casually with acquaintances and friends. Some of them had been invited to this little soirée. She hadn't, but then, she was just a woman. Who was going to take any notice of her?

She'd thrown a scarlet sash over her shoulders, hiding the scar. Her skin was still too light, but it was night-time, and already the guests had stuffed themselves with food and drink and were sliding under the tables with wine running down

129

their bellies. She'd just be part of the background blur.

Bloody typical. Bloody politicians. Filling their stomachs while Egypt fell apart.

She went to the door of the main hall, peered in. There were blind musicians playing, women dancing bare-breasted with great metallic spheres attached to their long pigtails, swinging and swaying as they moved. The air was a thick mixture of incense, perfume, alcohol.

The Pharaoh sat at the far end of the hall, on a raised dais. He was dandling a small girl on his lap. A woman, evidently the Queen, sat beside him. As Ace watched, she reached over, playfully tickled the child under the chin.

Pretty pretty. Happy families.

Just for a moment something bobbed to the surface of her empty mind. The image of a woman laughing, her embroidered sleeve in front of her mouth. A woman laughing because she'd been given an order, an order to do something silly.

She shook her head, and was empty again.

This was the first time Ace had seen Pharaoh. From what Sesehset told her, he was in the habit of making appearances with the wife and kiddies, being worshipped by his adoring subjects – while the soldiers looked on, making sure that everybody cheered.

It was simple. They went into the party. Ace waited for Pharaoh to leave. She followed him, overpowered his guards and bore him away under cover of darkness. Then the Setites would start to make demands.

In exchange, she had their help and protection, their knowledge of the rift.

And of course she had a share in whatever wealth or power the Setites obtained. She was, after all, a professional.

They'd talked money, standing in Peseh's kitchen, the Setites ogling topless girls making beer. Sesehset had laughed when she'd said, 'You scratch my back, I'll scratch yours,' and Peseh had tried to scratch her back.

With their help, maybe she could find Sedjet. Maybe even go home. Home. Home? This was home. But she'd find Sedjet. Maybe even find the monsters who killed the – it was a straightforward coup d'état. The priests of the other gods

130

would follow the Setites, restoring the power of their temples. The army hated the king; they'd fall into line once they realized what was happening. The common folk just couldn't understand what Pharaoh was up to. They'd do what the new leaders told them to do.

Everything would go back to the way it had been. Except that from now on, Set, the god of Chaos, would be on top.

Benny was smiling. Shock was making her drunk. She wanted a drink. She wanted a tin of mangoes in sugar syrup pureed and served over crushed ice. With a little umbrella and a shot of vodka.

Someone had been shot.

She smiled.

She wanted to get up and move around. She didn't want to move an inch. If she moved, the hoof beats in her shoulder would intensify. They were already pounding, fast and irregular, an itch she couldn't scratch. Her field of vision was red.

Oh. *She* had been shot.

She was leaning awkwardly up against a wall of the tomb, feeling the irregular texture of ancient plaster through her sweat-soaked shirt. There was dust all over her, all over everything. How long had she been here, becoming part of the find?

There was a human? movement in the low doorway nearby. 'Vivant?' Benny murmured. *'C'est toi?'* She tilted her head gently to see the face.

There was no face to see. The figure stood with its hands in its pockets, not cramped at all by the narrow space. Its face was smooth as warp shielding, white plastic. It wore black trousers, black vest and bow tie, white shirt and jacket, and a red (tulip? rose?) in its *pocket* that MADE Benny want to SCREAM!

She turned her head away from the burning flower, twitching. 'What is that thing?'

'This?' The White Lady's porcelain fingers brushed across the petals. 'This is the blossom that lured Persephone to Hell.' She reached into a pocket of her white jacket and took out a

131

small device. She pushed down on a button with her perfect thumb.

Benny's surroundings flared white, bright, a blank wall. 'Oh no,' she moaned.

'What is it?' said the White Lady, with interest. She picked up a long, slender stick.

'I hate dreams,' Benny said. 'I hate this Jungian stuff. Symbols and stuff. I detest every kind of virtual reality.'

'You edit your own diary.'

'Couldn't we just get on with the story?'

'This isn't a dream,' said the Lady. 'At least, it isn't your dream. Space-time's broken like a sheet of safety glass, full of cracks. Dreams can trickle through those breaks.'

'Maybe I'm just someone else's dream,' muttered Benny, sleepily. 'If I pinch myself, will they wake up?'

'What a mundane philosophical observation,' said the White Lady. 'And whose dream might that be, dear?'

'I did not know then whether I was a man dreaming I was a butterfly . . .'

'What's that?'

'I don't know,' said Benny giddily. 'I just heard it somewhere, I think. Who are you, anyway? Not the Ghost of Christmas Past, I hope.'

'Christmas,' said the White Lady. 'How quaint. Do you celebrate it?'

'My mother was Catholic.'

'Oh yes, your mother. She was killed fetching your doll, as I recall. Vaporized by a Dalek plasma blast. You must hate your child self for that.'

Bernice shook her head, angrily. 'My mother was stunned by the blasts, she didn't know what she was doing. I understand that now, I saw that on Belial, I know it wasn't my fault.'

'There is no more pain?'

'Yes .'

'Then consider this: your mother was killed by the first Dalek beams. How could she have been stunned?'

Bernice opened her mouth, and closed it, two sets of memories clashing in her mind, two sticky yellow labels stuck over one another.

132

Her voice was choked. 'Who are you?'

The White Lady pressed her device's button again with a flourish. 'Figure 1,' she said.

The Egyptian tomb was gone, replaced by something similar but different – Babylonian, thought Benny, no earlier, very early indeed, Early Sumerian. Inside of a temple.

Time was frozen. There were people everywhere, stopped in position: people with swords, bloodied, shouting. 'It's a hologram,' said Benny.

'It's my slide show,' said the White Lady. 'I hope you like it.'

She swept the stick into the three-dimensional tableau and pointed. Benny gaped up at a huge woman, a snake, no, a Giger woman-snake, her silver flesh imprinted with fantastical circuit designs.

The she-monster's palm was flat against Ace's forehead. The teenager was screaming – teenager, the original Ace, Ace the way Bernice had first met her. Screaming with her mouth open and her hands clawing at nothing.

'Oh God,' stammered Benny, 'what's happening?'

'The details aren't important.' The White Lady swung her stick again, pointing across the room.

The Doctor was being held by two huge guards, all hair and sweat. The little man was caught at an odd angle.

Benny stumbled to her feet before she knew what she was doing. The flare of pain in her shoulder precisely matched the brilliant blossom in the Lady's pocket. 'Hey,' she said.

The Lady took her arm and helped her hobble over to the Doctor. Now she could see the twisting tension in his shoulders, one hand reaching out as he tried to turn his hips, the balance of his feet. He was trying to break free of the warriors' grip, desperately, wrenching forwards towards Ace. At the same time his eyes were closed, his head bowed, as though he couldn't bear to look.

Benny touched his hair with a trembling hand. Ace was being tortured, but Benny wanted to comfort the Doctor, tell him it was going to be alright.

'It must have been alright,' she muttered. 'This must have happened long before I came on board. Whatever happened, it was all alright in the end. It's just some adventure or other.'

'Figure 1,' said the Lady again. 'The Doctor unable to prevent his companion's pain. A leitmotiv. Perhaps the reason he hurts her deliberately is because it gives him some control.'

'He doesn't hurt her because he wants to.' Benny was piping like a little girl, the Lady's hand tugging on her as she tried to pull away. 'He doesn't hurt anybody because he wants to.'

'Doesn't he?'

'He had to do it. He's too clever. Don't you understand? Too clever. He always sees the best thing to do, the right answer. So he – he doesn't have any choice, does he?'

'Does he?'

'How can you have any free will when you know the future?'

'Can you?'

'What is all this, anyway?' Benny sank to her knees. Her hand trembled over her heart. 'If you're the Grim Reaper, just reap me, okay?'

'I'm not Death,' said the White Lady. 'Though some people wish that I were. Figure 2.'

She pressed her button again, and the world changed. A new image – a dark English night, the air full of smoke, at the foot of a castle wall.

The Doctor lay on the wet grass, back arching, mouth open, eyes open, his whole body twisting in raw physical pain.

Ace was there, and a young man, and Benny saw the body language that connected them like an electric current, even in their panic. They were just about to see that the Doctor's shoulder was dislocated, but in that snapshot moment they didn't know why he was screaming.

And now it was Ace that Benny wanted to comfort, wanted to assure that pain couldn't kill you, it didn't last forever. Ace, helpless in the face of the Doctor's agony.

The White Lady swept the pointer down, traced a line across the Doctor's chest, just below the damaged shoulder. 'There's a major ganglion here,' she said, moving the stick in a small circle. 'A great nerve cluster, almost a tiny, separate brain. A manner of switching-box. It allows a Time Lord fine control over their own metabolism: respiration, core temperature, blood chemistry. A blow to that tissue can render the

134

Time Lord unconscious as their heartsbeat and breathing abruptly slow. Other damage can cause excruciating pain. Stimulate that ganglion, and every nerve in the body reacts. As we can see from Figure 2.'

'Why are you showing me this?' Tears were running out of Benny's nose. She wiped them on her sleeve. 'Why are you?'

'Perhaps you need this information,' said the White Lady. 'And anyway, it's my job.'

'It's your job,' said Benny hotly. 'You're a torturer, a torturer!'

The White Lady sighed sharply. 'Really, your subconscious does not even begin to contain the cultural information necessary to understand this dream. I no more torture people than Death kills them. The first time the Doctor met me, it was entirely of his own volition. My job is to bring home to you something you already know – that the Doctor plays with people as though they were pieces in a game. He is too old, too callused, too callous. He will sacrifice anyone for advantage.'

She leaned down, bringing her featureless face close to Bernice's. 'And that is why you are dying in a dusty Egyptian tomb, an impossible distance from your home. There is nothing more for you.' She plucked the blossom from her lapel, and stretched out a pale hand. 'The Doctor has abandoned you here, and you must give up now. Just give up, now.'

There was a long silence. The flower was an inch from Benny's nose. It smelled of scarlet and crimson.

When she answered, she could barely hear her own voice.

'It's not true. He's one of the pieces too. He would sacrifice himself if he had to. He's done it. I saw it.' Benny felt some strength come into her trembling body. 'I saw it.'

Benny was stooped over the Doctor, frantically trying to get a response out of him. Blood was trickling from his mouth and nose, sluggishly. His eyes had flickered shut.

The White Lady shook her projector switch, irritably. The flower was gone from Benny's field of vision. 'It's my slide,' sobbed Bernice. 'And you can't change it. You can't change it.'

And now there was a song, somewhere in the distance, an elusive melody. She closed her eyes, tilted her head, but she

135

could only make out a few notes of the tune. But the words were clear. *Come here, come here.*

She sniffed, blinked, looked up.

'Mlle Summerfield,' said Vivant, 'The work will not be done if you simply lie about, now, will it?'

Ace's chance came sooner than she thought. Akhenaten laughed, swung his daughter into the air, gave her over into her mother's arms. He was an odd-looking bod, Ace thought, even as she meandered into the hall, doing her best to look like just another sodden party-goer. He was skinny, but with a pot-belly. His face was long and his smile was weak. He didn't even bother to go lion-hunting to keep himself in some sort of shape.

He stalked out of the hall, followed by three guards, count 'em. They'd be good, too, top quality stuff. For a moment she wished she had her combat suit. Give 'em a twist, a flick of the wrist, no muss, no fuss.

She wandered out after Pharaoh. When a guard tried to stop her in the hallway, she kicked his left kneecap loose and stomped on his larynx when he fell down.

Hmm. Maybe she wouldn't need her suit after all.

The cannons were distant tonight. Midnight found the Doctor in the kitchen, very slowly peeling another of Thierry's apples with a knife.

He was letting events flow by him, carelessly caught up in the river. There wasn't much else to do besides letting Kadiatu bundle him about like a pile of old clothes. He sighed, looking down at the rag-bag he was wearing. He missed his silk shirt. He missed his hat.

He missed Ace. He missed Ace very much indeed, Had she survived Cold Storage? Was she still alive, on the other side of one of the Ants' temporal crevices? Or had the metal insects got to her? If a scout had come for him, what about her?

I say, old bean, what about me?

He looked up, to where an imagined Bernice was grinning at him, perched on a kitchen stool and tossing her newly blonde hair out of her eyes.

'Ace had hibernation sickness,' he said. 'She might have been blinded, or had brain damage. If the thawing was uneven, the ice crystals might have burst her heart –'

I came to rescue you both, said Benny, more seriously. I know what I'm doing, don't worry.

'But we were separated in the rift. I felt it happen, felt you lose your grip. The damaged areas of space-time are full of powerful, random forces flinging us off in different directions.'

Which is why you have to stop the Ants. Stop the forces leaking out of the cracks and destroying the universe. What are you going to do about Kadiatu?

'She seems to have learnt her lesson as far as the time experiments are concerned.'

But do you trust her?

'Why not let her think she's in control for a while?' The Doctor had made a long snake of apple peel. He put it carefully down on the table. 'She's trapped. And trapped animals are the most dangerous.'

We're all trapped, Doctor. You included.

'At University,' said the Doctor, 'they warned us never to talk to the dead.'

There was a single wail, rising and falling into silence. It came from somewhere downstairs – the cellar – a woman's voice echoing eerily from the bricks. Scuffling, furniture noises, the sound of a blow landing. Silence again.

Listen to us. It's up to you to set us all free. Ace picked up the strip of apple peel and swung it around in the air, playfully. *So get on with it, eh?*

For instance, said Benny, raising an eyebrow, *you might want to stop talking to ghosts. I only mention it.*

'I can't help it,' said the Doctor softly, and now the pain was back again, the sharpness in his shoulder he had been ignoring. He repulsed the insane urge to stick the knife in the itching pain, cut it out of his body. 'I'm not myself.'

Must be something you drank, said Benny pointedly.

What did they add to you? said Ace curiously.

'Do you remember the organic matter that infected the TARDIS, after we repaired it with Goibhnie's protoplasm?'

137

Hell, that was a long time ago. I remember. The cat tried to warn us.

'And then I was in two minds, as it were. For months. I couldn't talk to you properly because I was fighting the virus that had infected the TARDIS' mind. My mind.'

Is this like that? said Ace.

Evidently not, said Benny. *In fact, he's positively chatty.*

'That virus altered my biology. It changed the way I thought. It was a subtle form of possession.'

Ace spun the apple peel slowly from her fingers. *The Ants' technology is organic,* she said. *To them, we're the machines. And you're wondering what tinkering they might have done under your hood.*

'They would understand Kadiatu perfectly,' he said, biting into his apple. 'Nerves for wires, genes for programs.'

Bernice was shuddering. *Possession,* she said. *It seems to be a bit of an occupational hazard.*

Nature of the universe, said Ace, *people are always trying to turn you into what you're not. D'you think they did something to you while you were aboard Ship?*

'No,' he said, 'it must have been afterwards.'

And now you're not yourself.

'No.'

That's Kadiatu's excuse, isn't it?'

The Doctor looked up at Ace, sharply.

'Am I out of my mind? Would I know?'

You're the one talking to yourself.

'What if this – Paris, Kadiatu – is all an illusion? A sanctuary I've created inside my own mind? How would I be able to tell the difference?'

Ace laughed, a silent, imagined laugh. *Been there, done that, bought the postcard. Go stub your toe on a rock and see if it hurts.*

'Hold on. I'll come for you,' he promised. 'I'll come for you both.'

And if it's too late? said Bernice. *Will there be white lilies at the funeral?*

Never mind, Professor. Ace winked at him. *When you're short of everything except the enemy, you know you're in combat!*

In the kitchen doorway, the littleboy was watching the Doctor talk to himself. The child looked about five years old: red hair, perfect skin, a precise spattering of freckles. It was not wearing nightclothes, but the same little suit it had worn during the day. It still clutched the red ball. Sitting at the table, slowly chewing on his apple, the Doctor did not even notice the child's cool stare.

Perhaps, a little while later, he looked up at the vague sensation he was being watched. But the littleboy had gone to its bedroom. There was nothing but a solitary mouse skittering along the floorboards until something went *snap*.

In the morning, it was Thierry who found the Time Lord curled up under a tree, a mile and a half from the mansion. Dew was forming on his hair and coat. The Frenchman knelt and gently shook the Time Lord's shoulder.

'Oh dear,' said the Doctor. 'Did I escape again?'

Chapter 10

Please Do Not Step on the Butterflies

Time goes, you say? Ah no!
Alas, Time stays, we go.
(Austin Dobson, *The Paradox of Time*)

Pharaoh sat with a bowl of wine in his hand. From time to time he took a sip. This evening, at this moment, the wine tasted especially good.

A woman was fighting his trio of guards, turning and twisting like a dust devil. She was silent, making no sound when a blow struck, even when the tip of a *khopesh* cut a long gash in her leg.

Pharoah had wondered briefly if this was some sort of audition. He'd heard about a foreign woman who fought like a soldier, and who wanted to join his army.

That was before she killed the first guard, ripping his own sword out of his hands and slamming it right through his chest. The hooked point protruded from his back, and he stumbled backward, gurgling, and fell onto a table. A pair of wine jars shattered beneath his body, and redness spread onto the floor around him.

She fought the way a dancer might fight. She ducked and wove, almost too quickly for his eyes to trace her movements. His bodyguards' bulging muscles and heavy swords were no use in such close, agile combat.

She jammed an elbow into the throat of one of the remaining guards. In the instant he spent being startled by the pain, she had flicked the arch of her foot into his groin, twisted her hips as she slammed her knuckles into his bruised windpipe. He fell, knocking his companion down.

140

The remaining soldier scrabbled away from the woman, snatching for his fallen sword.

'Who fails the test,' said the woman, 'feeds the Devourer.'

She grabbed the *khopesh* away from his groping fingers and slashed it through the air, once, twice. The third arc sliced through the guard's cheek, cutting a second mouth. She had slit his throat with the point before he was even able to scream.

The battle finished, she straightened, turned to Pharaoh. Her hair was wild and stuck to her forehead and face, her pale skin was flushed. She held her blade like a butcher.

Pharaoh started to laugh.

Bernice lay on a stretcher in Vivant's tent. He had been watching her around the clock, sleeping beside her on a military cot, bringing her water and changing the dressing on her wound.

She had been sleeping solidly for two days – or was it three? There had been no dreams. Good. There was only the song in the back of her mind. *Come here, come here, come here.*

She stirred. Vivant was by her side in moments, laying a wet compress on her forehead. 'Don't try to get up,' he said.

Benny felt around her shoulder. 'How bad is it?'

'Not very bad at all,' he said soothingly. 'Our surgeon says that the bullet struck at an angle, and did not penetrate deeply. The skin is torn, there was a lot of blood, but it will not be necessary to amputate.'

'Amputate!'

'*Une plaisanterie,*' said Vivant. 'Just a joke. Do lie still.'

'My diary!' she said. 'Oh no, Vivant, they took it. They killed those poor men. They smashed the wall, they took the sketch I made.'

'They also killed the bartender – perhaps because he told me where you had gone. *Qu'ils aillent au diable, ces Mahométans*!

Benny shook her head, angrily. 'They're not Islamic. They're some sort of Dynastic survival. An underground cult dedicated to the return of Set survived into the twentieth century.'

141

'Is that so?' said Vivant. 'Perhaps you should have another glass of water.'

'Er, yes,' said Benny, blushing.

Vivant sat down next to the stretcher. 'I have seen to it that a payment has been made to the murdered handlers' families. Bonaparte will not miss a few hundred francs.'

'I should have gone alone. It's not fair to put anyone else into danger. None of this is fair! How are we going to find the Graffito?'

Vivant helped her to sit up. Her shoulder was sore, but she was obviously going to live. 'There's some medicine in my bag,' she said, 'it'll help prevent septicaemia.'

'The surgeon says there's no sign of poisoning of the blood,' said Vivant, but he picked up the travel bag anyway.

Benny opened the zipper, clutching the bag to her chest so that the artist couldn't see inside. He watched as she pulled out some strange pills and swallowed two of them. 'Do you know, Mlle Summerfield,' he murmured, 'you are a very mysterious woman. I would like to know more of your secrets.'

Benny looked at him over the top of her travel bag, hesitating. Their eyes met for a long moment.

'Now, if I told you them, they wouldn't be secrets any more, would they?' she said softly, and tugged the zipper shut.

'You could at least have the common courtesy to be afraid.'

Ace's face was lit from beneath by a brazier. The warm light barely reached the walls of the cave, casting deep red shadows that faded into blackness. She sat cross-legged, her *khopesh* balanced across her lap.

Pharaoh raised an eyebrow at her, but said nothing. His hands were tied in front of him, and he sat awkwardly with his back against the wall. He looked just like the sculpture she had vandalized, long face, full lips. His eyes glinted with a very nasty sense of humour.

She'd trussed him like a chicken and chucked him into a chariot and sped off even as the alarm was being raised. The Setites contributed to the chaos by milling about shouting

142

nonsense, tripping people up and asking stupid questions. The palace had sounded like a receding circus as her horse pelted across the desert, following a trail of torches. Each time she passed one she shot an arrow into it, knocking it from its stand and extinguishing it.

The horse had taken a tumble a klick from the cave, breaking its leg in a deep hole. She and Akhenaten had been thrown from the chariot, rolling over the stones. She'd put an arrow through the horses' head, untied the bruised Pharaoh's feet and dragged him to the cave.

The cut in her thigh wasn't too bad. In fact, given her opponents, she had done exceptionally well.

She ought to be proud of herself.

'I understand,' said Pharaoh.

Ace had been staring into the brazier. She looked up at Akhenaten. 'What?'

'You want to make your name part of history. To be written down in the records as the one who killed Pharaoh.'

Ace shook her head. 'You don't look dead.'

'Don't be obtuse. Your allies aren't going to keep me alive any longer than they have to; as the legitimate ruler, I'm too much of a threat to them.'

'They plan to exile you. Establish a new Dynasty.'

'Of course.' He was smirking! 'That's what it's all about. History. Nothing ever changes here. Egypt has no history – just a list of kings, a scribbled record of wars. I'm not going to be just another name on that list. And neither are you.' His lips curved into a half-smile. 'Who's paying you?'

'It –'

'No, let me guess. The army promised you a position if you'd kill me.'

'This isn't a game.'

'Then perhaps the Amunites offered you what's left of their fortunes to dispose of me. A foreign, female assassin. Very ostentatious, I like it.'

Her face twisted. 'You're a tyrant. I wreck tyrants. You won't let anyone worship the way they want to.'

'Pharaoh is always a tyrant. Because it's Pharaoh's task to keep Egypt in order. Do you really think we could do without that order, without measurements and records and laws?'

'Maybe you overestimate their importance, mate.'

'There are three hundred and sixty-five offering tables outside the palace I built for my Father. One for every day of the year, heavy with food and drink. That bounty is the direct result of my rule. I'm the vessel through whom Aten gives the people life.'

'The people don't worship Aten, you know. They still worship the gods you've banned.'

Akhenaten's eyes were hard in the red light. 'It hardly matters what superstitions the peasants entertain. My religion is for Pharaoh, not for them.'

Ace's sigh echoed. 'You talk too much.'

'I've been talking since I ascended to the throne. Explaining, over and over.'

'Why explain anything to an assassin?'

'Ah,' he said. 'You used the word.'

Ace stiffened. 'I meant –'

'You're worth talking to because we're equals. Equals in the eyes of history. I am the most extraordinary Pharaoh who has ever lived.'

'I'm not here for your crukking autograph.' There was that glint in his eyes again, like metal. 'You are crazy.'

He grinned, fleshy lips pulling back from his teeth. 'I'm a god.'

'I've met lots of gods,' said Ace. She stirred the coals in the brazier with a stick. 'They're boring. They never have any depth, like cartoon characters. Not like real people at all.'

'The priests don't worship me. They hate me for taking away their power.'

'Look, shut up, alright? I'm not interested.'

'The army hates me because I'm not running about conquering hairy nomads in the desert.'

'You just let foreign princes walk in and take whatever they like!'

Akhenaten shook his head. 'You don't know anything about it. Egypt's foreign lands administer themselves, they have their own armies. I need my troops here. Where they can keep an eye on the priests, and I can keep an eye on them.'

'You should have kept a few more then, shouldn't you?' said Ace pointedly.

Pharaoh laughed. 'But I was expecting you.'

'You what?'

'The Setites have been plotting on and off for months. They were just waiting for someone disposable to come along. Someone who'd follow their orders.'

Ace roared and was on her feet, clutching the *khopesh* in furious hands. He just sat there chuckling. She was losing control, she could feel it.

No, she had already lost control. She had let herself be controlled. Like a good soldier, she was only following orders.

Her head buzzed and she held the sword, held the sword. She could work out what to do, she could work it out. What would she do?

What would the Doctor do?

Why, he would stop her, of course.

When aliens or time-travellers tried to change Earth's history, he stopped them. Put things back the way they were supposed to be.

Ace sat down on the floor of the cave, hard. Glowing coals scattered from the overturned brazier. The *khopesh* clattered away out of her hand.

'Lost your stomach for history?'

Ace grabbed at her sword, dropped it again.

'You see,' said Pharaoh, 'war is easy. Any fool can flail about on a dusty plain, killing at random. It's much more difficult to make precise changes.'

'What am I doing?' said Ace.

Akhenaten stood up, back to the wall. 'I'll make you a deal,' he said.

Kadiatu, Thierry and the Doctor were having wine for breakfast when the soldiers banged on the front door. There was no sign of Mme Thierry. With an expression of resignation, Thierry scooped up some bread and cheese and a cobwebbed bottle. 'This ought to placate them,' he said, 'and perhaps they'll give me a little intelligence in return. Mlle Lethbridge-Stewart, be sure they don't see you! *Attendez*'.

Hot summer sunshine was coming through the window, lighting up the kitchen in orange and white. Kadiatu was onto her second loaf of bread, smearing great slabs of salty butter onto the slices. The Doctor was pulling a piece of cheese into smaller and smaller fragments. They sat in silence for a while, listening to Thierry cracking jokes with the soldiers. After a while the apple merchant lead them out onto the front lawn to polish off the bottle of wine.

'It's a principle of war,' said the Doctor, 'that one doesn't assume the enemy won't come, but instead one must be prepared for their coming – not to assume they won't attack, but instead to make one's own position unassailable.'

'Who said that?' said Kadiatu.

'Sun Tzu. Chinese general, Fourth Century BCE. That was shortly before we fell out.'

'You've known a lot of soldiers.'

'Rather too many, for an aging hippy like me,' said the Doctor, with a rueful smile. 'I can't seem to avoid you.'

'I'm not a soldier,' said Kadiatu, around a mouthful of bread.

'You'll be surprised,' said the Doctor. 'You'll be surprised. It happens to you. It comes with the job. The healer and the warrior.'

'What happened with Sun Tzu?'

'It was the little matter of his killing two of the Emperor's wives. He only did it to win an argument.'

'What'd the King do?'

'He banished Sun Tzu for a few years, but as soon as the country's borders were threatened again, he called the old general back. I wasn't much of a military adviser – I kept holding conflict resolution seminars.' Kadiatu laughed. 'I can't spend all my time putting flowers down gun barrels.'

'What about this war, then?'

The Doctor shrugged. 'The usual combination of bad timing, bad planning, breakdowns in communication, and naked greed. Genuine injustices being exploited for the sake of power. The Commune could have righted many wrongs, but it lost its chance in poor organisation and casual violence.'

'I feel paralysed,' said Kadiatu. 'As though I could wreck

146

history if I breathe the wrong molecule of air.'

'The forces that drive history are as complicated as the forces that move the air. A butterfly's wings cause a hurricane, which causes a drought, which causes the starving farmers to work together to use what water they do have, and to count and keep records. That was how Egyptian civilisation started. But it doesn't matter which butterfly's wings start the hurricane.'

'There must be individuals who change history. What if someone got in a time machine and killed Hitler?'

The Doctor had made a pile of tiny fragments of cheese. 'Much of history is cast in concrete, but there are disequilibrium points – assassinate the wrong individual at the wrong moment, and history could unravel like a scarf.'

He raised his hands, as though looking for the right place to start a complex lecture. 'Have you ever seen a flock of birds, waiting to migrate?' Kadiatu nodded, chewing. 'Imagine the riot at Montmartre. One person is jostled in the crowd, shouts in anger. Someone else hears, shouts out a slogan. More people start to yell, move about. And once a certain initial peak of energy has been passed –'

'– the crowd turns into a mob and shoots those two generals from Versailles.'

'The war coalesces from small events like that. It's so difficult to predict just where the disequilibrium point is. You and I have a special responsibility, Kadiatu.'

She was frowning. 'I was just wondering how many Hitlers you've disposed of over the years.'

The Doctor shook his head, yawned suddenly. 'I put things right. When someone comes from outside history and tries to derail it, I put it back on the right course.'

'That's not entirely true.'

The Time Lord looked at his hands. 'It's very difficult to keep the human race on the straight and narrow,' he conceded. 'And the more changes I make, the more changes I have to make.'

'Round and round like a hamster in a cage.'

'That's a horrible simile.'

'Listen, while I'm asking lots of questions . . . The Earth

would have moved between my arrival and yours – and the Ants'. How could we have appeared at the same place?'

'Perhaps someone glued the exit point in place.'

Visions of warp equations danced in her head. 'That's nonsense.'

'Hmm.'

'Just one more.'

'Mmm?'

'After the Ant tried to read your mind, why did you curl up like that?' His eyelids were flickering now, and he dragged a hand across his forehead. 'You thought I was going to beat you up. Didn't you? Is that what they did to you? Punished you because they couldn't read your mind?'

'They're not interested in punishment,' he slurred. 'They're all brute force and no elegance, they'd knock down a wall instead of opening a door. I want the pieces of that Ant. And your handscan. Bring me the pieces. Excuse me, I think I'm going to go to sleep now.'

He managed to fold his arms under his head before it hit the table.

Kadiatu watched him for a full minute, listening to the sound of his breathing. Carefully, she took his wrist. His pulse was a complex double twitch, slow and steady. For some reason she was suddenly reminded of the first time she'd picked up a frog when she was a child – the cool skin, the knowledge that she was holding something inhuman.

She stood up and peeked through the door. The soldiers were gone; Thierry was sitting on the porch, drinking the dregs of the wine.

'I'm going to Paris,' she told him. 'When will Nicolas next be here?'

'He's due at noon,' said Thierry. He blew across the top of the bottle, making a mournful, echoing note. '*Et le Docteur*?'

'Best to let him sleep,' she said. 'You've got to step down the dose, Thierry.'

'You were the one who said he was dangerous.'

'He's going to work it out. He's probably already worked it out.'

'*Vraiment?*' Thierry leaned back in his chair and squinted

148

up at her. 'Why has he not said anything about it?'

'You don't know him.'

'And you,' said the Frenchman, 'are not getting to know him any better.'

'Listen.' Kadiatu raised a hand, counted symptoms off on her fingers. 'Psychogenic amnesia, flashbacks, irritability, exaggerated startle response. He can't remember what they did to him, but he thinks it's going to happen again. He has shell shock, Thierry. Post-traumatic stress disorder.'

'*Ah oui, bien sûr. J'aurais dû savoir ça immédiatement.*'

'At the moment, I really don't think he's a danger to anybody.'

Thierry pulled his hat down over his eyes. 'Best to let him sleep,' he echoed.

But the kitchen was already empty, dust motes dancing in the orange light.

Chapter 11

Open Wide! Come Inside!

POLONIUS: What do you eat, my lord?
HAMLET: Worlds, worlds, worlds.
           (William Shakespeare, *Hamlet*, non-existent folio)

The TARDIS stood in a courtyard of the palace, humming softly to itself.

Ace fell against the warm, rough side of the blue box, pressing her cheek to it. She imagined she could hear the tune it was making, the gentle rising and falling of its engine pulse.

Akhenaten watched, dispassionately. 'This was found at the same time you were,' he said. She turned to look at him. 'Yes, I have spies everywhere.' He patted the TARDIS' surface, gently. 'I knew there must be some connection between this magical object and the foreign woman of Set.'

'I thought his name was forbidden.'

'Set is nothing more than a name. I have wiped him from the face of the Earth. Scratched out all the names and replaced them with my own. I will live forever and never be forgotten.' He ran an incurious finger over the TARDIS' surface. 'What is this thing?'

'This is – this is the ship of millions of years,' breathed Ace. 'I should have known, I should have known it all along. This is why I can speak Egyptian. Why didn't I see that before?'

Akhenaten shrugged. 'We can put a great deal of effort into deluding ourselves, when our need for illusion is deep.'

She looked at him, awkwardly. 'Don't apologize,' he smiled. 'Take your ship and go.' He strode away. Not afraid to turn his back on her.

The door opened for her, as she had known it would. Ace went inside the console room. The humming here was subliminal, like the sound of her own blood flowing through her body. She closed her eyes. The door shut silently behind her, cutting off the party sounds, the smell of dust and roasting flesh.

She leant her back against the inner surface of the TARDIS doors and sank slowly to the floor.

She felt heavy, the way you feel heavy when all the water has drained out of the bath. She felt as though she could lie down on the floor, the warm white stuff, draw her knees up to her chest and curl up and never, never get up.

It had been a long time since she had felt like that. She remembered coming home from the hospital, once all the papers had been signed and the phone calls had been made and her father was dead. Her mother had gone downstairs to drink warm tea laced with whisky.

Little Dorothy had curled on her bed, eyes open, listening to the rain coming down the window outside. Empty except for that sound. It was her right, to be still and silent and to have no responsibilities. She had earned it. She could go mad now, if she wanted to.

After a while she got up off the floor. 'Oh,' she said, out loud, 'I am covered in blood.'

She went for a shower.

The Doctor watched Thierry through one of the second-floor windows. The Frenchman was quietly getting plastered on several bottles of homemade wine. When he was satisfied his host wasn't going anywhere for the moment, the Doctor left the spare bedroom and went down the stairs.

The door to the cellar wasn't locked. He knocked, quietly, waited for an answer. Nothing. Carefully, he pushed the door open, and padded down the stairs.

It wasn't dark; a single tallow candle lit the cellar with ghost-story light. Low ceiling, not much space. Brick pillars and wooden wine-racks outlined in the pale yellow radiance. Soft light, soft sound: a woman sobbing.

Gently, gently. The Doctor allowed himself to make a little

noise, just enough that she'd realize someone else was there without being startled. She stifled her crying, looking around her in the dimness.

'It's alright,' he whispered. 'It's just me.'

Mme Thierry was sitting up on an improvised bed, just a mattress and sheets stacked against the wall. She was primly dressed, but her hair hung down over her face in limp curls, and her shoulders were slumped in exhaustion. '*Que voulez-vous?*' she murmured.

He came close enough that they could see each others' faces. The bruises were mostly on her shoulders and arms, where they'd be less likely to show under the bulky nineteenth century clothing. She drew her shawl around herself, but she was staring at his face, and the Doctor realised that she was looking at the purple mark on his left cheek.

He sat down, making no sudden movements, his back to one of the brick pillars.

'You shouldn't be here,' she said, after a while.

'Why don't you summon your husband?'

She was too tired even to smile.

'Do you need medical attention? I'm a doctor.'

'I know that,' and now she did smile, with irony. Her face was much older than it should have been, and there was a strength in her eyes that flashed in the candlelight. 'I am not seriously hurt. But I am ashamed.'

The Doctor shook his head. 'Sometimes you can't help it. Sometimes, no matter how hard you resist, they can still do things to you.'

'It is not that. *Je rêve*,' she said, in a low voice. 'I imagine – terrible things.'

His eyes were pulling the explanation from her, but she looked away, became silent again. The Doctor said, 'Killing your husband?' A tiny, bird-like nod of the head. 'Why do you stay?'

'Because,' sighed Mme Thierry, 'he would kill me if I left. He has told me, many times. And even if he did not, where would I go? I would starve, or be blown apart by a shell. There is no sanctuary, he is doing nothing unlawful, nothing wrong.'

152

But the Doctor was shaking his head from side to side, agitatedly. 'You should leave, you should go, just go and keep going –'

She stretched out a bony hand, touched him lightly on the wrist. He looked into her eyes. 'You have been tortured. Haven't you?'

'Dozens of times,' said the Doctor dismissively. 'Captured hundreds of time, escaped hundreds of times. It's like saying the same word over and over; it stops meaning anything after a while.'

Mme Thierry nodded, nodded with understanding. 'Perhaps one day he will hit me until I lose my mind,' she said grimly. 'And then all my dreams may come true.' She raised a finger. 'You must not drink any of the wine he gives you.'

'I know that too,' smiled the Doctor.

Mme Thierry hesitated, then reached under the bed and drew out a strongbox. She pushed it across to him, and he picked the lock with a bit of wire.

The box was full of gold. He pulled out a bracelet that had to have come from Mesopotamia, pieces of eight, a cheap gold watch from the twentieth century. The Ants had plundered history to pay their servant. Given their power, Thierry was thinking very, very small.

'What about you?' said Mme Thierry. 'Why don't you leave?'

'Sometimes you have to do nothing.' He slammed the lid down until the box locked, pushed it back under the bed. 'That can be very, very difficult to do.'

'When he hits me,' said Mme Thierry, closing her eyes, 'I try to stay still and to make no sound. It gives him no excuse to hurt me further. And after a while, he stops.'

They sat in silence for a little while.

'Tell me three things,' said the Doctor.

'*Oui.*'

'The child. Is he yours?'

Mme Thierry shook her head. 'François brought him home one evening and told me we were to adopt the boy. I do not even know his name,' she added. 'He is such a strange, cold child. I have never heard him speak a word.'

153

'Are there any weapons in the house?'

'There is a pistol kept loaded in the drawer in the upstairs bedroom,' she said steadily. 'What is your third question?'

'What's your name?'

'Madame Thierry.'

'No. Your name.'

It was a few moments before she answered, as though she were trying to remember. 'It is Genevieve.'

Ace went into her bedroom with a big flannel towel wrapped around her. The dust of the desert was gone from her skin and her mouth, and a little of the Sisterhood's salve had gone a long way towards soothing her burned skin. Her hair was untangled, hanging down around her shoulders in a smooth wave.

She sat down on the bed. The room seemed so empty. Most of her stuff, what little of it there was, was tucked away in a foot locker underneath the bed. But someone had changed the sheets, and turned the covers down neatly. A pair of jeans and a denim shirt were tidily laid out on the bed, along with clean socks and knickers and a small felt bag.

A quarter of an hour later she walked into the console room, stretched, hovered at the controls. She raised her hands.

She could go anywhere. Anywhere. It was just Ace now, Ace and the TARDIS. The machine was humming to her, as it had often hummed to her, the first mind it had touched as it uncurled from its long hibernation. They were like sisters now, ready to have their own new adventures.

Slowly, she let her hands fall back to her sides.

A moment later, she was typing instructions into the visualizer. Scanner data coruscated on a flat screen beneath her chin, forming patterns and diagrams, sending spirals of colour over her face.

After a while, she smiled.

Kadiatu had expected at least a guard. But her house was unwatched, empty. No-one had bothered to wash away the blood on the road outside.

She hadn't left any of the soldiers alive to report in; it was entirely possible that the looters had gotten to the bodies before the Garde. Or perhaps corpses were so common that four more just didn't make a difference.

She stood in the lounge for a while, making a mental note of the things which looters had already taken – furniture, mostly, bulky wooden items which would make good firewood. There were splinters all over the carpet where the chaise longue and the piano had been broken up on the spot, the easier to transport. The stealing didn't bother her, it was natural for unattended stuff to go missing. They'd left the grandfather clock, still slowly counting out the seconds.

Would they really have not cared about the people she'd killed? She hadn't been paying much attention, had a hazy, generic image of war built up from TV news and warvids. Her parents and their friends used to pop over for a drink and the worst rental tape they could find, and laugh themselves stupid. Kadiatu spent those parties trying to trick people into giving her sips of beer.

She remembered when her brother was first shown in public, six days after his birth, her father handing out gifts to the midwives at the party. They'd taken the umbilical cord, wrapped in plastic sheeting in a wooden box, and buried it somewhere where evil spirits wouldn't find it.

She'd reached over the edge of her brother's cot, the wooden bars coming up to her armpits, and his tiny hand had closed around one of her fingers. She asked her mother whether there'd been a party when she was born too, and her mother said of course there was, she had just been too young to remember it.

The cellar door was still intact, humming very quietly to itself. Kadiatu used a sonic key to switch off the electric fence she'd wired across the door, the tiny conductive threads invisible in the dim light. The small device squealed a series of notes, killing the humming, and she tucked it back into her sleeve.

She'd dropped the pieces of Ant through the hole. The head was dented, half-hidden by the wooden stairs where it had rolled. Its eyes hung loosely on their stalks, regarding her mournfully.

She picked up the severed leg and examined it with an engineer's eye. These things were big, but they weren't particularly well-constructed – lightweight instead of armoured, not meant to take a shot. Overconfidence? No, they really were just designed to fetch and carry, weren't meant for combat.

She sat on the bottom step, tugging uncomfortably at her dress, and stared up at her nameless ship. Beached on the shores of time. She wished she could just get in, press a few buttons, zap herself back to Makeni for some proper food and a pair of jeans. Or Lunarversity. Anywhere familiar. She wanted to explore familiarity, now, take in the tiny details she had missed, taking it all for granted.

And the Doctor wasn't going to get her back, that was becoming more and more obvious. Her parents had had to explain to her about some of their friends, not to make loud noises around them. The bursts of anger, the memory loss, that sudden, instinctive curl into foetal position. This time she was on her own.

There was a sudden sizzling in the air, an ozone smell. Kadiatu was half-way to her feet when the ship vanished.

It just disappeared, like a television picture that had been switched off. Her mouth hung open.

'Shit!' she said, at length.

Thierry's desk was covered in paper: receipts, orders, business letters. A fountain pen stood in its stand, a glass shape with a coral in it held down a mass of unpaid bills. There was a case of butterflies on the wall, dusty and forgotten, pinned bodies dried and shrivelled behind the glass.

The littleboy watched with pale eyes as the Doctor quietly slid open a drawer. The pistol had not been used for years. The Time Lord spent a few moments examining it, making sure it would still work. He rummaged in the back of the drawer for ammunition.

The littleboy watched and watched. The Time Lord could feel those pallid eyes burning into his back, as though the child's vision somehow cooked a corridor through the air, as though the room itself bent around him in some way.

'I believe it was Anton Chekhov,' said the Doctor at length, 'who said that if you plan to fire a gun in the third act, you have to load it in the first.'

He turned to face the littleboy. The child's face held no emotion. The skin was perfect, unworn; he had never smiled, never frowned, never tripped and fallen in the dirt.

He was still holding the red ball. 'There aren't any other toys in the house,' said the Doctor. 'That's just for show, isn't it? You wouldn't know what to do with a toy. That's not what you're for.'

He put the pistol into the pocket of his coat. 'See you in the third act,' he said, and went out of the room.

The guard snored and stirred, hands laced over his fat belly. Benny stepped right over him, her shoes in one hand, moving silently across the desert sand.

The Setites' camp was a small circle of tents – Benny counted three, plus a fourth shelter cobbled together from tarpaulins and branches. A single palm tree stood overhead with a dozen horses and camels tethered to it. The wind sang eerily through the huge leaves.

They'd spent a week on camels tracking the Setites, skirmishing with bandits and pockets of resistance fighters. Benny's shoulder had healed more quickly than she had expected, which made her wonder what else might have been in the antibiotics.

She moved closer to the improvized shelter. Surely no one would be sleeping in there, not with all those gaps and holes and the uneven shape – which meant that was probably where they stored stuff.

She gestured to Vivant. He was half-hidden behind a boulder at the edge of the camp, watching nervously as she tiptoed towards the tent. He worried about her so much, the sweet thing. If she really were stuck here – accept it, Summerfield, why can't you just accept it – she could think of far worse people to be stuck to.

She raised her hands above her head and brought them down sharply. He nodded and moved towards the animals.

Bernice peeked into the tent. No-one home. She slipped inside, amongst pots and pans, blankets and boxes, and drew

157

herself into a small shape that wouldn't be visible from outside.

It wasn't long before an irritated whinny broke through the night air, and then suddenly three shots, crisp as ice.

The camp erupted into shouting, scrambling life. Through a frayed rip Benny watched the Egyptians running to catch up with their bolting animals. A few more shots – Vivant encouraging them on their way?

Benny saw men, young boys, but no women. She wondered if the Setites were like the Thuggee, passing the religion on from father to son.

No-one thought to check the supplies tent. She heard more shots and held her breath, hoping that Vivant and his men were alright. It wouldn't do for Denon to survive the Terror and then get shot at random in Egypt. If nothing else it'd put archaeology back a century or so. God, how did the Doctor handle this kind of responsibility?

She slipped out her flashlight, turned the beam down low, shone it around the tent. There were a few boxes, none of them locked. Her diary wasn't anywhere to be found.

She slipped out of the tent. The camp was empty. Not too bright, these Set worshippers – falling for such an obvious distraction. Even the snoring guard had woken up and joined in the chase.

She nipped over to the largest of the six tents. It had to be the tall man's. God knew what he'd made of her diary. Hopefully he just thought she was insane.

She pulled out her pistol and went inside. There was a low table, a cot bed, a rug on the floor, a couple of scimitars – a table.

Benny threw back the tablecloth. It was a chest. She shot the lock off and pulled it open.

Her diary was inside, sitting on top of a pile of neatly folded silk. Probably stolen goods. She reached for the book.

'Stand up slowly,' said a voice behind her, 'and drop your gun.'

Benny stood up slowly and dropped her gun. 'Do you want me to put my hands above my head?'

'Why not? Turn around.'

158

Benny turned around, lacing her fingers on top of her head. The tall man looked her up and down. He had a large, rather unstable looking pistol in his hand.

'You are a most interesting woman,' he said. 'A woman from the future, looking for the treasures of the past.'

'Oh dear,' said Benny. 'You didn't actually believe all of that, did you?'

'Why else would you write about it in such detail, if it weren't true?'

'Would you believe I'm trying to beat Shelley to the invention of science fiction?' The tall man looked at her blankly. 'No?'

'The sacred writings contain different passages regarding the way in which Sutekh will return,' said her captor. 'One passage speaks of a hole in the air, through which a man might step into the time of the ancients, or forwards into the unseen centuries to come.' He gestured with his weapon. 'I want you to show me where that hole is. Or better still, show me the ship of time.'

'You must be joking,' said Benny. 'I'm not letting a loon like you loose in history. It was bad enough with the three of us running around.'

'Then this time I'll make sure I don't miss.' He pointed the pistol at her heart.

Benny dropped to her knees. 'Oh please, please don't shoot me!' she begged, her voice turning into a terrified squeak. The tall man looked down at her, bemused. 'I'll do whatever you want, just please don't –'

She reached down and jerked the rug out from under his feet. He fell backwards with a curse. Benny had already snatched up a scimitar and swung desperately at his hand, cutting into his palm and knocking the gun away.

The tall man tried to punch her, managed to hit her in the injured shoulder. She yelped and fell onto the cot bed, trying to regain her balance. The tall man grabbed another sword, slashed down, trying to cut her in half as she twisted frantically aside. His sword tore a great vertical slit in the tent wall. Benny elbowed him in the face and jumped out through the tear.

159

The tall man was hot on her heels. She turned as he thundered up behind her, bringing up the scimitar to parry – and again – and again – each blow she caught sent a ringing pain through her injured shoulder.

He was driving her backwards, backwards across the sand. She wanted to look around, to see if Vivant was there somewhere but she couldn't take her eyes off the tall man. She was just barely managing to hold him off. She could have fought properly, if the light were better, if she were more familiar with the weapon, if she weren't injured –

She hit something, stumbled backwards, and was suddenly falling, her leg caught in one of the storage tent's tarps. Half the tent collapsed with her, saucepans clattering, boxes tumbling, a pile of blankets overbalancing.

She lay on her back, dazed, holding the scimitar over her. But the tall man was reaching into the debris of the tent, pulling something out.

Another gun.

Benny bit her lip, closed her eyes. *Doctor! Ace! Here I come!*

There was a single shot.

Benny's whole body jerked.

The tall man fell like a tree. He collapsed on top of her and started bleeding on her shirt. She yelled and pulled herself out from under him.

Vivant was standing over her, holding a smoking pistol. Around him, French soldiers were moving into the camp, the Setites in tow, cuffed and cursing.

Denon reached down to her. '*Es-tu blessée*?'

She took his hand, let him pull her to her feet. Suddenly, she grinned all over her face. 'Life could not better be.'

Sesehset was watching the sun come up. He sat alone in the desert, just sat in the dust. It was probably his last sunrise, and he wanted to see it.

The Setites had scattered. Peseh was selling his lands, moving to his estate in Punt. Senef had disappeared altogether. The others had various plans, places they could hide. Sesehset had no employer, nowhere to go.

160

He sat under the stela they had defaced. Last night their plans had been as sharp and certain as the cuts in the rock face. Now they were nothing more than the chips of stone in the sand, scattered, meaningless.

There was a terrible sound. Sesehset sprang to his feet, startled out of his angst, looking around frantically. He had expected to have more time before it started.

The noise was echoing up from one of the caves in the cliff face. Sesehset's heart beat furiously. Perhaps it was just a rockfall happening underground. Not the Devourer.

Who fails the test feeds the Devourer.

A figure came striding out of the black shadow. It wore unfamiliar clothing something covering its eyes.

'Tepy,' breathed Sesehset. 'Are you a ghost?'

She stopped perhaps ten feet from him. He saw that she was carrying something long and slender in her hand, perhaps a staff.

She turned slowly, looking back at the stela, the grotesque figure of Pharaoh smiling up at his faceless god. 'That's why he changed the style of the art. He wanted to be remembered properly.'

'Did you kill him?'

'I didn't kill him. He didn't kill me.'

The priest realized he was trembling. 'What now?'

'You set me up.' Ace laughed. 'Set up. I ought to be angry, Sesehset. But I'm so used to it by now.'

The priest was shaking his head, but she was saying, 'You lot just wanted everything cosy again, back the way it was when you were rich and powerful. I could really have brought it all crashing down. No Ace, no Audrey, no Kathleen . . . no Bernice.'

Faster than lightning, she was grabbing his robe, the thing on her eyes reflecting his terrified face like black water. 'I want you to open the hole in space for me, Sesehset.'

'I can't!' He stumbled backwards, but she kept her grip on his robe. 'I don't know how, it isn't –'

'I watched that place for weeks. The only time the rift opened up was when you were there. Now, how do you explain that?'

'I –'

'And that's not the only thing. I didn't notice it before. I was stupid.' She let go of his front and raised her arm. Sesehset saw that the arm was covered in fine goosebumps. 'I haven't felt that since fighting the Time Soldiers. The TARDIS sensors agree with me. You're the key, Sesehset. The key that opens the door in time. Right? Start walking.'

He turned to try to run away.

Ace lashed out with the cattle prod, catching him on the arm. Sesehset squealed and fell over, squirming in the dust.

'You alien monster bastards,' snarled Ace. 'Who are you?' But his face was blank. 'Start walking,' she said again.

They went through the desert in the hot dawn. Twice more the ex-priest tried to run away. Ace brought him down with the prod each time, watching dispassionately as he twitched in the dust.

'Listen to me,' she said, when she saw he was looking around a third time, wondering in which direction to bolt. 'You work for the people who killed the Doctor. I have no mercy for you, Sesehset. Nothing. Not even anger. Run away again and I'll squash you like a bug.'

When they got to the desert valley, it was noon. The back and armpits of Ace's shirt were soaked. Her socks were probably welded to the inside of her sneakers. She felt the tingling in her hands and feet, the knot in her stomach. She remembered lying in the dirt here, waiting to die. She remembered Sedjet's strong arms lifting her.

Sesehset turned to look at her. There was nothing human left in his eyes at all.

'Do it,' she said.

The rift exploded outwards, instantly, like a great white flower unfolding in the air.

Sesehset just stared into it like the machine he was. His eyes reflected the burning light of the breach in reality. The rift distorted, expanded, blew the sand away in a stinging hurricane as it dug into the ground.

Ace took a deep breath, threw her arms over her head, and jumped into the void.

* * *

'Lend me your gun, would you?'

Vivant handed Bernice his weapon, absently. His eyes were fixed on the inscription, carved deep into the cliff in lines of anger. The message had survived endless years, lifetimes, millennia.

He was unpacking his cardboard box of art equipment, preparing to sketch the stela and the extraordinary inscription at its foot.

Benny's first shot ricocheted. Her second exploded amongst the words, spraying shards of limestone in all directions.

Denon looked up in astonishment. Benny calmly shot the inscription three more times, until there was nothing left but a series of shallow gouges. And the persistent voice, louder than ever, singing *come here*, *come here*.

'*Mon Dieu*,' said Denon. 'After all the trouble we took to come here.'

Bernice was shaking her head, impatiently. 'There must be something else here. Leave your pencils for a moment, Vivant, and help me find it!'

Slowly, he put down the box. 'It has been my goal to preserve the antiquities of Egypt,' he said, 'before time or human violence could destroy them. I'm not at war with the Mamelukes, but with oblivion.'

'Vivant,' Benny said, 'that inscription should never have been left there. Trust me.' He looked at her, strangely. He had done so much for her, without ever asking awkward questions. 'Trust me,' she said again. 'Please, Vivant. I know I can trust you.'

It took them a quarter of an hour to find the tomb entrance. No peasant pottery this time, just ancient chips of limestone, a heap of workings, blown an ancient colour by the wind.

Benny leant in and peered down. There was a shaft perhaps ten feet deep, leading down into the cool dimness. Vivant started to hammer a tent peg into the rock, tied a rope securely around it. Benny lowered it carefully into the shaft, pulled on thick leather gloves.

Obeying an ancient tradition of archaeologists, she took off the Doctor's hat and laid it carefully on the stone chippings at the top of the tomb. 'Won't be long,' she said.

'Mlle Summerfield,' said Vivant, 'there's so much you've kept from me.'

Benny hesitated at the top of the shaft. 'Yes. I know.'

'You know a great deal more than you have told. I don't understand how you have come to possess so much information. It is as though you can tell the future as well as uncover the past.'

Benny turned serious eyes on her benefactor. 'It's a bad habit I picked up from an old friend,' she said. 'Only now perhaps I understand why he played his cards so close to his chest . . .' She cursed, silently. Vivant was trying hard not to look hurt. 'I've shown you and told you more than I should have already.'

'I would like to know so much more about you,' he said.

Benny shut her eyes. In the distance, she could hear the handlers discussing the weather and someone shouting abuse at a stubborn camel. The wind was rushing past the cliff face.

Come here, come here.

Oh, God. She could understand Arabic.

A huge, crazy grin spread itself over Benny's features. Vivant tried to match her smile, but he knew he had lost her.

'Wait here,' she said.

He nodded. Benny took hold of the rope and swung herself carefully over the edge and into the pit.

The TARDIS was waiting for her in a half-finished tomb, a cave whose walls had been half-smoothed before being abandoned. Part of the cave roof had fallen in; she kicked rocks and dust out of the way of the door. It opened at her touch.

The console room was dark. Immediately she stepped inside, a pale luminescence started to trickle from the walls. Benny closed her eyes for a few moments then opened them again, getting used to the dim illumination.

'How long?' she breathed. 'How long have you been waiting here for me?'

There was a note taped to the console, perfectly preserved:

Dear Doctor or Benny,

Thought you could use this more than me. I'm coming through the rift.

XXOO

Dorothy

Denon sat in the dust at the top of the shaft, eyes closed. Above him, Akhenaten's ancient stela loomed, adorned with long columns of incomprehensible language. And yet it was not so strange or mysterious as the woman who had brought him to this place.

'Vivant!' came a shout from below.

'Mlle Summerfield?' he called down, barely able to make her out in the dimness.

'Throw me down my hat!'

Vivant picked up the Fedora. He carefully brushed the dust from the brim, held it to his face for a moment. The scent of her hair was in it.

He held it over the edge of the pit and let it go.

'Don't worry about me!' came her voice. 'Just go back to Bonaparte and get on with your job!'

'*Ne m'oubliez pas!*' he shouted, and the handlers looked up as his voice carried in the morning air.

'Believe me, Vivant Dominique Denon, you won't be forgotten!'

The Doctor stooped to examine the soil in Thierry's orchard. There was a great scoop taken out of the trees, a hollow surrounded by shattered trunks and fallen limbs. Tiny brown lumps – long-rotted apples – peppered the ground around the site of Kadiatu's impact. Great shafts of golden afternoon light streaked down between the trees.

None of the broken trees had been removed. Grass and weeds were starting to peek up through the churned soil. Nothing had been disturbed at all.

In point of fact, no-one had come to disassemble and drag away Kadiatu's spacecraft.

The Doctor heard a tiny sound behind him. A standard issue French military pistol being cocked. He went on with his examination of the soil, watching a tiny, pale green blade of grass uncurling itself. If he stared at it hard enough he imagined he could see it growing.

'Stand up,' said Thierry.

The Doctor stood up and turned around slowly, pushing his hands into the pockets of his coat.

166

Thierry towered over him, the pistol held at the end of a completely straight arm, the barrel moving in tiny circles as his aim wavered. '*Oui*,' he said. There was an alcoholic quaver in his voice. '*Vous êtes un imbécile au plus haut point!* I have been working for your enemies all along.'

'Yes, yes, yes,' said the Doctor irritably. 'I was just wondering how you moved Kadiatu's ship.'

If Thierry was taken aback by the Time Lord's casualness, he didn't show it. He reached down with his free hand to tousle the hair of the littleboy, who stood next to him, eating a bar of chocolate. 'The Ants moved it, *bien sûr* Using one of their machines.'

The Doctor glanced towards the house. 'Brand-new clothes, new furniture, plenty of food. Wealth in the middle of devastation.'

'There is a war on,' said the Frenchman, 'if you hadn't noticed. We have as much right to stay alive as anyone else. If it's any consolation, Doctor, you are not being sold for some false ideal, some philosophy of the rabble, but for the purest of reasons. For survival.'

He took something out of his pocket. It looked a little like a cactus, green and pulsing with quiet life, covered in stubby spines and tiny etchings.

'We've just been waiting for the right moment,' said Thierry. 'We needed to see whether you would trust us, tell us anything voluntarily, since the Ants had so little luck in drawing information directly from your mind.'

'How much do you understand about their technology?''

'Very little. But then, I am not a veterinarian, and I understand horses well enough to ride them. On the other hand, you understand the Ants' machines very well. They want your knowledge. I want it.'

The Doctor said cheerily, 'You can't always get what you want.'

Thierry, infuriated, shook his head. 'They were far too gentle with you. I am not afraid to cause you damage.'

He fired a single shot from the pistol.

The Doctor did not react, even though the bullet whizzed past within an inch of his ear.

167

The Frenchman grinned nervously. 'This little engine will summon Kadiatu's ship. Then we shall open and stabilise the rift her arrival created. The Ants will have a permanent tunnel through space and time.' He raised the organic device.

The Doctor closed his eyes. 'I wouldn't do that if I were you.'

Thierry tried to laugh like a villain, waving his gun about. 'They can use her ship to punch further tunnels through the ether, stabilising each one. They will plunder as they please. That power makes this war look tiny, pitiful.'

'I meant,' said the Doctor, 'that I wouldn't summon Kadiatu's ship here.'

Thierry gave him a look of furious indignation and pressed his thumb into the device.

There was a whump and a crash, and suddenly the ship was standing in the orchard, just where it had come to rest after sliding on its belly through half a kilometre of trees. A second and third wave of thunder rippled through the air, and the ground trembled with the sudden displacement.

'Oh, dear,' said the Doctor, starting to back away.

'Stay where you are,' growled Thierry, punctuating the order with a wave of his pistol. 'The Ants want you as much as they want Kadiatu's ship.'

'I had expected,' said the Doctor, 'that they'd take Kadiatu's vessel directly on board. But evidently not. Ah, well,' and he kept backing away, 'the best laid plans –'

'Stop!' shrieked Thierry, but even he could hear the sound coming from the ship now, rising in pitch.

'Let's see,' said the Doctor. 'I could stop and be killed in the explosion, or I could run and be shot. Given the odds –'

The little man turned and dashed away across the field.

Thierry screamed and followed. But not fast enough.

The light seemed to curve around the Doctor's body as he ran, blanking out everything in front of him and trying to drag him backwards into its searing heart. He couldn't hope to out-run it.

Then the ground was gone from under his feet, and he was tumbling, falling, blinking the burning spots from his eyes. He felt soil underneath him, sliding and loose, a fierce grip on his coat. The dreadful sound didn't register for several seconds, and he suddenly clapped his hands to his ears, far too late.

Genevieve was lying atop him, shaking violently, her hands clawing at his coat. She had dragged him into one of the fox-holes in the lawn.

They lay there for several seconds. Then the Doctor gently untangled himself from her, popped his head up above the surface of the ground and surveyed the damage.

The ship had undergone a massive spatial implosion, taking a huge, irregularly-shaped chunk of the orchard with it. The air was still sizzling with the after-effects, tiny fires springing up in the undergrowth, flickering and dying again.

'Blast,' he said.

'What happened?' said the Frenchwoman.

'That was meant for Ship.' The Doctor blew out a long sigh. 'Thank you, Genevieve.'

'Will there be any more explosions?'

'No. No more.' There was no sign of Thierry; the blast must have drawn him in, like an aeroplane passenger being sucked out through a window. The Doctor wondered whether or not to tell his wife. It could wait.

A small red ball rolled up to the edge of the hole, right under the Doctor's nose.

The Time Lord climbed up out of the hole. 'Stay here,' he told Genevieve, 'and whatever you do, don't look.'

The littleboy was standing on the lawn, perhaps twenty feet away. The Doctor walked slowly towards the child.

The first ripple in the time field was a tickling at the top of his spine, drawing quivering fingers up the back of his neck. Like someone walking over his grave. He kept walking.

The second ripple crashed out from the littleboy in a wave. Time slipped a groove, just a fraction of a second, enough to turn the Doctor's stomach and make tiny fish swim in his field of vision. He started to take the pistol out of his pocket.

With the third ripple time shorted out, stood still, ran back-wards and forwards. The Doctor was holding the pistol, it was still in his pocket, he was taking careful aim at the red-headed child standing on the lawn in front of him, he was taking the pistol out of his pocket.

A great ball of searing light appeared in the air directly above the child, blanketing the countryside with a roaring, hissing silence. The ball of light floated down, surrounding the child in a carousel glow. In the centre of the light was a jagged hole, growing larger and larger, becoming more defined.

The Doctor filtered out every sense until all he could see was those pale eyes watching him. He aimed carefully between them.

Then time came bursting out of the hole, gushing out like blood from a cracked clock-face, shattering in his skull like a lightbulb. His hearts misfired, syncopated, forget-getting which beat was supposed to to come next as reality stut-stuttered.

He started to lose his grip on the pistol. He started to lose his grip on the pistol. He start-started to lose lose his grip on the pistol.

Something heavy slammed into him. He lost his grip.

Third Piece

On a Wing and a Prayer

The skilful fighter wins by making no mistakes. That means having already established that victory is certain – conquering an enemy who is already defeated.

(Sun Tzu)

Chapter 12

In which Ace Traverses a Tunnel Through the Space-Time Vortex, Unprotected by a Force Shield and Uncertain of Whether the Walls of the Tunnel Will Collapse

Fish! Was this how oil on a puddle, FISH out of puddle erupting in rainbows water felt? Colour swirling away, spinning hands and feet TOO FAR away, swirling away, too far away – her HEART was fluttering. God! Swirl flutter by flutter by – Oh, God! Oh, mother! Oh, GOD!

Chapter 13

Intersection of Three Sets

> The Healer and the Warrior
> Were walking hand in hand;
> The Warrior asked the Healer
> If he knew what he had planned.
> 'To see the future and the past,' she said,
> 'It must be grand!'
>
> (Lewis Carroll, *Through the Looking Glass*,
> non-existent manuscript)

She broke through the surface tension at the tunnel's end and burst into air and sunlight and flopped on the grass, gulping air, tears streaming down her face. Her jittering hands were afire, her whole body glowed like a ghost, the air cracking and popping around her.

She dragged her head up, forced herself up onto her knees. Her heart was trying to rip its way out of her chest. Nearby, a young boy – five? six? – was regarding her incuriously, hands in his pockets.

The Doctor stood not ten feet away. He was going to shoot the boy.

With a wordless shriek, Ace threw herself at him and thwacked him with the cattle prod.

They tumbled to the ground, both weapons bouncing away across the grass. Jesus, some of the things she'd seen the Auxies do, but you didn't kill children, you didn't kill kids!

She slapped him across the face, once, hard. 'What are you doing?' she shrieked. 'What the cruk do you think you're doing?'

But he just laughed, his pupils expanded to huge black

circles, a look of giddy ecstasy crossing his features. Ace realized she couldn't hear him laughing.

His head lolled back suddenly. She let go of his lapels.

The rift was still open. Worse, it was getting bigger, blowing up like a balloon, bringing the rushing chaos of the Vortex with it. The air was full of butterfly colours and a raging noise so loud she hadn't even heard it. Her linen dress was no protection against the slicing wind.

The Doctor lay limp on the grass, hyperventilating. There was dew or condensation forming on his face and hands. Time twisted and twitched in Ace's belly.

She found the pistol in a hollow in the lawn. Late nineteenth century.

The rift was a swelling sphere, throwing up clumps of seared grass and soil as it bit into the ground. Its edge blew outwards, towards the Doctor. The Time Lord rolled onto his side, still laughing – but there was something about the way the air was crumpling and his body was twisting and space was folding up around him and he thrashed soundlessly and clawed the air, a piece of animated origami, assaulted by time, drowning in it – and the Ants were going to come through and she had to stop it, she had to stop it, all she had to do was –

Ace snapped up the pistol, took careful aim, and shot the five-year-old child between the eyes.

Benny ran out into a storm of colour and sound. The wind almost slapped her off her feet. She grabbed for the TARDIS and leant hard on it, trying to take in her surroundings.

There was a gaping hole in the air, flickering fitfully, on and off. It was closing, snapping out waves of random energy: scarlet, aqua, gold, white, heliotrope, lime, vermilion. She ripped her eyes away from it.

She was just a few seconds too late.

The Doctor, Ace, and a small child were lying in a strange triangle on the grass. Bernice started running to them through the dying timestorm. She stopped short when she saw that the boy wasn't going to need her help. Just a few seconds late.

Ace was trying to push herself onto her knees, the pistol still in her hand. Benny marched over to her and pulled the weapon out of her fingers. 'Doctor . . .' said Ace indistinctly.

Benny hurled the gun away and hauled her to her feet. She was freezing cold, condensation all over her flesh; the grass underfoot was covered in frost, as though the rift were trying to suck all the heat out of its surroundings.

There was suddenly a woman at Bernice's side. Period dress – continental. 'What year is this?' shouted Benny.

The woman didn't hear. 'I'll take her inside,' she shouted, leading the dazed Ace away towards a country mansion.

At last, with a tremendous pop, the rift closed.

Benny blinked rapidly, trying to get the spots out of her field of vision. She knelt beside the Doctor. There was ice in his hair and a thin layer of frost on his face. He was trying to roll over, hands pressed to his ears, wearing a crazy grin.

She took hold of him, helped him into a sitting position. 'Doctor,' she said sharply, 'Doctor!'

His eyelids flickered. 'Hello, Bernice,' he said, the words blurring together. 'Is that you? I was trying to daydream, but you know, my mind just kept wandering . . .'

'Shut up, you git,' she said, 'you're half-frozen.'

'Is that all?' She hefted him to his feet, and caught him as he stumbled. 'I thought I was caught in the chronon backwash of an interdimensional implosion. Just shows how wrong a person can be. It's good to see you.'

'You too. Now be quiet.'

The woman in the dress had come back outside. She averted her eyes from the dead child lying on the lawn.

'Oh God,' said Benny. 'Was it yours?'

The woman shook her head. Wordlessly, she helped Bernice take the Doctor inside the house.

Nicolas was eating something in the kitchen. Kadiatu had interrupted his usual rounds; she needed to get back to the farm. She sat in the living room, gnawing the haunch of a horse and thinking.

There was nothing left of her vessel but a large empty space. She rubbed the back of her neck, absently. Ship should have been destroyed. But it wasn't. Why not?

The Doctor probably had a good idea.

176

He was part of her family's stories. Her great-great-grandmother had written a book about him – well, about UNIT, but the two were difficult to separate. She had heard all about him as a child, read all about him as an adult. But she'd never expected to run into him on King's Cross Station.

Just imagine. If the transit system hadn't decided to get the two of them together, she wouldn't be sitting here eating this horse.

She put the hunk of meat down, closed her eyes. It had been Aunt Francine who'd made her realize who the little man was, Aunt Francine and her X-ray eyes, seeing past the human facade into his alien physiology – the physiology she had read about in the Stone Mountain archives, using a borrowed icebreaker to access the classified files stored from the first grandfather's time.

And there had been more.

A second Time Lord had been on Earth in those days, but he wasn't stranded the way they were stranded without her prototype vessel. He was coming and going freely, just to spite his old rival. UNIT's priority A1 order had been to watch for him.

She had read the surviving parts of her ancestor's diary entries, snaffled by the Official Secrets Act over the protests of his widow. A lot of it was lost or destroyed, but she'd even found yellowing, two-dimensional photographs, and tried to imagine the people moving and speaking, as though she were the projector that turned them into holograms.

It had been in the empty gym, with all the soldiers down in the mess for a drink, their voices echoing across a rainy concrete courtyard. In those days the Doctor had been very different-looking, taller, with a taste for impractical fashion and terrible army tea.

'Just in case we run into him again,' the Doctor had said, 'there's something I want to show you.'

He had caught hold of the Brigadier's hand – Kadiatu imagined the man being a little taken aback by the unfamiliar touch – and had run the Brigadier's fingers along his left collarbone. 'There's a nerve cluster here,' he said. 'If you're going to hit him, hit him there. It should render him unconscious with a minimum of fuss.'

The Brigadier must have nodded, seriously. 'I take it you want me to keep that piece of information to myself.'

'I'd prefer it weren't generally known.'

And Alistair had kept it a secret, and so had his descendants. Until his great -grand-daughter broke into his records.

But she wasn't his descendant at all. Was she?

Someone had to look after Earth, to match the Doctor's ability to drop in whenever he pleased. That was what Project Butterfly Wing had been all about. For every action, there is an equal and opposite reaction. The Doctor had poked and prodded the human race until it had hit back. With her.

It was possible that in the patchwork of her genes was something of her adoptive father's. He'd been a Thousand Days' War supersoldier, body and mind edited to fight the Martians. It was from the augmented soldiers that her DNA had come. If one of Brigadier Yembe's chromosomes was present in the mix, it would be the only information he had left her, keeping her in the dark for so long. Her parents had kept her away from doctors, which hadn't been hard – she never got sick – never needed a vaccination. Never got into a fight with other kids, never ran a race.

If it hadn't been for the Doctor, she might never have known what she was.

She could give it up, tell him everything, let him sort it out. But then, he was probably the one who had mucked it up.

She had dismissed her *gens de maison*. Better that they didn't get caught in any extraterrestrial cross-fire. And yet, without her salary, were they going to be worse off? It was so hard to know what to do.

Kadiatu picked up the horse's leg and sank her teeth into it. 'Time for Plan B,' she said.

After a while she realized she was lying on something warm.

Ace blinked and stretched. A proper bed, with proper bed-clothes. Light was leaking in through a curtained window, soft, summery morning light. She felt warm.

She was lying next to the Doctor; actually, she was lying half on top of him, one arm thrown across his chest. She could feel her hand rising and falling with his sleeping breath. She was only wearing her bra and knickers.

'I hope Bernice doesn't catch us like this,' she murmured. The Doctor did not stir.

Yesterday started to filter into her mind, backwards.

She remembered Bernice and Mme Thierry fussing over her and the Doctor. Benny had made her get into the bed with him. He was in his shirtsleeves now. Classic hypothermia treatment.

She remembered shooting the boy in the face. The axe-and-cabbage sound, the – she folded up the image and packed it away in her mind, where she could deal with it later. She could handle it.

They were buried in a huge pile of blankets. She sat up and pulled on her shirt.

She remembered hitting the Doctor, trying to stop him from shooting the child. There was a long, purple line under his left eye. Had she done that? No, she had seen it before, on the ship –

There was a great purple bruise on his left cheekbone, the impact of a human fist, the skin split open with the force of the blow.

Which meant – which meant – he hadn't died, he was still alive, he –

Ace's hands went to her mouth. Her vision blurred. She forced it down, she could handle it, she could –

The Doctor's soft blue eyes were open, looking up at her. He gave his head a tiny shake. 'Let it out,' he told her.

Ace sobbed into his shoulder, her hands clutching the fabric of his shirt, her arms and chest jerking violently as she cried. A little awkwardly, he put his arms around her. He held her, held her, even after the sobs and the movement had diminished into silence.

'Are you alright?' she mumbled.

'Of course I'm alright. I'm always alright.'

'The boy,' she said, 'the little boy. You wouldn't really –'

'He wasn't a little boy. He was a machine. I doubt he could think much beyond calculating coordinates.'

'But if you had to –'

'I'm not like that.'

'You are,' she said. 'You would if it was important.'

'How do you know?'

'Cos I would.'

The Doctor sat up. Ace snuggled up to him, and he put a gentle arm around her. 'I met another one at the other end. A man. He could talk, and think . . . He must have been the deluxe model.'

'To Ship, we're all machines. Humans, Ants, everyone.'

'God, it's good to see you.'

The Doctor didn't say anything, just held her a little more tightly.

She reached up and tickled him under the arm.

He jumped as though something had stung him. 'What are you doing?' he said, wriggling under the blankets.

'A-ha, the all-powerful Time Lord can dish it out, but can he take it?' Ace pounced and started to mercilessly tickle her victim. He yelped and nearly fell out of the bed, but the sheets were tangled up around him, so that he ended up suspended over the side.

'You're giggling!'

'I do not giggle!' The Doctor, grinning all over his face, reached up and grabbed Ace's arm. They both tumbled onto the floor, shouting with laughter.

At this point Benny walked in the door. 'What on Earth is going on in here?'

'Benny!' they both shouted.

'What a memory!'

Ace said, 'Tickle machine is out of control!'

'Right,' said Benny. She snatched a pillow off the bed and boofed Ace in the head with it.

Ace reached out and grabbed Benny's ankle, tripping her up so that she fell onto the bed.

The Doctor scrambled out of the way as Ace started throwing cushions at Benny, who deflected them with her pillow. 'Stop this at once!' he protested.

Ace chucked a cushion at him. Benny took the opportunity to thump her again with the pillow.

'This has gone on long enough.' The Doctor picked up the

other pillow and beat them mercilessly about the head and shoulders.

Ace grabbed hold of his arms, and Benny pulled away the pillow, laughing, but Ace's giggling was turning into sobbing, great gasping sobs. 'Shit.'

The Doctor cradled her while she cried, properly this time, hanging onto her as though she were a life preserver on a very wide and cold ocean. Benny, looking embarrassed, sat down on the floor and tried to stuff some of the feathers back into the misshapen pillow.

'I'm sorry,' said Ace, 'I'm sorry, I just, they were hu-hurting you and I co-couldn't make it stop, I couldn't make it stop!'

'Shh.' He rocked her back and forth, gently. 'That's all over with now.'

'I couldn't do anything, I couldn't do anything, I couldn't stand it!'

'Shh. It's over.'

Benny gave him a look that said, Is it?

He reached out a hand to her, and she joined in the hug. 'I had a plan,' he said. 'It didn't exactly work.'

'Oh, that's a first.'

'Time for plan B.'

'Run?'

'Where to? Eventually, Ship will succeed in stabilizing one of the rifts. Then it will be able to duplicate that rift, over and over in different places and times, an infinite self-similar set – and the universe will disintegrate around it.'

'I was joking,' protested Bernice, sitting back down on the floor.

'Are you alright?'

She crammed a fistful of down into the pillow. 'I thought you were dead. No, I knew you were dead. Both of you.' She pulled the Doctor's fedora off and plonked it down on his head. 'This is going to take some getting used to.'

Ace blew her nose on the Doctor's hanky. 'I feel like such an idiot,' she said.

'What about you?' Benny asked. 'Did you know we were alive?'

The Doctor said, 'The TARDIS knew. She kept track of us, kept us linked, at least subconsciously.'

Ace wiped her eyes. 'Yeah. Alright. Now what?'

The Doctor stood up. 'Conference,' he said.

Benny wanted to be alone.

Funny, that. Now they were back together again, she just wanted some time to herself. She fished around inside her head, looking for the reason, the way she fished for half-remembered facts, or the reason she had gone into a room.

They'd talked in the kitchen, trading stories, comparing notes. Afterwards she'd gone out to the TARDIS and put on banged-up jeans and a blue Glomesh shirt she'd pulled out from under her bed. She'd cut her hair down to the dark roots, a couple of inches long. Bugger the anachronism, she just needed to be herself for a while.

Right now she was sitting on a chair on Thierry's lawn, drinking port and listening to the distant sound of guns.

She hadn't told Ace or the Doctor about her nightmare.

She wondered what Vivant had made of her disappearance. He hadn't got a proper goodbye. Without Denon, she would have starved, but now she felt slightly embarrassed by how much she had had to rely on him. It reminded her of how reliant she was on the Doctor. Powerful friends.

She snatched up a mental fish. The memory glimmered, silver flashing in the sunlight. The silver badge on her father's hat, glittering as he promised he'd be back. She hadn't had a proper goodbye either, he had gone away and he hadn't told her whether he was alive or dead. It wasn't fair!

She wondered for the hundredth time whether the Ants had taken him.

The sound of hoofbeats brought her out of her reverie. She tilted the hat back. A horse and cart were clopping up the long driveway to the mansion. A portly young man was driving it. As the cart drew up, a woman sat up in the back and pulled the tarp off.

'Hi,' said Benny. 'Remember me?'

Kadiatu uncoiled from the cart and was pelting across the ground towards her, lithe and single-minded as a leopard.

Benny caught her breath and stayed where she was. Where was she going to run from that?

Kadiatu stopped short of Benny's chair, perfectly still. She gazed at the white woman, as though trying to see through her skin and, make sure the right soul was inside. She was dressed in French clothes, men's clothes, her muscles showing through the cloth. She looked older and her hair was shorter. She looked as thought she could rip phone books in half.

'Where's Thierry?' she said.

Benny picked up the port bottle and took a slow suck. She needed it. 'The place is under new management now,' she said.

'Where the hell did you come from?'

'Language,' chided Bernice. 'I brought the Doctor's TARDIS.'

'What happened to my ship?'

'Rather a lot has happened in your absence. The Doctor will explain everything. Mmm. Actually, that's pretty unlikely.'

'Where's my ship?'

'It's gone.'

'What!'

'I'm afraid it blew down.'

'It blew up?'

'No, it imploded. I'm afraid M Thierry was caught in the implosion.'

'Killed?'

Benny nodded. 'He was working for the Ants, you know.'

Kadiatu shook her head, slowly. 'You have wrecked everything. I don't believe it. You have mucked it all up.'

Benny waved the port at Kadiatu, but the tall woman just shook her head. 'I don't get drunk,' she said. 'If you'd just let the Ants take my ship, they'd have been destroyed. That was what I planned.'

'That'd be a bit of a surprise,' said Benny, 'given that you're working for them too.'

Kadiatu's hand went to the back of her neck. 'When'd he work that out?'

'Good question. You get used to it after a while, you know.'

* * *

183

'I'd stay where you are if I were you,' said the Doctor, without turning around. Ace hovered on the cellar steps.

He was back in his white clothes, bent over a table they'd dragged down from the living room. A couple of muon lamps from the TARDIS were fixed to the table.

Ace sat down with her back to the wall, hugged her knees. They'd talked for hours in the kitchen, but she still didn't feel as though she were up to speed. And she hadn't told the Doctor or Benny about her nightmare. 'I want to ask you about the rifts,' she said.

The Doctor kept on doing what he was doing. She noticed he was wearing latex gloves, had a box of them on the table, like a box of tissues. 'Ask away,' he said.

'Is the rift you came through in 1871 the same rift that Bernice came through in 1789?'

'Rift's not quite the right word. The rift per se is a fracture running through a four-dimensional area of space-time. The exit point keeps changing its temporal coordinate.'

'It's drifting back and forth in time.'

'That's right. It sounds as though the exit point you encountered in Egypt was doing the same thing. Other rift exits will be moving through space but not through time – they will seem to appear in more than one place at once. And still others may be moving through both space and time.'

'But they appear relative to the same place on the Earth's surface. How's that possible?'

'They've been anchored. It's child's play, one of the basics of time corridor technology. But time corridors are temporary – they collapse when you cut their power. These holes will never seal up. Anything could come through them and threaten the Earth, future or past. And they put a constant strain on the space-time they pass through.'

'So it hurts space and time when the rifts move around like that?'

'Have you ever seen the magic trick where you slice a banana without peeling it first?' A scalpel flashed in the Doctor's hand, briefly.

'Tell me how it's done.'

'It's very simple. You use a needle and thread, moving the

184

thread in a zigzag pattern through the banana skin, slicing up the soft fruit inside. Then, when you peel the banana . . . Gaps appear in the walls of the rifts, like holes in a tunnel, and the Ants can pop out into random areas of space-time to do a spot of piracy.'

'So how're we going to stop them?'

'It's not really a them. It's an it. Ship is a computer with a program that's gone haywire. How would you stop a computer?'

Ace thought for a moment. 'Unplug it,' she said. 'Is Ship drawing power from the Vortex?'

'Very good.'

'Oh, thanks,' said Ace sarcastically. 'Then you have to change its programming. Find the right command to stop it. Or introduce a virus.'

'Very, very good. The only trouble is, organic computers are experts at dealing with viruses. They have to be.'

'I've used puters with organic components – protein wafers and whatever – but a whole spaceship made out of living matter?'

'An organic computer is a big advantage when trying to negotiate the Vortex,' said the Doctor. 'Like a living mind, the TARDIS can handle mathematics that would distort a normal computer.'

'Is Ship a TARDIS?'

'No. It's from the very far future. An Earth colony at the edge of the galaxy. Their planet was destroyed. They decided to leave before that happened.'

'How was it destroyed?'

He hesitated, half turned. She saw the purple scar on his cheekbone, standing out sharply in the fierce light. 'I'm not exactly clear on the details. We haven't spoken often.'

'Why is it doing this to people?' whispered Ace.

'The colonists created a computer into which they could upload their minds. They wrapped a spacecraft around the computer, to take it away from the dead world. And then this Ship fell into one of the rifts Kadiatu created. It was badly damaged. It could have happened to anyone, really.'

'Why didn't they just leave in the spaceship?'

'Their bodies were dying.' He put down his scalpel. 'Only their minds could be salvaged, stored in the gestalt of Ship's computer. Many of them opted to stay behind.'

'I'm not surprised.'

'The group mind wouldn't let them. The Ants were the colony's workhorses. Ship used them to drag the others on board and process them. '

'Oh my God.' Ace opened her eyes. 'Ship is still trying to assimilate all the colonists.'

The Doctor nodded. 'That's all it does, that's all it knows how to do. As far as it's concerned, the rifts just give it better access to material which needs to be processed.'

'What about the people, the slaves?'

'More flexible and smarter than the Ants. Better machines.'

'Why don't they just stop? Oh. Because they're scared. If they all stopped at the same time, Ship would be helpless.'

'But it's the prisoner's dilemma. If just one of them goes on strike, that person gets processed. Their best option is to co-operate with Ship. But if they cooperated with one another . . .'

'Are you finished yet?'

The Doctor nodded. 'Let's get out of here.' He snapped off his gloves and pushed them into a bucket.

Ace hesitated on the steps. 'Listen –'

He shook his head. 'There's no way of knowing whether your Egyptian friend is still in cold storage, or whether he's been processed.'

'It's my fault he was taken. I have to get him back! I want to go there! I want to kill Ship!'

'I'm not ready yet,' said the Doctor.

She grabbed his arm. 'You're not ready?! There are people dying up there – out – wherever they are! Being tortured and dying! What are you going to do about it?'

'I don't know,' said the Doctor. 'I've forgotten.'

'You what? Have you lost your marbles?'

For the first time, she saw a hint of panic in his face. 'I did know, but I made myself forget. When the Ant came for me in Paris, it couldn't work out what I was planning, because I don't know myself.'

'You've finally done it,' Ace snorted. 'You've even managed to bamboozle yourself. Well, can't you figure it out?'

'Not yet.' His hands fidgeted. 'It must be a good plan, or I wouldn't have bothered to hide it. Kadiatu's been trying hard, but she hasn't managed to figure it out either.'

'You make it sound like she's the enemy.'

The Doctor raised thumb and forefinger. *Just a tad.*

'If she's on their side,' said Ace, 'I'll kill her.'

'I wouldn't advise that.'

'Hey?' said Ace. 'You don't have any objections, any moral problems – you just wouldn't advise it?'

'Take a close look at her. Trust me, Ace.'

He pushed past her and up the stairs.

Ace reached into her pocket, felt the tiny bag, heard glass clinking on glass. It couldn't be that simple, could it? She started up the stairs after him.

She couldn't help looking behind her.

The littleboy's components were neatly stacked in pieces on the table.

She managed to get outside the house before she threw up.

Kadiatu came loping around the back of the house, stopped at the edge of the yellowing lawn.

There were trees that had grown backwards into saplings, flowers that had blossomed out of season. There was a huge crater in the lawn, smooth-edged, as though something had nipped a bite out of the Earth. At its edges, Thierry's orchard was a mess of apple blossoms and ripe apples and rotting apples. There was no sign of Thierry. The Doctor's TARDIS stood at the edge of the crater.

'Shit,' said Kadiatu, with feeling.

A woman had just finished throwing up in the crater. She backed away from the edge, wiping her mouth with little, rodent motions, and turned around.

They stood perhaps twenty feet apart.

The woman was short, stocky, her muscles the hard muscles of real use. There'd be scars under that denim, some of them deep. She was white, with big brown anime eyes. Kadiatu looked at her eyes and saw one of those people her parents had warned her not to make loud noises around. Best to be careful of this one.

Ace looked back, saw the shape of Kadiatu's body, the way she held her arms and head when standing still. In magazines you saw bodies like that, thanks to computer reimaging – it took at least as much technology to create them in the real world. Somewhere under those French riding clothes was a serial number, probably picked out microscopically in light-coloured skin.

She'd fought alongside a few of the engineered, mostly people from colonies at the edge of the expanding bubble of human space, where the technology was still legal. They were like grenades, great weapons, but you didn't want to be too close to them when they exploded. Best to be careful of this one.

Genevieve was baking bread. She hummed a little tune as she floured the pan, plucking bits of sticky dough from her fingers and wiping them on her apron.

The three *voyageurs* had sat around her kitchen table, telling impossible stories. It seemed bizarre, the familiar surroundings, the quiet sunshine, the tales of hurtling through centuries to the Pyramids or to meet Napoleon himself. Some of it she hadn't understood. But when she did not believe, she glanced out the window, to where a fifty-foot crater had been bitten out of her back lawn. To where she had last seen that *salaud* François and his *salaud* littleboy.

The Doctor sat at the kitchen table, peeling and slicing apples into a ceramic bowl. Genevieve pushed another pan of bread into her oven. A hot, yeasty breath blew out into the kitchen. She smiled and pushed the door closed.

'What will you do?' asked the Doctor.

She started tugging at her apron strings. 'I have my freedom now,' she said. 'I suppose I could sell the estate and go away.'

She sat down at the table with him. 'Perhaps I will stay. I don't feel as though I have earned the right to leave.'

'Earned it?'

She picked up a piece of his apple peel and bit a piece of the end. 'The explosion was an accident, *n'est-ce pas*? I did not do anything.'

'Do something now,' said the Doctor.

Genevieve gathered up the dish of apple slices, took them to the bench, where a bowl was already lined with thick pastry.

Kadiatu ducked under the door frame. Genevieve stopped humming.

'You'd better have something clever up your sleeve, because I've run out of ideas,' said the tall African woman.

The Doctor pulled a bag of barley sugars out of his pocket, unwrapped one with great care and popped it into his mouth. 'It's going to take patience.'

'We've got no time,' said Kadiatu urgently. 'Now that these two are here –'

He shrugged his left shoulder, massaging it as though to relieve a cramp. 'Not twice this day inch time foot gem,' he said, 'as Takuan put it. An inch of time is worth a foot of precious stone.

There was a dreadful mechanical sound outside. Genevieve went to the window, clutching her bowl of apples. The Doctor's blue box was fading away, like shadows disappearing in the morning sun. She blinked. It ought to be *extraordinaire*, oughtn't it? Perhaps she would never be surprised by anything ever again.

'Where's it gone?' said Kadiatu, alarmed.

Where the Ants won't be able to get their grubby little mandibles on it,' said the Doctor.

'Surely they wouldn't be able to use your TARDIS?'

'No. But they might learn a lot by pulling the old girl to pieces. They know too much already, they learn so quickly – as soon as they try an idea they're adapting it, expanding it.' He looked at her. 'They must have found you fascinating.'

'If you'd just let them take my ship aboard . . .' She raised her hands, in a gesture that was almost pleading.

The Doctor shook his head. 'They suspected a booby-trap – that's why they sent the vessel here first. This way, they still think you're on their side.'

'Do they? How long will that last? What's your plan, then?' insisted Kadiatu.

'Oh, there is one,' said the Doctor, 'I just –'

The back door creaked open and Ace came in, trying not to look ill. She went up to the Doctor, holding something out. 'Are these yours?'

The Doctor opened the little bag and let the marbles inside fall into his palm. For a moment he stared at them in bewilderment. Then he closed his hand, closed his eyes, a look of relief crossing his face.

'Of course,' he said. 'That was it.'

Chapter 14

The Oncoming Storm

> History is time's way of preventing everything from
> happening at once.
>
> (Graffito, Prydonian Academy)

They rode in the hay in Nicolas' cart, with the top down.
Twice they were stopped. Twice the Doctor had a quiet word
and they were allowed to drive on. Ace grinned at Benny and
said, 'The Force gives me power over weak minds.'

They bumped along cobbled streets, passed parks in which
not one tree had been left standing. A house stood in ruins,
smoking softly. Some cafes were still open, tired Parisians
drinking coffee on the pavement. From time to time, the
Doctor shook his head. '*Paris, sa grand' ville,*' he muttered.

They climbed out of the cart at Thierry's city house.
Kadiatu paid Nicolas while Benny plucked splinters from her
clothing. There was no-one about to give them strange looks,
just the sounds of distant shouting and smoke in the afternoon
air.

'I'll have to take care of some of Thierry's business,' said
Kadiatu. 'Make yourselves at home.' She went inside.

'Are we assuming she's on our side, then?' said Ace.

'Oh yes.' The Doctor nodded. 'She would have stranded
herself, using her vessel as a weapon against Ship.'

'How about us?' said Ace. 'Are we stranded?'

'If Ship succeeds,' he said, watching Nicolas trot away, 'it
won't be possible to be stranded. The barriers that separate
one moment from the next will come crashing down. All
places, all times squashed together like a cosmic blanc-
mange.'

'Doctor,' said Bernice, 'are you saying the universe will come to an end?'

'Nevermore a butterfly,' he breathed.

Ace puffed out her cheeks. 'Best not to screw up then.' She went into the house.

Benny pulled something out of her pocket. She had to tug the Doctor's sleeve to get his attention; he was peering into nothing, as though trying to see something suspended between two molecules of air.

She held it up to the light. It was a gold ring, a wedding ring. 'It was in the cart. Just mixed up with the hay.' There were initials engraved on the inner side. 'It doesn't belong to anyone we know.'

'Perhaps you should follow Nicolas,' said the Doctor, without much interest.

'I'd like to know what he's about, maybe ask him a few questions. Is Kadiatu qualified to fight monsters?'

'It's important to work out which people the enemy has sent to spy on you – and to bribe them to serve you instead. Said Sun Tzu. You don't trust her.'

'With the entire universe at stake, I'm not sure I trust anyone,' said Benny.

'What about me? Do you trust me?' His eyes suddenly pulled into sharp focus, raking at her face. 'Have I been taken over by some alien entity?'

'You *are* an alien entity,' said Benny. 'And your lack of a formal degree in fighting monsters is adequately substituted for by practise in the field. I wish you could tell us your plan, though.'

'Sorry,' he said. 'This is something I have to do myself.'

Benny grimaced. 'Surplus to requirements as usual. I can't follow Nicolas, he's scarpered.'

The Doctor pulled out a notebook and scribbled down an address. 'How'd you know?' she said.

'Written on the side of the cart. Off you go.'

Off she went, throwing a worried glance over her shoulder. What had that been all about?

'How is Ship these days?' said the Doctor. The roses on

Thierry's mantle had withered and blackened, hanging down over the side of the bowl. 'Long time no see.'

Kadiatu was rummaging through Thierry's desk, having wrenched it open, snapping the lock with her fingers. 'It's a sick ship.'

'Not ship-shape?'

'There is a virus going around.'

'Well,' said the Doctor, 'to the vector belong the spoils.' He unwrapped another barley sugar.

'There were power fluctuations. Some personalities broke free from the gestalt. They were suicidal, attacking Ship's systems. The ones which couldn't be reintegrated were destroyed.'

'Mm. They can't have been very well integrated in the first place.'

Kadiatu shook her head. 'Ship was only designed to hold a few hundred minds. There must be several thousand packed in there now.'

'How many angels can dance on the head of a pin?'

'They've had to stop gathering more subjects while they sort out the problems.'

'Good.'

'Cold storage is empty. Ship's slaves have started on one another.'

The Doctor bit down on the barley sugar with a *crack*.

'Ship manages,' said Kadiatu, 'to keep an eye on everything regardless.'

She turned, held up the hair at the back of her head with a gesture that might have been casual. The Doctor walked idly across the room, glanced at the skin on the back of her neck. No scar – but a blur of displaced cells where the surgery had been healed. Sonics? Nanotechnology?

'Oh yes,' he concurred, 'a finger in every pie.'

'Ship likes to keep track of its components.' She tapped him lightly on the collarbone.

'Yes. The walls have ears. Literally.'

'Your post-traumatic stress disorder. You faked it.'

The Doctor hesitated. 'Yes. Of course. I didn't want Ship thinking I was still dangerous. Yes.' He pushed the heel of his

193

palm into his collar bone.

'You don't want to go back there.'

'I'd have to be dragged back.'

Kadiatu nodded. 'We understand one another, then.'

'Yes,' said the Doctor. 'I think we understand one another.'

'Good. I've got to run some errands and clear Thierry's things before the Versaillais arrive. I've put the pieces of the Ant back in the basement.'

He stopped massaging his shoulder. His eyes were distant, distracted. She knew how he felt: the constant pain made you unfocussed, panicky. 'Sorry you had a wasted journey.'

'Aren't we all.'

'They're about to have a war here, aren't they?'

'They've already had one, actually.'

Ace was sitting on the stairs of Kadiatu's basement. 'But this whole place is in a state of siege. There's war in the air, it's gonna happen soon. How soon?'

The Doctor put down the piece of Ant he was examining, carefully laying it alongside the others on a blanket. He seemed rather small in the enlarged basement, sitting cross-legged in the dust, his bag of barley sugars to one side.

He got out his pocket-watch and flipped it open. 'Tonight, as a matter of fact. One of the city's gates has been left completely unguarded. Someone will spot this pertinent fact and signal the army outside.'

'Hmm. They're not very organized, are they?'

'Within a week, there'll be nothing left of the Paris Commune. Except memories. Parisians will be shouting *Vive la Commune* again in 1968.'

'Why's it called a Commune, anyway? Are they Communists?'

The Doctor picked up the Ant's head, turned it around slowly, pivoting the antennae in their joints. He was working by lanterns. Ace wondered how he could see clearly enough. 'Socialists. The "Commune" is the government elected by the Parisians. It isn't the first Commune, nor the first time Paris has broken away from the rest of France, but in fact, similar rebellions have happened all over the country. At any rate, you're right, they're tremendously disorganised. Too much enthusiasm and not enough forward planning. The Versaillais are going to march in here and shoot at anything that looks even vaguely red. Semaine Sanglante.'

'How many people?'

'About twenty-five thousand.'

'More than the Templo Mayor.'

'Hmm.' The Doctor had pried open the robotic head, was poking around in the circuitry inside. 'It'll be especially dangerous for unaccompanied women. Milkwomen will be shot because their bottles *might* contain petrol.'

'Why don't we stop it, then?'

He looked up at her. 'What?'

'We could stop it. We know exactly when and where the attack starts, right?'

The Doctor sat back. 'You're not serious.'

Ace shook her head. 'You don't understand. *Why* don't we stop it?'

'You tell me.'

'Something else would happen to cause the war.'

The Doctor nodded. 'This siege can't go on forever.'

'So no matter what we did, things would happen just the same.'

'Not quite. We're playing with different scales, different magnifications.'

'Close up?'

'We might save a life here and there, ease some suffering.'

'A little further back?'

'We can't stop the actual war, not without tremendous effort, and not without endangering all of Earth's future history. The Russian Revolution was partly inspired by the Commune, they learned a lot.'

'Further away,' Ace answered herself. 'We've got a universe to save.'

Silence for a bit. The Doctor kept mucking about inside the Ant's head, pulling out components. To Ace's eye it seemed modular, the bits and pieces independent little lumps of technology.

'What did you do in Ancient Egypt?' asked the Doctor.

'Kidnapped the king.'

'Ah.'

Silence for a bit.

'I didn't kill him. I think I was going to. Actually, I think I was a little out of my skull.'

'I know what's it like. I was stranded once myself,' said the Doctor.

'Did you get that feeling like you were caught in a big trap?'

'Oh, yes.'

'Like when the electricity's off in a storm, and you think, I can't watch TV, so I'll listen to a record, but you can't do that either. You can't do anything, really. Like that.'

'So,' said the Time Lord, 'why didn't you?'

'Sorry? Oh – well, he talked me out of it. The people I was working for were just using me. I was just following orders, right?'

'I'm listening.'

'I must've been out of my head. I thought they were into anarchy, right? But they just wanted to get into the palace and I just wanted to do something.'

'Something must be done, this is something, therefore we must do this?

'Yeah. I didn't tell you before cos – because I thought you'd be really pissed off, actually.'

'What am I going to do, send you to bed without supper?' He grinned up at her. 'You're old enough, you're experienced enough to make your own decisions. I'm just glad you're on my side.'

'Ditto,' she laughed. What happened to Akhenaten, anyway?'

'He died, and his revolution died with him.'

'The Setites got him?'

'No. He just died. His religion was suppressed, his monuments were destroyed, his name was chiselled out of the records, and his city was abandoned and fell into ruins. And he was forgotten about for a couple of millennia. No-one even knows where he is buried. If he was buried.'

'Cruk.'

'Indeed.'

'Like the Commune. History repeats itself.'

'Not precisely. History is quasi-self-similar. The same patterns happening over and over, never quite the same. You're beginning to see them, aren't you?'

Ace met his eyes. 'Yes. It's all patterns to you, isn't it? Patterns that other people can't see.'

'Sometimes patterns which aren't even there. That's what faith is for. Faith in Time, faith that things will work out the way they're supposed to.'

Ace messed up her hair. Old, yeah, yes, she was getting old; there was probably some grey in there now. 'So even if I had killed Akhenaten . . .'

The Doctor had picked up one of the components, was prodding it with a piece of wire. 'Time heals all wounds. Particularly her own. Oh!'

Ace was on her feet before the little component hit the floor. The Doctor was clawing at his left shoulder, his hands clenching in spasms. He fell backwards, banged his head on the wall.

She was by his side. 'What is it? What do I do?'

He tried to speak, but all he could do was gasp, breathless syllables of distress. His whole body was jerking. She wrenched him clear of the brickwork, got his hands away from his collar bone, unbuttoned his shirt as his fingernails scrabbled at her jacket.

There was nothing there. For a moment, in the dim light, she thought she saw a blurred circle in the flesh – but there was no wound, no scar. Then what – ?

She twisted her head around. The machine! She lowered his trembling frame to the floor and plucked up the tiny device. Its little lights were flashing and winking. Right. She raised it above her head.

'Gn!' The Doctor was reaching out his right hand. 'No!'

She pushed the component into his palm, closed his fingers over it. He held it in both hands, did something to it. The flickering lights went out.

He relaxed suddenly, and the little device rolled out of his grip. 'Doctor!' Ace shouted, shaking him. 'Are you alright?

Can you hear me?'

His eyelids flickered. He looked up at her. 'Oh yes,' he said, 'I remember the first time we met.'

'What? Yeah, it was in that cafe, I was wearing a stupid black and white uniform, and – listen! Are you listening?'

The flutterwing was three metres long, a slender, legless insect. He didn't dare touch the fabric of its wings, which were unbelievably fine, little more than a sheen of colour stretched over the rocky hillside. The stuff just went on and on, draped over scree and boulders, maybe twenty metres wide, maybe thirty.

He crouched beside the body, a small boy run away from home, lost in the landscape outside his house. Flutterwings were born in the sky, lived in the sky – they never touched the ground. Did the outsiders eat them? He looked at the long, thin body. It looked like a length of computer cable. The arrow seemed impossibly large. The creature trembled, sending a shimmer through its broken wings.

The arrow was distressing it. He tugged gently on the feathers at the end, and the arrow slid easily out of its body. There was no blood on the tip.

There were no medical facilities here, no drugs or equipment. Was the flutterwing dead? What was it thinking? Did it hurt?

He wondered what it felt like.

So he turned the arrow around and stabbed it into his palm.

Ace was gently stroking the Doctor's hair. 'And then you said, "There are three rules. One –"'

His hand jerked out of her grasp. 'Is that all?' he muttered.

'Nah, there were two more, you –'

'Is it that easy?'

'Hey,' she said. 'Anybody home?'

He focused on her. 'How long?'

'Only a couple of minutes. You're okay? What happened, then?'

He sat up and buttoned the top buttons of his shirt. 'I evidently found the part of the Ant which allows it to communicate with Ship.'

'So it was putting out a signal? Did they trace it, do something to you?'

He shook his head. 'They did something to me a long time ago.'

Ace put her hand against the Doctor's collar bone, gingerly, as though expecting to feel a kick. 'Oh, God. They *installed* something, didn't they?'

'Their mistake. It makes everything so much more convenient.'

She gave him a long, critical look. 'What are you planning to do?'

'Wouldn't they like to know.' He smiled sweetly. 'What goes bang thud, bang thud, bang thud?'

There was a queue outside a butcher's shop. It wasn't moving. Benny joined the end of it, listened to the dialogue between the tired women. Empty baskets gripped in dusty hands. They didn't say much, didn't even complain about the wait.

She had been there almost an hour when Nicolas's cart pulled up. She watched his reflection in the shop window. He was a big bear of a man. Eating too well, not like the stick-figure soldiers, the skinny women.

He hefted a huge rolled carpet from the back of the cart, handling it awkwardly. Benny's mouth was a little dry.

The building had been badly damaged by shellfire. A wooden sign hung at an angle over the front, the letters LACE TAPI visible through the plaster powder. The front doors and one of the shattered windows had been boarded up. Nicolas disappeared through a side door.

He re-emerged into the sunlight ten minutes later, still carrying the carpet, which seemed to have become lighter. He loaded it aboard, tied down the tarpaulin on the cart, and trotted away.

The ladies in the queue watched his horses with hungry eyes. Benny crossed the street while they were distracted. The side door was locked. She glanced back at the women, but they weren't interested.

Carefully, she slid the Doctor's Chinese lockpick out of her sleeve. It took a couple of minutes to get the door open.

199

The shop inside was musty, full of grubby carpets standing in tall cylinders. Like forgotten totem poles. Not a lot of carpet selling was going on here. In one or two places the ceiling gaped open, beams of light striking down into the room, dancing with dust motes.

No high-tech security device on the door; hopefully no booby traps inside. Stairs went up to the second floor – probably living quarters, if they were still useable. Benny checked for doors. The kitchen, unlocked; a cupboard, unlocked; the front door, a mesh of boards covering it on the outside.

Basement door, locked. She flinched as she opened it, but nothing vaporized or otherwise killed her.

It took a moment for her eyes to adjust to the new lighting. There was a gentle glow coming from the basement, illuminating the foot of the stairs. A reddish-green glow. A slow, pulsing sound.

'If you want me,' she muttered, 'I shall be in the spleen.'

She hesitated half-way down the stairs. The walls were covered in thick, green gunk. Nodes of it gave off bright green light. There was a constant rustling, a whispering, the sound of jungles or forests. Patches of the floor were still flagstones, but ridges and layers of the living stuff had reached across it. Around the walls there were massive pods or maybe blisters. Great sacs filled with softly luminescent green goo, taller than she was.

As she came closer, she saw that the sacs were translucent. She could make out shapes inside them. Heads and limbs and . . .

There was a bench in the centre of the room, a small pile of folders at one end. Tiny sacs were growing all over the bench. There were shapes inside them as well, hands and heads and embryos, but also irregular, coiling things, no part of the human body. Nicolas had left his burden on the bench. A soldier, a man from the Garde Nationale, the bloodstain on his jacket already gone black with time.

'Right,' said Benny. 'I flatly refuse to throw up. I deny all nausea. Otherwise I'm going to be useless for the entire rest of this adventure.'

Ace shrugged and fidgeted, stuffed into one of Mme Thierry's dresses and into the back row between two women who were knitting. The room was packed with women. Most of them were wearing red belts, some with pistols stuck into them. Children milled about as best they could between the tight seating, or howled in their mother's laps.

The two knitter's elbows moved back and forth, nudging Ace. She could barely see the front of the room for cigarette smoke. A table was piled with books and papers. Several women with red belts and sashes, faces drawn and concentrated, sat there.

Ace closed her eyes. She was tasting the dust of the desert again, the dust of history: how many of these people would be alive in a week's time? The Doctor had called it *La Semaine Sanglante*, the Bloody Week, and it was going to start tonight. Why had she even bothered to come to this meeting?

'Men are cowards!' The speaker was young, angry, with large eyes and long brown hair. 'They say they're the rulers of creation, and then they complain they have to fight. Well, let them go and join the traitors at Versailles, and leave the defence of the city to us! We've got more to lose than they have. We've got petroleum, we've got axes, we've got strong hearts. We'll be the ones on the barricades. We'll show them that they can't tread us down any more!'

She sat down, breathless. There was scattered applause and murmurs. The woman on Ace's left snorted a huge pinch of snuff.

Ace opened her eyes again. She startled. The young woman was looking right at her – no, she was just looking into the crowd, to see who had clapped and who disagreed. She couldn't be twenty yet. And she'd be lying in the gutter by Friday, her anger silenced.

Another woman had taken the stand. 'It might not be necessary to fight on the barricades. But we won't make our grandmothers' ghosts ashamed of us. We'll bring the wounded soldiers back home, and save their lives. We'll cook and sew for them. We'll make sure the Versaillais won't be able to live off the sweat of our backs any more. For too long, we've all been cogs in the machinery: soldiers, workers, women, literally parts of the machines in their stinking factories. Now the

Versaillais must be made to understand that they cannot treat us like machines!

'*Citoyennes*!' boomed a third woman. 'This is all so much hot air. What we need is action, immediate action. Get your men to follow the right track, to fulfil their duties. We must put our backs into it! We must strike without mercy and destroy those who are undermining the Commune! Men must cooperate or be shot! If tomorrow we sent a hundred cowards before the firing squad, you can be sure that the next day a thousand would come forward to serve the Commune.'

'You don't have the day after tomorrow,' said Ace loudly. 'You don't even have tomorrow.'

There were shouts and murmurs. The women on either side of her stopped knitting. 'Order!' someone called from the table at the front.

'And you know it. You know there's no time left. No one's made proper plans to defend the city. What have you managed to accomplish? What about all the incompetence, all the screwing around? What have you really done?'

'War widows have been adopted by the Commune, married or not – they won't starve,' said one of the women behind the table.

'There are plans for a girl's industrial school. Plans for nurseries, so that poor mothers can earn a crust. Plans to organize women workers so that they can share in the profits generated by their labour.'

'Plans, plans,' said Ace. 'If the Commune disappeared tomorrow, all your plans would be forgotten.'

'That doesn't excuse us from the duty of making those plans.' The young speaker got to her feet.

'What's the point?' Angry murmurs were moving through the crowd, but it didn't matter. None of it mattered. 'It's like Akhenaten, it's all going to be torn down anyway. What's the point if you're all going to be shot?'

And now she saw the weariness in the young woman's eyes, felt the desperation of the crowd. 'If that is our destiny, we cannot escape it.' said the young *citoyenne* quietly. 'No matter. One day there will be schools for women. One day we will be able to work as we please, and be no-one's slaves.

Even if we die, we will not be forgotten.' The crowd hushed. 'The Commune may not last one more day, even one more hour. But it has already planted the seeds of a hundred revolutions. Even if it is only a temporary arrangement, that makes it no less valuable. Not unlike life itself, Mademoiselle'.

There was another smattering of applause. The women were getting up, picking up hats and children and heading for the doors. 'She knows her stuff, that one,' said the woman on Ace's right, packing away her knitting.

Ace sat down, closed her eyes again, tasting the dust of the desert. *Even if it is only a temporary arrangement, that makes it no less valuable.* It did count. It did matter.

The young *citoyenne* was surprised when the *Anglaise* came up to her, a rifle slung across her back. 'So,' she said, 'what's the plan?'

Kadiatu came down the stairs, cradling the child's body in her arms. Hiding it in the bolt of tarpaulin had seemed like a pointless exercise. The bloodbath that would start tonight would make counting corpses just as pointless, moral nitpicking.

The child had been dead a day; the sooner she got it into storage, the better. She unrolled the little girl from the tarp, picked her up by the scruff of her shirt and stuffed her into an empty sac hanging from the wall. Green liquid overflowed down the walls of the blister, lifting the girl's tiny hands, soaking into her dirty clothes and highlighting her painfully thin face in a soft reddish glow.

Kadiatu sealed the blister, strode to her research bench, reached down behind it and twisted her fingers in Benny's hair.

The woman was trying to dart aside, moving like a hologram with the playback speed set too slow. Like an insect caught in treacle. That was happening more often, more easily. Would there come a time, Kadiatu wondered as Benny struggled in slow motion, when she saw everything at this unnatural speed, when it took her a week to have a conversation?

She let reality wind back up to normal. It would only take a moment to kill Benny in any case, a flick of the wrist that would snap her neck. 'Do it! Why don't you do it!' the woman was shouting trying to turn to look at her assailant. 'It'll just be another dead body!'

'Don't you judge me,' growled Kadiatu. 'Don't you dare judge me. You have no idea of what's going on. No idea at all.'

She let go of the woman's hair. Benny stayed still in a half-crouch, but she couldn't stop the words. 'You're killing people!'

'Our roles are reversed.'

'Is that it, then? Are you possessed by some alien? By Ship?'

Kadiatu rubbed the back of her neck. 'Not possessed. One of Ship's possessions. But not any more.'

She backed away, giving Benny space to straighten up. 'You've made some kind of deal with it, haven't you!' said Benny. 'You're killing people for it! Killing children!'

Kadiatu looked at the little girl, floating in her vegetable womb. 'She died of starvation. I bought the body from her mother. The money might keep *maman* alive, if she survives the *Semaine*.'

'Why?' insisted Benny. 'What *for*?'

'Ship showed me how its technology works because it needed help from a time traveller. It downloaded so much stuff into me, so much information. And then it put something in my neck. Around my brainstem. So it would know what I was doing.'

'A bug?' said Benny, horrified.

'I can talk to you now,' said Kadiatu, 'because I've killed it. Ship built this lab so I could work on solving its time travel problem. We built the littleboy; we anchored the rifts so the Ants would emerge on Earth instead of the middle of space. But that turned out not to be as efficient as taking spacecraft.'

'My father disappeared in space,' exploded Benny.

Kadiatu just raised a hand. 'Shut up,' she said. 'I don't have long to talk. I also created a virus specific for Ship's tissue.'

'Did it work?'

'I injected myself with it. I'm full of virus. It killed the implant. I should kill you.'

204

'Why?'

'If Ship catches you, it'll know everything you know.' Kadiatu raised a hand. Benny flinched, backed up against the bench, trying to look her in the eyes.

'I didn't think it would be like this,' said Kadiatu. 'I didn't think it would be so complicated.' She lowered her hand, slowly.

Benny breathed out, hard. 'Why did you do it, then? Why build a time machine?'

'Why do you travel with him?'

Benny pushed her sweat-soaked fringe out of her eyes. 'To see the universe. But you always get caught up in something along the way. There are always Ants to spoil the picnic.'

'The Ants exist because of me. That's why I have to destroy them, destroy Ship.'

The fear had gone from Benny's face. 'I want to talk to you,' she said. 'Properly.'

'There's no time. There's never been any time. They've always been watching.'

'What is it they want?'

'Ship wants to carry out its program. It wants to process everyone.'

'Everyone?'

'Everyone.'

'*Everyone?*'

'Everyone.'

'But why? What's the point?'

'There is no point. Ship's just running on automatic.'

There was a soft puff of air. Benny whirled. There was an Ant standing behind her.

Kadiatu picked her up and hurled her at the wall.

Benny rebounded from the spongy stuff and rolled onto the floor. The Ant scrambled over the bench at Kadiatu, its forelegs rearing up. She grabbed them, wrenched them apart. She was tired of fighting. She couldn't be bothered to fight. But she had to keep up appearances.

The Ant's antennae reached for her face. She let the itching in her brain build until it filled her up, static blotting out everything.

* * *

The Doctor had his distant face on. Ace found herself peering into shadows and straining her ears. The enemy was listening. But they weren't in the shadows. They were lodged in the Doctor's shoulder, over his collarbone. He was bugged, but it didn't seem to bother him.

Benny waited impatiently at the top of the stairs. Ace stifled a sneeze. The Doctor was peering about, not focussed on anything, as though trying not to give away what he was really interested in by being interested in everything. He absently held on to Kadiatu's lab notes, the folders full of dog-eared pages, filled with scribbly student writing.

'Fascinating cult, the Setites,' he muttered, around a couple of barley sugars. 'They kept going until the early twentieth century, you know, passing the little bits and pieces of Osiran technology down the line.'

'Yes, yes,' said Bernice, almost stamping her foot with impatience.

'Sutekh killed the last of them. And then I killed him. He wasn't forgotten, though. Set-worshippers turn up again in California in the seventies, on Eridani in the twenty-fourth century.' The Doctor ran his finger along the top of the counter, coating his fingerprint with thick dust. 'The enemy. The outsider. A powerful archetype.'

'It depends,' said Ace, 'on what you're the enemy *of*.'

The Doctor swivelled. 'You ended a sentence with a preposition. You can't *do* that.'

Ace slowly grinned.

They had reached the top of the stairs. 'It's a sort of laboratory,' said Benny. 'Kadiatu said she had developed a virus.'

'No, she didn't look well.'

'No. She planned to –'

The Doctor held up a finger. 'Loose lips sink ships,' he said. Benny frowned, but stayed silent.

They looked at the bodies and the body parts, the blisters of green fluid, the writhing things and the growing things.

The green light helped, thought Ace. The colours of the battlefield were missing, the red, the pink and grey. And the butcher-shop smell, always startling, always new. Instead, it was green, as though they were in some deep forest and not a continental basement, green and smelling of greenness, the smell of mucking about in the front garden as a small child, making the leaves and sticks have wars with one another.

She found herself looking at her fingers, bending them back and forth. Imagining the components underneath, the tendons and bone and nerves.

The Doctor was wandering about the lab like a kid in a particularly gruesome toy shop. He gestured at half-formed bodies, bumpy spheres like giant peas, lumpy machine-creatures growing on fat vines. 'Gatekeepers,' he said, 'Seekers. Hoppers. Communications devices. All based on a fusion of human and Ship flesh. Much of it's meant to be grafted onto a human user, on a temporary or permanent basis.'

'Hoppers?'

The Doctor pointed out a huge, crablike organism, pulsing slowly against a wall as though it were asleep. 'For short transdimensional hops. Ship's advanced so much . . .'

'By stealing technology.'

'Yes. And four thousand heads are better than one. Fortunately, there's still one thing it hasn't worked out how to do.'

'Kadiatu said it wanted to process everyone who ever lived.'

'And to do that you'd need a TARDIS. And a lot of patience.'

'What if we just waited?' said Ace. 'Wouldn't Ship just explode or something, once too many minds had been stuffed into it?'

'The damage to space-time would already be done.' The Doctor had stopped at a fat brownish-green lump, sitting on a chair in the corner. 'A-ha.'

'What's that?'

'It's a model of Ship's brain,' he said. He knelt down beside the chair, pulled out a fountain pen, poked the thing. It quivered like a plateful of jelly. 'Just what I'm looking for.'

Benny and Ace sat in Nicolas's front room while the Doctor did squishy things with his pet brain. Benny was perched on the counter, legs dangling over the side. Ace sat on the floor.

'We'll get him back,' said Benny.

'Hmm? '

'Your Egyptian chap.'

'Yeah.'

'What was – what's he like?'

Ace shrugged. 'Nothing special. He saved my arse, though.'

Silence for a bit.

'What's he planning, do you suppose?'

'Hmm?'

'The Doctor. I suppose he is planning something,' said Benny. 'In the great tradition of planning something.'

'And not telling us about it. Yeah. Definitely.'

Every inch of Kadiatu's skin was covered in the green stuff. Tiny green fibres, twitching, moving – alive.

'Do you know what it is?'

'Nah. Only that he expected me to give him those marbles. That's why he left them for me. He filed the plan away at random in his head, and used the marbles as a mnemonic to retrieve them.'

They crawled – they crawled and crawled, over her, under her and into her. Her mouth was full of them. She would have to scream through a jungle if she wanted to scream.

Her body was riddled with the virus. The tentacles should be shrivelling, dying. They weren't.

'Clever trick.'

'Yeah. Did Kadiatu tell you what she was up to?'

'Creating a virus to kill Ship. She killed the implant they put in her.'

'Of course – that's why the Ant came for her. They like to tinker, don't they? They put an implant in the Doctor, too.'

'Grief! They did what?'

'That's why he didn't want you to tell him anything.'

Benny eyed Ace. 'Are you kosher?'

'I'm fine. But I think I've guessed Kadiatu's plan. Ship kid-

208

naps her, and she infects it with the virus.'

Benny nodded. 'That's what I think she was planning.'

Half a dozen Ants watched the process. She was suspended perhaps ten feet above the floor, at the centre of a twisty mass of little tentacles, all alike. Why wasn't it working? And they were doing something, doing something to her, changing her–

Modifying her!

I'm not a machine! she tried to shout. *I am not a MACHINE!*

'It's a sort of competition,' said Ace. 'Which one of them will beat the bad guy first?'

'This is no time for games,' said Benny.

'You're right.' Ace swung her legs over the edge of the counter, jumped down. 'I'll go and see what he's doing.'

Not a machine, I'm not, I, machine not, I –

Ace opened the door of the lab a crack. Inside, the Doctor was sitting in lotus position, meditating. The living light of the room stained his face green, picking out the lines of tension.

It took her a moment to realize that he was hovering an inch or two off the floor. Carefully, she closed the door.

After a while the Doctor realized he was sitting on the cold floor, head resting in one hand. He opened his eyes, massaging his forehead with the tips of his fingers.

That was everything he could do. It was up to Kadiatu now.

Almost silently, with just a tiny *bamf* of air, she materialized in front of him.

He was moving even as he took in her new appearance. She wore a sleeveless hired hand coverall, her long arms exposed. Bright green threads ran down the lines of her muscles, like streaks in marble. One of her eyes was brilliant green, almost luminescent in the shadows of the lab.

He rolled and was on his feet. She was reaching down to grab him, moving like electricity, fingers raking cloth as he shrugged his jacket off and fled across the lab.

Fast, faster than human, but not fast enough.

She caught up with him as he reached the cellar steps, closing a hand on his shoulder like a metal clamp. She spun him around.

He was still trying to pull loose when she smacked the heel of her palm into his left collar bone.

He went utterly limp, only her grip holding him vertical. She wrapped an arm around his waist and hoisted him into her arms. The cellar door was opening, slowly, then faster, speeding up as her brain slowed back into normal time. A silhouette: Ace was coming through.

Kadiatu vanished in another puff of air.

Ace ran right through where she had been standing.

'Cruk!' she shouted, stumbling on the floor of the lab.

Benny came through the door behind her. 'What happened?'

'They got him! Kadiatu came and got him! She's taken him back to that little ship of horrors!'

'Cruk!' Benny picked up the Doctor's jacket. 'Double cruk! We shouldn't have left him alone!'

'We thought they were on the same side, remember?'

'We still shouldn't have left him'.

'They'd done,' said Ace, her face twisting in revulsion, 'they'd done something to her. She was part, she was part vegetable.'

'Oh God. That's what they're going to do to *him*.'

Ace looked around, grimacing, desperate. 'One of these. I'll use one of these.' She went to the wall, unhooked the hopper.

'That's crazy!'

'I'm not –'

'I'll come with you.'

'I think it's only for one person.' Ace struggled with the loops and tentacles of the hopper.

'It looks like Giger threw up on it,' said Benny. 'Are you sure you know how to –'

Ace's head snapped back as the hopper closed on her body, wrapping its ropy tentacles around her chest. She grunted through clenched teeth. Benny grabbed at the organism, but it

210

had settled across Ace's shoulders like a malevolent back-pack.

'No, no, it's alright,' Ace coughed. She stood for a moment, working out how to breathe in the grip of the thing. 'It's supposed to do that.'

'How do you know?'

'It just told me.' Benny looked at her in horror. 'You'd better stay here in case either of them come back.'

'Just a –'

'And anyway, if it's Kadiatu, better I go than you.' Ace drew an evil-looking gun out of her jacket – a flechette-thrower, the one she called her Flash Gordon gun.

'Don't be stupid, you've seen the way she moves! She's genetically engineered, she probably knows forty-one ways to kill you with a paper-clip.'

'She's not going to be expecting me to follow her,' said Ace. 'And neither is he.'

'Look, you shouldn't –'

'Benny,' said Ace, 'I'm going to do it.'

'Good luck,' said Benny lamely.

'Luck,' said Ace, 'has nothing to do with it.'

Chapter 15

Hurt/Comfort

> Q.
> What goes bang thud, bang thud, bang thud, bang thud,
> bang thud, bang thud, bang thud, bang thud, bang thud,
> bang thud, bang thud, bang thud, bang thud?
> A.
> A Time Lord committing suicide.
>
> (Graffito, Prydonian Academy)

The Doctor woke up.

His wrists were bound behind his back. It felt like electrical wire. He was lying at an odd angle on the floor. Living floor, tasting of salt and vegetation. Kadiatu's fingerprints were bruised into his shoulder.

He shrugged, trying to get more comfortable. Oh – ankles tied as well. She wasn't taking any chances.

He was wearing a uniform. The dun fabric was coarse against his skin.

Oh, no.

It had all been a dream, hadn't it?

He pressed his cheek against the cool floor. He had never left Ship. He couldn't escape outwards, so he had escaped inwards. Saving Ace, meeting Kadiatu, all of it, a pitiful fantasy.

Then the ganglion in his shoulder burst into life. He twisted in his bonds, tiny flashbulbs going off in his field of vision.

That had been done to him after he'd left Ship. Afterwards.

It had been in Kadiatu's cellar – they'd used hoppers to transport the medical equipment. They'd implanted a tiny seed in the ganglion, a little fleck of Ship's living matter. The living thing had grown, slowly coiling itself around the sensitive nerve cluster, sucking sugar out of his blood. And now it was ready to germinate.

He could have wept with relief.

The hopper's movement felt like being shoved through a wall. But it was better than the free fall through the raw stuff of the Vortex. Ace stumbled across the rough floor, the machine convulsing around her chest.

Ace looked herself up and down. All her bits were where they should be. She turned quickly, arm loosely bent, pistol aim taking in every corner of the room . . . no corners. It was a great curving hall, the inner wall studded with tall neon tubes.

Empty. Silent. No. A sound like little bells – dripping water.

The air was crisp, like the puff of dampness as you opened the fridge. Oh, yes, she had been here before.

Benny was stooped over the Doctor, frantically trying to get a response out of him. Blood was trickling from his mouth and nose, sluggishly. His eyes had flickered shut.

They were going to do the same thing to the Doctor that they did to Kadiatu. She had to be there. She had to stop it. And yet, the pit of her stomach was still spinning – not from the jaunt through the ether, but from the knowledge that she wasn't going to be able to stop it. Because he meant for this to happen.

Benny and she had sometimes joked about switching off the gas in the TARDIS in case he tried to shove his head in an oven. But she'd been in that dark three a.m. place herself, and sometimes she wondered if he was old enough to hope, somehow, that this time he might actually be killed.

She squeezed her eyes shut for a moment. The feeling she'd had in Egypt when she threw up on Sedjet's front lawn, the insane feeling, it was coming back to her.

She went to the tubes. Each was the right size to hold a large human being. There were hibernation controls at the base – surprisingly similar to the ones she'd seen aboard the *Admiral Raistrick*. Maybe they'd picked up an IMC ship in their travels and pinched the technology.

The first tube she checked was empty, and the next, and the next. Surely there'd be someone here, he was here somewhere, she might be able to get the machines to work, she might be able to save them –

She realized she'd been running around the curve of the wall, shouting. For how long?

Every tube was empty.

She was too late. She'd failed. She hadn't saved him.

A black blossom of pain erupted in her chest. She started to crumple it up, stuff it down – no, hang onto it, hang onto it –

She sat down on the floor, took deep breaths. She stopped, hand cramping around the hilt of the gun. No-one had heard her yelling or come to kill her. Or take her away to the funny farm. Oh, God, was she coming apart at the seams?

Ship was empty because it had processed everybody. Everybody except the Doctor, and he was next.

The burning erupted through her. She came to her feet, grimacing like a panther. 'You monster!' she shouted at the walls. 'Monster! You alien monster bastards! You took Sedjet away, you took Alan away, you took Jan away, but you're not going to take the Doctor away!'

The Doctor got out of his bonds and out of his cell and he ran.

His shoulder was electric, burning, but he made the pain drive him on. There were no alarms, no guards, only Ship, the curved walls surrounding him. He felt their attention as he fled, Ship sensing him, watching him.

It was like the bad moment on a roller-coaster, just before the top of the first dip, when you realize you've left it too late to get off. In a moment you'll be falling, falling –

Chest heaving, he stumbled against a wall. The layout of the corridors was different to the pattern he remembered. Ship had rearranged itself – was probably rearranging itself even now, its interior becoming a labyrinth to trap him. He imagined he could hear it breathing.

Half a dozen thick green vines leapt out of the wall and snatched at him. He sprang back. The vines were growing out of the living stuff of the corridor, lashing out, blindly groping for him.

He bolted, turning down another passageway where the light was redder, twisting back on his course. He didn't know where he was going, he just had to keep going, keep going, keep going –

The thing in his shoulder *squeezed*.

He collapsed in mid-stride, lay on the spongy stuff of the floor with his knees drawn up to his chest, face white as paper. He did not move. He barely breathed. His heartsbeat was an agonizing motion in his chest. He wished it would stop.

While he lay there, the tendrils quietly grew from the wall behind him, slowly looping over and around and beneath him until he disappeared inside the solid cage of vines.

Neither of them said a word.

Kadiatu was waiting for Ace when she exited cold storage. Ace was in firing position the instant she saw the African woman. She hesitated. Perhaps she hesitated because she'd personally killed exactly three hundred and ninety-nine sentient individuals. One more would make it four hundred. Perhaps she was just tired. But no matter what happened, she had to save the Doctor.

Kadiatu's body kept trying to leap into combat speed, her arms and legs jittering with the urgent need to move, to fight. No matter what happened, Ace could not be allowed to save the Doctor.

Kadiatu's gun arm jumped up into firing position and the bolt leapt across the short space between them and a coruscation of light exploded in Ace's midriff and around her and she fell sideways, hair flying, shades spinning away, her body still following the arc of the dodging motion she was trying to make. Her gun stuttered, peppering the walls and ceiling with flechettes.

The shot should have turned her into a wisp of vapour. Perhaps Kadiatu's aim was a little off.

Kadiatu's arm jerked down forty-five degrees, covering the woman lying on the floor.

She lay there.

She lay there.

215

She lay there.

Kadiatu turned and walked jerkily away.

And neither of them said a word.

The Doctor opened his eyes. The agony in his shoulder had diminished to a dim thrumming. He was lying awkwardly on his side, twisted in a mass of green tendrils.

He tried to move. There were vines drawn tight around his legs and arms, across his chest. One was looped across his throat, forcing his head back. As he watched, a long spiral of green wound itself around his left wrist.

There was a figure standing over him. She was smooth and white as porcelain. But much more durable. Even before Death had come to life as the first creature fell on the first world, she had existed, as essential and as intolerable as her younger sister.

'I have come,' said Pain, 'to make sure you keep your side of our bargain.'

It ought to hurt.

Ace was hunched against the wall, breathing hard. Her mind had come sharply back into focus. She knew just what to do.

She did not fumble with the combat kit, even though her hands were shaking. The hopper had climbed off of its own accord, half its tentacles singed into flaking black wires. Perhaps it would die.

She unzipped the kit and pulled out the military handscan with her left hand. Very basic things, used mostly for triage; they told you whether you were dead or about to die.

Okay, she'd caught the edge of a plasma burst at extremely close range. There were extensive burns – probably second-degree – to her right side and arm.

She ought not to be able to move. It ought to hurt, really.

The handscan prescribed two military endorphin derms. She pressed them to her arm, added a third one for good measure. If it didn't hurt now, it was going to start hurting soon.

She unpackaged a fourth derm with shaky fingers, put it on her shoulder. Traumatized blood vessels would have leaked fluid – how much, she wouldn't know, and in any case she wouldn't be able to replace the stuff until she got to a very non-existent medical facility. The derm would help fight off the shock.

She struggled to her feet. The endorphins already sloshing about inside her, giving her a buzz like exercise or combat. They could not completely mask the burning.

So long as she could keep the pain away, she'd be alright. She just had to keep moving until she found the Doctor.

Nicolas burst in through the door of his shop, chest heaving. Benny was asleep, slumped over the counter. She woke up with such a start that she fell off.

They glared at one another across the counter.

'*De rien,*' he said. 'The tricolour's flying over the Arc de Triomphe. It's over, it's all over.'

'Alright,' she said suspiciously.

'Where is everyone?'

'Fled,' she fibbed, yawning. 'Looks as though it's just you and me.'

'Soon it'll be just you. I'm getting the hell out of Paris.' He stopped, considered, and asked in a surprised voice, 'Do you want a lift?'

Benny shook her head. 'I have to wait for my friends here.'

'You suit yourself, mademoiselle, but they're rolling barrels down the Champs Elysees to make barricades. It's more like the pit of hell than the fields of heaven. Everything smells of petrol. I had to escape press-gangs twice – they're just tearing the streets apart and pulling up the cobblestones to make walls.'

'I heard the cannons,' said Benny. 'But I have to wait.'

'You suit yourself. I don't know what your friends have been doing all this time, what it's all been about, and I don't care. I'm going.'

Ship guided Kadiatu through the passages until she found the Doctor, cocooned in a tangled mass of greenery. Ship's nerves. A flock of repair butterflies was crouched on the vines, antennae twitching, unable to get to the damaged component inside.

His eyes snapped open. Kadiatu started and jerked back. As though she were the one in trouble.

'I have nothing to say to you,' he said.

Kadiatu took out her handscan and slowly waved it over him. 'The first step was making the gatekeepers, the time machines that looked like human beings. We grew them using scraps of DNA, from real human beings and from Ship. Then the hoppers.' She closed the scanner, put it away. 'And this is the third step.'

'That's the old cliché, isn't it? It won't hurt if you don't fight it.'

'Are you listening to me?' She squatted down on the floor opposite him.

'Relax and enjoy it. What nonsense.'

'You wrecked Ship's plan to use the gatekeepers to stabilize the rifts. It could have tried again. But it realized there was a way to give itself the power to travel through space-time.'

'Where's your sister? I thought she'd be here.'

Kadiatu leaned back on the wall. She was alone, and he wasn't even listening to her, he was having a conversation with someone who wasn't even there. 'Look what they've done to me . . .' she whispered.

'Don't imagine I'm afraid of you. Familiarity breeds contempt.'

'It could have been me, you know. Or Bernice, or Ace. All it takes is a time traveller. But I convinced the Ants that you were the best candidate. You've crossed the time field more often than any of us. You may be the most experienced time traveller the universe has ever seen. All Ship has to do to access that experience is to install you.'

The vine around the Doctor's left wrist tightened suddenly. The tip of the vine nosed against his skin, splitting into finer tendrils. One by one, they began to push their way into his flesh. He struggled in his green bonds, going into convulsions as Ship's stuff began to fuse with his nervous system.

The vines pulled tighter, holding him still. The tendrils burrowing into his wrist began to shove their way up the nerves of his arm. His teeth were fiercely clenched, his head rolling and rolling. He did not scream.

'The whole process won't take more than an hour,' said Kadiatu. Soothingly? 'Once the tissue makes its way into your central nervous system, you'll be an inseparable part of Ship.' She looked down at her hands, the fine green lines winding their way down her arms. 'And then we'll be able to go anywhere in space-time. Anywhere at all.' She sighed, sleepily. 'I just want to go home.'

'Click your . . . heels together,' the Doctor snarled.

The butterflies, shaken free by the trembling vines, flapped ponderously away down the corridor.

Ace heard a sound. It took her a moment to work out what it was: a familiar voice, moaning. The sound rose, was cut off. God. For a moment she didn't want to turn the corner.

At first, all she could see was a great mound of vines, green stuff spun like thread from the corridor wall. It was trembling, alive. Then she saw a hand, and a hint of dull fabric underneath. She walked slowly around the heap on the floor, right arm curled to her right side, and squatted down beside it.

The Doctor was in there, deep inside the vines, eyes tightly closed. His hands were drawn up to his chest, curled into claws. One of them twitched hideously. Ace watched with road accident fascination as the green stuff around his wrist pushed itself a little further into him.

The Doctor had given it his best shot, and he'd failed. Ship was going to make him part of itself, and then it was going to harvest the universe.

He mustn't die alone.

She stood, soundlessly and sighted down the barrel of the flechette thrower, left-handed. Temple shot would be the easiest; he'd never know what hit him. Her aim shook only very slightly.

Ace couldn't believe how calm, how cool she felt. Was this how the Doctor had felt when he'd blown up Skaro, when he'd trapped the Timewyrm, when he'd let Jan die?

With a tiny motion of her thumb, she flicked off the safety.

His eyes snapped open. They were bright green, the same colour as the vines that surrounded him. She started, but he couldn't see her, his blind eyes searching the corridor for the source of the sound.

Oh, God. Ace's aim wavered.

Think about it. Give yourself ten seconds, and fire.

Ten.

'But there are three rules. One. I'm in charge.'

'Whatever you say, Professor.'

Nine.

'Kill her.'

Eight.

'Ace. Come back. Come home.'

'What's happening to me, Doctor?'

'It's alright, Ace. We're going home.'

Seven.

'You're so clever, you little shit. I'm never gonna play your games again . . . never get manipulated again.'

Six.

'Two. I'm not the Professor. I'm the Doctor.'

'Whatever you want.'

Five.

He saw the searing Blue in her eyes, the glitter of the obsidian blade in her hand. He threw his arms around her, as though she were the one who needed protection, as though she were the sacrifice. And then she slammed the knife up and into his chest, and suddenly his knees buckled and she was the one holding him.

Four.

'And the third?'

Three.

'Scream, I'll save you later.'

Two.

'Well, I'll think up the third by the time we get back to Perivale.'

One.

No.

She wasn't going to sacrifice him.

That was the third rule. That was it. That was her rule. No one deserves to be sacrificed. Not her, not Jan.

'Not even you, you old bastard,' she said out loud, and pu

her gun away.

Astonishingly, he winked a chlorophyll-coloured eye at her. Then he threw back his head and screamed.

Nicolas had stuffed a travelling bag with clothes, money, some food hidden in a cupboard in the shop. He ran to the cellar door, flung it open, hesitated at the odd green light and the thick, sour hothouse smell. Well!' he cried. 'Are you coming?'

The Englishwoman appeared at the bottom of the steps. 'You're leaving?'

'*Bien sûr!* I don't fancy hanging around for the justice of the Versaillais.'

'What time is it?'

Nicolas glanced back at a cuckoo clock on the wall. 'It's eight in the morning. It's already warm, going to be a scorcher.'

'I'll say. The Communards will set Paris alight to try and stop the advance of the troops. And the Versaillais are going to shoot everything that moves.'

'You're very well-informed.'

'Yes.'

'So let's go!'

Benny was coming up the steps. 'Do you know what's down here?'

Nicolas shook his head. 'I thought, perhaps a medical school, without a license. She needed the bodies for dissection.'

'How many bodies did you bring here?'

'Perhaps a dozen. Perhaps a score.'

'Why are you trying to save my life?'

'*Comment?*'

'How many people did you kill? For how much money?'

Nicolas backed away from the cellar door. 'If you don't want a lift,' he growled, 'you can stay here and burn!'

'How many, Nicolas? As long as you got your money, it didn't matter how they died, did it?'

'You can stay here and burn.' He stomped out, bag slung over his shoulder.

221

Benny listened until she heard his horses' hooves on the cobblestones. 'I wasn't going anywhere anyway,' she said, and went back into the cellar.

Ace was screaming too, now, because the Doctor was thrashing in the vines, his tenor howl skittering up into a surprisingly high shriek. She tried to reach him, but there was too much vegetable matter in the way, looping and snaking, trying to grab her hands.

Suddenly his cries were cut off. His chest heaved, a tiny trickle of blood made its way out of his mouth. Ace's ears rang, but the only noise was the desperate sound of his breathing.

With a crunching sound, the flower exploded out of his shoulder. She screamed again as she was sprayed with alien blood. The blossom uncurled itself just below the Doctor's left collar-bone.

Ace frantically wiped sticky hair out of her eyes. The flower's roots were thrust deep into his chest, wrapped around the ganglion. *Don't throw up, don't throw up, you've seen worse stuff than this, haven't you? Haven't you*? The blossom pulsed redly into life, its petals rushing with the double rhythm of his hearts. It was a communications relay, connecting his central nervous system directly with Ship's.

And then Ship died.

The corridor trembled once, its light flickering like a sick fluorescent tube. The sounds of the living vessel whispered away into nothing. The air hung thick as treacle.

The Doctor's body hung limply in the mass of tendrils. Blood was pooling beneath him. The flower's pulse was still beating, but erratically, as irregularly as the slow sound of his breathing. As Ship slid into death, it was taking its newest component with it.

Ace got out her Draconian army knife, grabbed a handful of vines, and started sawing at them.

He shouted with pain, making her jump backwards. 'No,' he wheezed, 'Cut the root . . . closest . . . the wall!'

Ace scrambled behind the mass of vines, found a single

thick cord where they converged, leading back into the stuff of the wall. It was already starting to wilt. She sliced through it.

Now it was easy to cut through the vines. She knelt and heaved the Doctor out, with more force than was needed. He leaned heavily on her. 'Are you alright?' he said.

Ace would have laughed if she hadn't been so nauseated. His shoulder was a bloody mess. She took hold of the wet, warm flower to cut its stem, but he raised a hand between the blade and the blossom. 'Leave it,' he begged. 'Just leave it.'

His eyes were still green, still blind, the optic nerve jammed with plant tissue. 'You're injured,' he gasped. We have to . . . get out of here!'

'Kadiatu barbequed my hopper.'

'Then we'll use the rift.'

'How?' There was a great creaking noise, and the floor lurched underneath them. 'Doctor,' said Ace. 'Are we going to die together?'

'You shouldn't have followed me,' he murmured.

'*Rien de rien,*' she said. 'I think I'll enjoy being dead. I could use the rest.'

Chapter 16

Set, Game, and Match

> Getting a Purple Heart proves that you were smart
> enough to think of a plan, dumb enough to try it out,
> and lucky enough to survive.
>
> (US Army tradition)

Ship rocked, as though something had exploded distantly. Ace and the Doctor were thrown against a wall, tumbling to the heaving floor. They lay there for a few seconds, waiting to see if another quake would slam through the dying vessel.

The Doctor's blood was soaking into Ace's clothes. Her own pain was distant, like the sound of a phone left off the hook, like the big grey ringing in the back of her head, trying to suck her down. She hoped she didn't die suddenly, that could be awkward.

They dragged one another to their feet. Ace stumbled, started to laugh. 'I've sprained my ankle,' she said.

Cold storage. Repair butterflies crunched under their feet. The rift's light jumped and seared. One of the glass walls had collapsed, letting the unfiltered radiance into the chamber.

'Can we go through it without force shields?' said Ace.

The Doctor's blind eyes were half-closed. 'Where . . . controls?'

She guided him over to a panel in the wall, limping. The controls were a mass of tubes and knobs, pulsing coldly. He reached out and ran his fingertips over them.

'I suppose my combat suit is here somewhere,' said Ace.

'Storage,' said the Doctor. 'No time.'

'Forget it.'

The Doctor was doing things to the controls. 'Enough power . . .? Hope . . .' he coughed.

224

He turned suddenly. Ace's head snapped around a moment later. 'Is it –?'

'It's Kadiatu,' said Ace steadily. 'She's holding a blaster.'

The Doctor reached out to Kadiatu with a trembling hand. 'We need your help.'

Kadiatu's face contorted, jerkily, as though two different puppeters had hold of her strings. 'Get!' She tried to speak, but it was cut off. Her arm jumped up.

'Ship's got her,' said Ace.

'Fight it,' breathed the Doctor. 'It's falling into death, you can fight it.'

Kadiatu's hand moved wildly, trying to keep the weapon trained on them, trying to shoot the controls, the walls, anything.

Ace flinched as a ball of plasma pumped out of the gun. But the space was suddenly full of roaring light, glaring sound. There was a gaping melted hole in the transparent shield that held in the rift.

Ace stepped away from the Doctor. Give her a moving target. 'Come on, you bitch!' She shouted, waving her arm. Hot pain rippled up her side. 'Whose side are you on? Come on!'

Kadiatu's green eye moved wildly in her head, following Ace's movements. Ace risked a sideways glance at the Doctor. He was still doing things to the control panel.

Kadiatu came towards Ace. Her face was contorted in horror and fury. 'Come on!' Ace shouted again, edging towards the rift. 'Come and get me!'

'Between!' gasped Kadiatu.

Ace understood.

She stepped between Kadiatu and the rift.

With an inhuman roar, Kadiatu ran at her.

Ace flung herself aside at the last moment, and Kadiatu, turning her run into a jump, leapt through the hole and vanished into the light.

Ace tried to pick herself up, crawled to the wall, scrabbled at the rough surface until she made it to her feet.

'She's gone,' said Ace. 'She jumped.'

'Not stabilized,' said the Doctor. ' . . . might . . . anywhere ! 'I hope she has a soft landing. Sorry we couldn't . . .' He coughed sharply.

'It's okay,' she said. 'We can't save everybody.'

'Never . . .' His voice broke.'Thanks for . . .'

'Let's get the hell out of here.'

There was a sudden wash of energy. Benny leapt to her feet as the basement filled with it and was suddenly empty, echoing. She blinked spots out of her eyes.

The Doctor and Ace stumbled to a halt. They were clutching one another in an awkward A-frame hug. Both of them were covered in blood, mostly the Doctor's, deep orange-red. Benny put her hand to her mouth at the sight of the flower growing from his shoulder.

He turned eyes on her which were horribly green. 'Benny,' he wheezed, 'Ace is hurt.'

Abruptly, he collapsed, Ace snatching at him as his knees gave way. She fell with him, unable to support his weight any longer.

Bernice was beside them in a second, catching the Doctor and gently lowering him to the stone floor. He gripped her hand with bloody fingers. Ace, on her knees, took his other hand.

'*Adieu*,' He coughed. '"*Adieu*," *dit le mourant au miroir qu' on lui tend, "nous ne nous verrons plus* . . .'''

Then he stopped breathing.

Benny's agonized eyes met Ace's for a moment. She bent with pain, her fringe hanging down over her face, pressing his limp hand to her heart.

Ace just sat there, cross-legged, looking at the flower. It spasmed, started to wilt, suddenly turned completely grey. She reached down and plucked the dead thing from his shoulder. Its roots came away easily, limp and slick with blood.

Almost immediately, he coughed and took a deep breath.'Thought so,' said Ace weakly.

The Doctor's eyes fluttered open. They were already changing back to their natural blue. 'That feels so much better,' he sighed.

Ship's mind was made of bric-a-brac, bits and pieces from thousands of stolen minds. As piece after piece of the living vessel died, its collection of junk began to shake loose.

There was Sedjet's memory of the view from the top of the Great Pyramid, unravelled from the knot of Ship's group mind.

There was Ms Cohen's terror of hyperspace, a sharp sliver of emotion split away from the gestalt.

The junk tumbled from Ship's closet, faster and faster. There were memories of childhood and battle and sex, someone's talent for the harp, someone's taste for chocolate, someone's faith in their god and someone else's faith in the scientific method. A sunny day, a teddy bear, a hospital ceiling, a Draconian marriage, a school play, the Shi'wod dancing ritual, onion soup. Distilled moments of humanity and a hundred other species, blowing away into the Vortex like streamers of light.

The jagged, ragged remains of Ship rolled, convulsed, burst like a balloon, and were carried away on the wind into oblivion.

Chapter 17

Exit the Warrior

Heroing is one of the shortest-lived professions there is.
(Will Rogers, 1925)

Benny spent the night on the roof, watching Paris ripping itself apart. Someone, she thought, ought to stay on guard.

She wished she knew the names of the buildings. Huge palaces, museums, libraries – set ablaze, one after the other, great columns of smoke rising and spreading to blot out the brilliant stars.

At about one in the morning, the entire dome of a building was blown off, with a crump! even louder than the cannons and shells. Nicolas's house seemed far from the action, thank goodness, but the fighting was spreading slowly to engulf the entire city.

They'd have to leave soon. The Doctor said Ace couldn't be moved, not while the shot of nanites he'd given her were doing their job. Nicolas had long ago dragged his bed downstairs into a storeroom. The TARDIS had materialized next to it, drawn to Ace by the same impulse that had made it chase her to Ancient Egypt.

They'd gotten the first aid kit out of the TARDIS, and Benny had bandaged the Doctor's shoulder, tightly binding his left arm to his side. The bruise on his face was starting to fade. He had been in surprisingly good condition, given the jagged tear over his collarbone. Ace was in much worse shape.

'The nanites can regenerate a lost limb,' he had said, carefully pressing a hypospray to Ace's wrist. 'They use the patient's own DNA as a template to regrow damaged tissue,

228

to break down foreign material or organisms in a wound.'

'Will it hurt her?' Benny had said, gently pulling the covers over the young woman's unconscious form.

'As little as possible,' he said, putting the spray away. 'Time Lords aren't very good at pain, they never have to feel it. It is risky, because it's so rapid, but it's her best chance.'

'Kill or cure.'

'If you like.'

'That was a really stupid plan.'

He looked at her over the bed, agitatedly passing the hypospray from hand to hand. 'She wasn't supposed to follow me.'

'No. I meant it was stupid in the first place.'

'Kadiatu thought to kill Ship with a virus. I'd already tried that, Ship was far too strong, or it would never have survived falling into the rift. I had to have access to its central nervous system. And for that to happen, it had to have access to mine.'

'Was that why Kadiatu took you back to Ship?'

He nodded. 'She was told to, but she knew I had something up my sleeve. She was right out of her depth. She should have left it to me.'

'You would have died if Ace hadn't been there.'

'I know. It wouldn't be the first time.' His hands clasped the hypospray, hard. 'Kadiatu got what she wanted. She can travel anywhere, anywhen. I hope we meet again, I want the chance to talk to her properly.'

'You were too busy trying to outplot one another.'

The Doctor shook his head. 'Ship was always listening.'

'You should have worked together.'

'Maybe next time. The problem with the easy way out is that it has already been mined.'

'Who told you that?'

He reached out, brushed a strand of hair from Ace's forehead. 'She did.'

Dying.

You don't have to do anything when you're dying.

Ace was finding the whole death thing a lot easier to handle than she had imagined. For one thing, she was so tired that it was a pleasure to just lie still. For another, she was pumped so full of military endorphins she could have flown to the top of Everest.

She was dimly aware that her body was in terrible pain. There was a patch of heat all down her right side, and little nagging places here and there. Tranked as she was she had no way of telling whether they were minor bruises or crater wounds.

Not that it made much difference. They had put on all the derms and skin grafts and stuff, given her a shot to boost the little machines running about in her blood, but it wasn't going to be enough. So she just lay there, letting the delirium throw up whatever images it chose.

One of her very earliest memories was picking up a black kitten out of a litter of kittens, joking that it was sleeping too much and putting it on its feet. The soft thump as it fell over. Running screaming to her father.

Her father had died too. Obviously it was hereditary.

She had been too short to see the bed properly, but she remembered the hospital smell, the colour of the afternoon light, the soft sounds as he struggled for breath. The sudden silence. Running screaming to her mother in the waiting room, screaming to fill up the silence.

She remembered lying in bed with a cold, listening to her own heartbeat, knowing that it could stop just like her father's heartbeat had stopped. Mum made her stay in bed, and now Mum was downstairs having a fight with somebody. There were pieces of jigsaw scattered all over the floor.

'Daddy,' little Dorothy sobbed. 'Daddy.'

'I'm here,' said a voice, and a hand took her hand, another brushed the sweat-soaked hair out of her face. A coolness entered her body, a sweet emptiness as the pain went away.

'Daddy,' she said again.

'I'm here.'

Little Dorothy found the missing piece of jigsaw, plugged it into place. Happy picture, happy family. She snuggled down to sleep under her eiderdown, gripping her father's hand.

Bernice found them in the morning, Ace breathing slow and steady as her body healed itself, the Doctor asleep next to

230

her, their hands gripping tightly above the covers.

When Ace woke up, the burning was gone, inside and out.

The Doctor was sitting on the edge of the bed, wearing a strange little pair of spectacles and reading a small book. There was a bit of red ribbon hanging down from it. When he saw that she was awake, he carefully marked his place with the ribbon and closed the book. 'How do you feel?'

'Sane,' she said.

'Right then, we'll be off.' He slipped the book into his pocket.

'Doctor, I –'

He raised a hand, sharply, between them. 'Sometime today this whole building will be ablaze and they'll be shooting women at random in the streets.'

Ace was struggling out of bed. 'We have to –'

'Ace,' said the Doctor agitatedly, 'there's no time. Benny's already aboard the TARDIS, let's go.'

'Doctor, I –'

'No, no, don't –'

'But you –'

'Just –'

They stopped, stared at one another for a long moment.

'I want you to have this,' said the Doctor.

He handed her the book.

'This is your 500 Year Diary,' said Ace.

'I'll be starting a new one,' he said.

They embraced, awkwardly. Ace closed her eyes, trying to imprint the memory of him into her brain, so she would never forget the fabric of his jacket, the soft, alien smell of his hair.

'Go and keep going,' she whispered. 'Don't stop for anything.'

Slowly, very slowly, he let go of her. Slowly, very slowly, he turned away and went into his TARDIS.

A moment later, Benny came running out, clutching a denim bag. 'You're staying! You're crazy! You haven't even got a toothbrush!'

Ace tucked the Doctor's diary into her jacket. 'I managed Ancient Egypt, I'll manage Paris. When I was a kid I always

231

wanted to be in Paris in the 1880s.' She grinned. 'Wicked frocks!'

'You haven't had a fight? He hasn't done something or something?'

'No.' Ace laughed. 'Nothing like that.'
killed.'

'You can't stay,' said Benny. 'You can't stay here. You'll be killed.'

'I can't leave and let all these people be shot.'

'But you can't change history.'

'I don't want to change it, I just want to be part of it.'

'But the Commune's about to collapse. What's the point?'

'Benny,' said Ace, 'what's the point of any of it? Anybody we save just gets to die later on. The whole universe eventually dies.'

She saw Benny – not quite recoil, but she was taken aback. Not the same little girl, she was thinking, seeing Doctor stuff in Ace's eyes. 'I can't stop the Versaillais, but I can ease the suffering and save a few lives. I've already made plans with the Women's Battalion.'

'Why stay and be a soldier?' said Benny softly.

'No, no. I'm not a part of anyone's machine.' She folded her arms, suddenly awkward. 'The Doctor told me a story once, about this general trying to teach the King's courtesans to be soldiers –'

'Sun Tzu?'

'Oh, you've heard that one. Well, I kind of see why he told me it now. I'm not taking anybody's orders any more. I want to fight for something *I* believe in. That's what these people are doing.'

'They'll do crazy things,' said Benny. 'They're already setting the city on fire. You'll be killed.'

'I'll be alright. Hey, I survived Heaven and Olleril and Belial and Peladon and Antykhon, right? I even survived Perivale.'

Suddenly they were both laughing, laughing like sisters. 'Some things,' said Benny, pushing the bag into Ace's arms. 'Just some clothes and things, Ace.'

'It's Dorothy, actually.' Ace put the bag down on the bed.

'Thanks anyway.'

'My God! I can't believe you're going!'

'Hey,' said Ace. 'I got used to being on my own when I was in Egypt. Besides, it's not just the Commune. The rifts can't be repaired. Somebody's got to stay and keep an eye on them.'

'How are you going to do that?'

Ace grinned hugely. 'The basement's full of time machines.'

Benny grinned back, despite the lump in her throat. 'Look after yourself. I'll try to look after him. He needs someone to look after him.'

'Does he?' said Ace. She shook her head. 'Don't let him stuff you around.'

'Don't get into too many *liaisons dangereuses*, okay?'

They clasped hands. 'Watch your butt, Summerfield. It's a tough universe.'

'With you loose in it,' said Benny, 'it had better be.'

The Doctor stood in the brilliant light of the Console Room. His face was shadowed. 'I knew she was going to leave.'

Benny sniffled. 'The sorceror's apprentice. Someone's got to keep an eye on those rifts. Someone who's been out into the universe. Earth needs its champion.'

'No,' he said. 'I knew she ended up here, all along. I traced her family tree long before we went to Whitby.'

'Remind me,' said Benny tiredly, putting an arm around his shoulders, 'never to try and throw you a surprise party.'

'Will she be alright?'

'I've never seen her look so alright.'

He shrugged his injured shoulder, wincing. 'I suppose the wound will heal quickly.'

'I suppose it will.'

Chapter 18

The New Adventures

> I hate quotations.
>
> (Ralph Waldo Emerson, May 1849)

Place: Paris
Date: 5 October 1815
Ace's age: Twenty-eight

Baron Vivant Dominique Denon was sixty-eight years old. At the moment, he was feeling every minute of those sixty-eight years. He was writing his resignation as *Directeur-Général des Musées Impériaux*.

They'd managed to keep the British out of the Louvre for months. He'd written letters of protest and personally confronted the soldiers who turned up on the museum's steps. Finally Wellington had sent a Lieutenant-Colonel around to order Denon to surrender the art treasures he'd watched over for so long.

Well, ha! He'd given that *Anglais* a piece of his mind. He had twenty-five guards, and instructions to defend the museum to the last, and that had been exactly what he'd meant to do.

Even now, he felt he should have done something more to save the collection. It broke his heart to imagine it scattered over Europe – or carted back to England for the glory of the Empire. He'd faced worse dangers than stony-faced Grenadiers, bayonets fixed or not. He'd prevented Napoleon himself from burning Louvre paintings. He'd survived the Reign of Terror and the invasion of Egypt. Why, he and Mlle Summerfield had put paid to rougher ruffians than cocky British soldiers.

He smiled at the old memory. Whatever had become of that woman? Something *extraordinaire,* no doubt, something *magique.* He hoped she was still having wild adventures somewhere. While he had nothing left to do but to grow old gracefully.

There was a knock at his door. *'Oui?'*

'Il y a une jeune fille qui est venue vous voir,' said his housekeeper, with just a hint of amusement in her voice. *'Une Anglaise, je crois.'*

'Please,' said Denon, pushing his half-finished letter away. 'Show her in.'

He didn't know the woman – no, she looked familiar, but he could not place her. Nor was he feeling particularly well-disposed to the English. 'What do you want, Mademoiselle?'

'Well,' she said, in London-flavoured French, 'I just thought I'd let you know that Bernice is alright.'

It took him a moment to work out what she was talking about. 'Mlle Summerfield?'

'Yeah. She told me about having to leave you without saying goodbye properly.'

'Extraordinaire,' said Denon. 'Please, sit down. How do you know her?'

'That's complicated. I know she couldn't tell you very much about where she came from, who she was. But I do know that without your help, she would have died – or have been trapped, with no way of returning to her friends.'

Denon merely inclined his head. 'I cannot help but think I have seen you somewhere before.'

'Wellington took a painting of me from the Louvre. It will end up on the wall of Windsor Castle.'

Denon's mouth opened slightly. *'Jeune fille avec fleur?'* he said. 'But that was painted last century!'

She smiled, put a finger to her lips. 'I wanted you to know that, even if your collection has been broken up and scattered, the works themselves will survive. That particular painting will still be in Windsor in a century and a halfs time.'

'Extraordinaire,' muttered Denon again. He shook his head. 'It is as though you and Mlle Summerfield can see into the future.'

'And the past,' smiled his visitor. 'I predict you're going to open a famous studio, M Denon, and that people will flock to see your collection of antiquities and art objects.'

'But those are my very thoughts, my very intentions. When I was seventeen, a Gypsy woman told me I would go to court, that I would be beloved of women, that a beautiful star would shine upon me. Perhaps she also could see the future; two of those predictions have certainly come true. But now my precious Louvre is being sliced up by the British, and I have failed to stop them.'

'You won't be forgotten,' said the woman. 'Remember that.'

Denon sighed deeply. 'In the end,' he said, 'that is all any of us can hope for.'

Place: Glebe, Sydney
Date: 14 July 1993
Ace's age: Thirty-seven

'Well,' said the Doctor, 'if it hadn't been for your timely arrival, the population of the Earth would have been destroyed by the Voltrana plague.'

'One to the good guys,' laughed Dorothée. 'Though I reckon you probably would have escaped from that dimensional bubble after a while.'

'A Klein sphere,' he said, 'solid on the inside, invisible on the outside, so that you just walk into it without even noticing it's there. A nasty little trap, typical of the Voltranons.'

She drained the last of her vodka and Coke. The cafe was just as she remembered it, from half a dozen planets. 'Now they're gone,' she said, 'it's good to have a moment to catch up with you.'

'How's Count Sorin?'

'We see a lot of each other.'

'Will you be getting married?'

'I doubt it. The bloody laws are ridiculous. I'm doing a lot of work with the suffragettes.'

236

'That must be very rewarding.'

'I'm very optimistic.' She grinned. 'I've been testing the range of the hoppers. I only seem to be able to go a century in either direction.'

'That's enough to keep track of the Paris rift. Has it given you much bother?'

'Not really. Some bugs did pop through in the 1850s, nothing very serious. They got a terrible fright when I dropped your name. Packed their bags and left.'

The Doctor laughed. 'Oh dear, that reputation of mine! What else have you been up to?'

'I made it back to the Boston tea party. I sailed for a while with Zheng Yi Sao.'

'Mmm. You must be beginning to get a reputation yourself. Any sign of Kadiatu?'

Ace shook her head. 'I've been hoping she might contact me, somehow. She's out there somewhere, isn't she?'

'I hope so,' said the Doctor seriously. 'I really hope so.'

'I got as far forward as 2002. I visited Cristián and Ben.'

'How were they?'

'Father and son doing nicely. I did consider saving Manisha.'

'Oh.'

'But I didn't.' She squeezed her eyes shut. 'I couldn't do t.'

'Because you'd seen it happen.'

'And because I know better. Otherwise you'd never have et me loose on the universe. How do you stand it?'

He just shook his head, turning his glass around in his hands.

'I did arrange for a police patrol car to be waiting down the street.' She smiled tightly. 'They caught the three boys who did it.'

'Ah.'

'Doesn't seem to have destroyed the continuum.' Ace breathed out a sigh. 'I saw myself. I saw myself as a kid, crying outside her house, you know? Because I hadn't been there o save her. I wanted to give myself a hug. I suppose I'll have ome kids eventually. I'd really like to marry someone just

237

like you, Professor.'

'Oh?'

'Only handsome.'

'Oh.'

She grinned and touched the tip of his nose with her finger.

Place: Paris
Date: 28 May 1871
Ace's age: Twenty-six

She had seen a woman shot dead for waving a red flag at the enemy.

She had seen six children shot as suspected *pétroleuses*, their bodies left with all the others to rot in the street. She had shot the Versaillais soldier who did it before he could turn his gun on a seventh.

She had huddled behind a barrel full of sand, taking turns with a terrified young man to shoot at the enemy, holding them back while a crowd of women and children got to safety.

She had wrestled a can of petrol out of the arms of a crazed Communard who was heading for a maternity hospital.

She had seen a Versaillais Marquis picking out prisoners whose faces he didn't like and having them gunned down in the street.

Now she was huddled on a barricade in the Rue Ramponneau. It was morning, and the air was full of smoke. Everyone else was dead.

A trooper sprang from a hiding place, rifle at the ready. She put a bullet through his arm almost without thinking about it and ducked back down.

Five minutes.

The Communards had lost perhaps three thousand troops in the fighting so far. That meant that another twenty-two thousand people were going to be killed in the next few days.

She shot over the head of another Versaillais. When he didn't take the hint, she squeezed off a shot that knocked his hat off. *She who hesitates under fire usually* doesn't *end up getting shot.*

She'd fought with the Women's Battalion, slowly forced back along the Boulevard de Clichy, back and back until most of the survivors had surrendered at the Place Pigalle.

Ten minutes.

They'd slowed the advance of the troops, given people time to go into hiding, to get out of the city. She'd never know how many lives she had saved. The numbers would be tiny in the face of the massacre that was about to start. There'd be God knew how many orphans and widows to take care of, how much rebuilding to do. It was going to be a difficult decade.

Fifteen minutes.

She fired off a last shot and realized she was out of ammunition. She'd done everything she could.

The last defender of the Paris Commune got down from the barricade and calmly walked away.

Afterword

by Sophie Aldred

Last things last . . .

I'll let you get your breath back: time travelling Kate
Orman style is a wonderfully exhausting business. So, are you
sitting comfortably? Then I'll finish.

Doesn't time have a habit of doing peculiar things? It's five
years since the Doctor and Ace walked off the screen to that
great cup of tea in the sky; four years since the TARDIS
materialized in print in Mesopotamia, and John Peel asked me
to write the foreword for the first New Adventures novel.

I felt then that I should never be allowed to leave the
Doctor Who family, and although here we are now, with Ace
adventured out on videotape and now in ink, I feel more than
ever before that this Doctor Who thing is for life. I can't get
away from Ace even if I wanted to, and I don't.

People have asked me what it's like to read about Ace in
the New Adventures. It's been like standing on a crowded
tube station platform, and catching a glimpse of someone who
was once very dear to me, in the flickering half-light of a
through train. Mind the gap, that ever widening gap. For now
it's time to move on again.

There's a part of me that hates goodbyes, and it's my second
goodbye to Ace. Which reminds me of that day back in
October 1990 when the phone rang for me at the BBC North
Acton rehearsal rooms and Sylvester was on the other end of
the line.

'Are you sitting down?' he suggested. 'I've got some bad
news – they've cancelled Doctor Who.' He may as well have
told me they'd cancelled next year. I put a brave face over the
hurt one and went back to the all-singing, all-laughing

240

Corners rehearsals, saving my tears of disappointment for a more private moment.

And now it's goodbye, and I should be used to it by now. Kate has done us proud. Here's an Ace I would love to have played on screen: older, wiser, battle-scarred and feisty as ever. And the lump in my throat this time is for the end of the relationship between the Doctor and Ace, so touchingly portrayed here and just as I would have wanted in the TV series. My thanks to all the New Adventures writers for taking Ace to new pastures and new extremes, and also to all Ace fans who have followed her to the ends of time and back. Yes, it's time for a rest, and time for the Doctor to be called something other than Professor. So. That's all folks. Or is it? 'Time will tell; it always does.'

Already published:

THE LEFT-HANDED HUMMINGBIRD
Kate Orman

Someone has been playing with time. The Doctor Ace and Bernice must travel to the Aztec Empire in 1487, to London in the Swinging Sixties and to the sinking of the *Titanic* as they attempt to rectify the temporal faults – and survive the attacks of the living god Huitzilin.

ISBN 0 426 20404 2

.

CONUNDRUM
Steve Lyons

A killer is stalking the streets of the village of Arandale. The victims are found each day, drained of blood. Someone has interfered with the Doctor's past again, and he's landed in a place he knows he once destroyed, from which it seems there can be no escape.

ISBN 0 426 20408 5

NO FUTURE
Paul Cornell

At last the Doctor comes face-to-face with the enemy who has been threatening him, leading him on a chase that has brought the TARDIS to London in 1976. There he finds that reality has been subtly changed and the country he once knew is rapidly descending into anarchy as an alien invasion force prepares to land . . .

ISBN 0 426 20409 3

TRAGEDY DAY
Gareth Roberts

When the TARDIS crew arrive on Olleril, they soon realise that all is not well. Assassins arrive to carry out a killing that may endanger the entire universe. A being known as the Supreme One tests horrific weapons. And a secret order of monks observes the growing chaos.

ISBN 0 426 20410 7

LEGACY
Gary Russell

The Doctor returns to Peladon, on the trail of a master criminal. Ace pursues intergalactic mercenaries who have stolen the galaxy's most evil artifact while Bernice strikes up a dangerous friendship with a Martian Ice Lord. The players are making the final moves in a devious and lethal plan – but for once it isn't the Doctor's.

ISBN 0 426 20412 3

THEATRE OF WAR
Justin Richards
Menaxus is a barren world on the front line of an interstellar war, home to a ruined theatre which hides sinister secrets. When the TARDIS crew land on the planet, they find themselves trapped in a deadly reenactment of an ancient theatrical tragedy.

ISBN 0 426 20414 X

ALL-CONSUMING FIRE
Andy Lane
The secret library of St John the Beheaded has been robbed. The thief has taken forbidden books which tell of gateways to other worlds. Only one team can be trusted to solve the crime: Sherlock Holmes, Doctor Watson – and a mysterious stranger who claims he travels in time and space.

ISBN 0 426 20415 8

BLOOD HARVEST
Terrance Dicks
While the Doctor and Ace are selling illegal booze in a town full of murderous gangsters, Bernice has been abandoned on a vampire-infested planet outside normal space. This story sets in motion events which are continued in *Goth Opera*, the first in a new series of Missing Adventures.

ISBN 0 426 20417 4

STRANGE ENGLAND
Simon Messingham
In the idyllic gardens of a Victorian country house, the TARDIS crew discover a young girl whose body has been possessed by a beautiful but lethal insect. And they find that the rural paradise is turning into a world of nightmare ruled by the sinister Quack.

ISBN 0 426 20419 0

FIRST FRONTIER
David A. McIntee
When Bernice asks to see the dawn of the space age, the Doctor takes the TARDIS to Cold War America, which is facing a threat far more deadly than Communist Russia. The militaristic Tzun Confederacy have made Earth their next target for conquest – and the aliens have already landed.

ISBN 0 426 20421 2

ST ANTHONY's FIRE
Mark Gatiss

The TARDIS crew visit Betrushia, a planet in terrible turmoil. A vicious, genocidal war is raging between the lizard-like natives. With time running out, the Doctor must save the people of Betrushia from their own legacy before St Anthony's fire consumes them all.

ISBN 0 426 20423 9

FALLS THE SHADOW
Daniel O'Mahony

The TARDIS is imprisoned in a house called Shadowfell, where a man is ready to commence the next phase of an experiment that will remake the world. But deep within the house, something evil lingers, observing and influencing events, waiting to take on flesh and emerge.

ISBN 0 426 20427 1

PARASITE
Jim Mortimore

The TARDIS has arrived in the Elysium system, lost colony of distant Earth and site of the Artifact: a world turned inside out, home to a bizarre ecosystem. But now the Artifact appears to be decaying, transforming the humans trapped within into something new and strange.

ISBN 0 426 20425 5